THE BRIDE
BACKFIRE

THE BRIDE
BACKFIRE

KELLY EILEEN HAKE

BARBOUR
PUBLISHING

For more information about Kelly Eileen Hake, please access
the author's website at the following Internet address:
www.kellyeileenhake.com

Cover Design: Lookout Design, Inc.

Published by Barbour Publishing, Inc., P.O. Box 719,
Uhrichsville, OH 44683, www.barbourbooks.com

*Our mission is to publish and distribute inspirational products
offering exceptional value and biblical encouragement to the masses.*

 Member of the
Evangelical Christian
Publishers Association

Printed in the United States of America.

DEDICATION/ACKNOWLEDGMENT

For God, who gave me the words; my mother, who taught me what they meant; my editors, who make sure I used them properly; and the readers, without whom it would all be a waste!

CHAPTER 1

Nebraska Territory, March 1857

N ot again!" Opal Speck breathed the words on
a groan so low her brothers couldn't hear her—a
wasted effort since the entire problem lay in having
no one around but Larry Grogan.

Even Larry, despite having the temperament of
a riled skunk and a smell to rival one, kept the oily
gleam from his eyes when the men of her family
were in sight. No, the appraising leers and occasional
advances were Opal's private shame. Hers to handle
whenever he tried something, and hers to hide from
everyone lest the old feud between their families
spring to life once more.

"Figured you'd come by here sooner or later,
since Ma and Willa are making dandelion jelly."
Larry levered himself on one elbow, pushing away
from the broad rock he'd lounged against. He
gestured toward the abundance of newly blooming
dandelions bordering Speck and Grogan lands, but

7

his gaze fixed on her as he spoke. "Let's enjoy the sweetness of spring."

"No." Opal kept her voice level though her fingers clamped around the handle of her basket so tightly she could feel the wood bite into her flesh. Letting Larry know he upset her would only give him more power, and false bravery to match. *Lord, give me strength and protection.* "Not today."

"Look ripe for the plucking to me." Larry sauntered closer, but Opal wouldn't give an inch. Everyone knew that when animals sensed fear, they pressed their advantage.

"Dandelion jelly may be sweet, but it takes a lot of work to make it that way. Do it wrong, it'll be bitter."

"I like a little tang." He reached out and tweaked a stray strand of her red hair as he leaned closer. "Keeps things interesting."

Opal fought not to wrinkle her nose as his breath washed over her. Instead, she tipped her head back and laughed, the note high and shrill to her ears as she stepped away. "Then I'll leave them to you, Mr. Grogan."

"Wait." His hand snaked out and closed around her wrist, but it was the unexpected note of pleading in his voice that brought her up short. "Won't you call me Larry?"

"I—" Opal couldn't have found any words had they been sitting in the clearing. She and Larry both stared at where his hand enfolded her wrist. "I don't think that's wise."

"We can't always be wise." With a wince, he used

his other hand to trace the long, thin scar bisecting his cheek. His hand dropped back to his side when he noticed her watching the motion, but something softened in his face. "You must like me a little, Opal. Otherwise you would've left me to die like everyone would expect a Speck to do."

Not really, no. She didn't speak the words, her silence stretching thin and strained between them. Larry's sly innuendos were a threat Opal expected, but Larry Grogan looking as though he cared what she thought of him. . . How could she be prepared for that? *Why didn't I notice his advances only began after his accident—that Larry must have interpreted me helping Dr. Reed patch him up as something more than kindness?*

Surprise softened her words when she finally spoke. "I would have helped anyone thrown from the thresher." Opal's reference to the incident didn't need to be more detailed. The man before her would never forget the cause of his scar, just as she'd never forget it was his animosity toward her father that caused him to mess with that machine in the first place.

"Even a Grogan?" He shook his head. "I don't believe you."

She would've backed away at the desperation written on his face if she could. "Believe it, Larry."

"What if I don't want to?" His grip turned painful, bruising her arm. "I know you'd do anything to protect your family. Even deny your own feelings." Larry moved closer. "And I can prove it with one kiss."

"My family would kill you." She tried to tug her wrist free, only to have him jerk her closer.

"We both know you wouldn't tell them." Darkness danced in his eyes. "This is between you and me."

Panic shivered down Opal's spine at the truth of his words. The one thing she could never do was put her family in danger, and if she told Pa or her brothers, blood would flow until there wasn't a Speck—or a Grogan—left standing. She stayed still as he leaned in, his grip loosening slightly as his other hand grabbed her chin.

"No!" Exploding into action the second she sensed her opportunity, Opal sent a vicious kick to his shins with one work boot. A swift twist freed her wrist from his grasp, letting her shove her basket into his stomach with all her might.

She barely registered the crack of wood splintering as she sprang away, running for home before Larry caught his breath enough to catch her.

"Pa ain't gonna like this." Nine-year-old Dave poked his head around the stall partition like a nosy weasel sniffing out trouble.

"That's why you're not mentioning it to him." Adam didn't normally hold with keeping things from one's father, but telling Diggory Grogan that another one of their milk cows had fallen prey to the strange, listless bloat that had plagued their cattle for the past few years without explanation would be akin to leaving a lit lantern in a hayloft.

The resulting blaze would burn more than the contents of the barn.

"But didn't he say that the next time one of those Specks poisoned one of our cows he was goin' to march over there an—"

"We don't know that anyone's been poisoning our cows, Dave." Adam pinned his much younger brother with a fierce glower. "But we do know the Specks have had sick cattle, same as us. The last thing either of us needs is to start fighting again."

Confusion twisted Dave's features. "When did we ever stop fighting?"

"There's different kinds of fighting, squirt."

"I know!" Dave scrambled after him as Adam left the barn to go find the meanest rooster he could catch. "There's name calling and bare knuckles and knock-down-drag-outs and slaps—"

His list came to an abrupt end when Adam rounded on him. "That's not what I meant." He squatted down so he could look his little brother in the eye. "There's fighting for what you believe in, fighting to protect what's yours, and there's fighting just because you like fighting. That's never a good enough reason, understand?"

"Kind of." Dave squinted up at him when Adam straightened once more. "How come we fight the Specks, then?"

"A mix of all three." Willa's voice provided a welcome interruption. "Our granddaddies both thought the east pasture belonged to them. Then each of our families believed the other was wrong, and now we're so used to fighting that we blame each other when anything goes wrong."

"Like the cows?" Dave processed their sister's explanation so fast it made Adam proud.

"Yep." He didn't say more as the three of them each chased down a chicken, ignoring the angry squawks and vicious pecks as best they could. When everyone's arms were loaded down with feathers and flailing spurs, they headed back to the barn.

"Then I guess it's a good thing Pa and Larry are out hunting today." Dave spat out a stray feather. "So we can scare some of the bloat out of Clem before he finds out and blames the Specks?"

"That's right." Willa set her jaw. "Because no matter what Larry says or how Pa listens, the Specks aren't poisoning our cows. And the last thing we need is for him to stir things up over nothing!"

That was the last any of them said for a while, as everyone knew it was useless to try to talk over the sounds of a cow belching. Since Dr. Saul Reed had first tried the treatment two years ago on Sadie—when the bloats began—the Grogans had perfected the process to a fine art.

If a cow grew listless, went off her feed, stopped drinking water, and generally gave signs of illness, they watched for signs of bloat. When baking soda didn't help, the last hope for expelling the buildup of gas before it stopped the animal's heart was to get it moving at a rapid pace. On the Grogan farm, that meant terrorizing the cattle with riled roosters.

Dave darted toward the stall and thrust his bird toward the back, spurring Clem to her feet for the first time that whole morning. She rushed out of the partition, heading toward a corner plush with hay, only to be headed off by Willa, whose alarmed chicken made an impressive display of thrashing wings to drive the cow out the barn door.

From there it was a matter of chasing her around the barnyard and up the western hill—the theory being that elevating her front end made it easier for the gas to rise out—until the endeavor succeeded or the entire group dropped from exhaustion. Thankfully, they'd yet to fail.

To an outsider, Adam Grogan would be hard-pressed to explain why leading a slobbering, stumbling, belching cow back to the barn would put a smile on his face, but Willa and Dave shared his feeling of triumph. Sure, Clem might not look like much of a prize at the moment, but she'd been hard-won. Better yet, they'd averted having Pa and Larry ride over to the Speck place with fired tempers and loaded shotguns.

Much the way Murphy and Elroy Speck were riding toward them right now. Adam tensed, taking stock of the situation. With Pa and Larry out for the day, it was up to him to take care of things.

"Stay here." He snatched the shotgun from the wall of the barn and rolled the door closed, pushing Dave back inside when he tried to squirm out. "I said stay. And don't go up in the hayloft either, or I'll tan your hide later." With the door shut, Adam slid the deadbolt in place, effectively locking his sister and younger brother in the barn. . .and hopefully out of trouble.

He strode to meet the Specks, intent on putting

as much distance from their stopping place and his family as humanly possible. While Adam didn't hold with the idea of a feud and did everything in his power to maintain peace, he wouldn't stake the safety of a single Grogan on any Speck's intention to do the same.

"Ho." Murphy Speck easily brought his horse to a halt, followed closely by his second-eldest son. The two of them sat there, shotguns laid across their saddles, silent as they looked down on Adam.

Adam, for his part, rested his firearm over his shoulder, vigilant without being hostile, refusing to offer false welcome. Specks had ventured onto Grogan land; it was for them to state their business. Adam wouldn't put himself in the weaker position by asking, and only a fool would provoke them by demanding answers.

Good thing Larry's not here. The stray thought would have earned a smile under any other circumstance.

"Where's your brother?" Murphy's gaze slid toward the corners of his eyes, as though expecting someone to sneak up on him.

Not a good beginning. He sure as shooting wasn't about to tell two armed Specks he was the only grown Grogan around the place. Adam just raised a brow in wordless recrimination at the older man's rudeness.

"What Pa means to say," Elroy's tone held a tinge of apology, though his stance in the saddle lost none of its steel, "is that Pete's seen your brother on our land a few times this past week."

"Oh?" *I knew he'd been up to no good when he hadn't been helping fertilize the fields. Something else stank.* Adam's jaw clenched.

"Some of our cattle have the bloat." Murphy's statement held accusation, though his words didn't. The man walked a fine line.

"Ours, too." Adam lifted his chin. "Must be a common cause."

"Common cause or no, seemed maybe a re-minder was in order." Elroy's level gaze held a deeper meaning.

His father wasn't half so diplomatic. "The next time a Grogan steps foot on Speck land without express invitation, he won't be walking away from it."

Adam ignored the sharp drop in his stomach at the irrefutable proof tensions were wound tight enough to snap. "Good fences make good neighbors." He gave Speck a curt nod.

"Fences and family, Grogan." Murphy's parting words came through loud and clear. "Watch yours a bit closer."

CHAPTER 2

"What did you see, Pete?" Opal fought to keep her voice steady when she tracked down her younger brother.

"When?" At fifteen, Pete had shot up to top her by a solid two inches, his limbs long and coltish as he turned to face her.

"Whenever it was you saw Grogan on our land." Opal chose her words carefully. As of now, all she knew was Pete had seen Larry skulking around this week and diligently reported it to Pa, who'd gone over to Grogan land this afternoon to address the issue. Her heart skittered at the thought of Pa and Elroy riding onto Grogan lands for any kind of confrontation, but since she'd only found out after they returned home safe and sound, there were more urgent things to focus on.

Like whether Pete had seen Larry following her or had heard their exchange by the clearing that morning. If so, why he hadn't told Pa about it. *And how can I keep it that way?*

But these were questions Opal couldn't fire at her brother outright—not if all Pete had seen were glimpses of Larry hanging around. As long as none of the Speck men knew the real reason for Larry Grogan's visits, she could keep their blood safely in their bodies. So she didn't say another word, just waited for Pete to spill what he'd seen and what he'd said about it.

"Two days past I saw someone in the brush bordering the southeast field but couldn't make him out. He beat it too fast for me to get a good look, but this morning I saw him again." Pete's young face hardened, making him look older. "Caught a glimpse of his face, and it was Larry Grogan. Like I told Pa, I could tell he was spoiling for a fight and he'd made it past the meadow."

He followed me. Opal sucked in a sharp breath, drawing an approving nod from her younger brother.

"He turned back when he saw my gun, but that's too close to the house." Pete jerked his chin toward their soddy. "We don't want the likes of Larry Grogan getting anywhere near you, Opal."

A humorless rasp of laughter scraped her throat. *He doesn't know. They can stay safe as long as I don't tell them.* She closed her eyes for a precious second as the knowledge flowed over her. *Thank You, Father, for protecting them. Thank You, too, for having Pete see just enough of Larry to make Pa warn him away. . . .*

"You did well to put a stop to it." She stretched out to net Pete in a swift hug before he squirmed free. "I'm so relieved Diggory and Larry didn't try to start something when Pa and Elroy went over to discuss it." Another not-so-minor miracle to add to her praise list that night.

"You and me, both." The martial light in her brother's eyes took her aback for a moment. "I didn't like it when Pa told me to stay home in case things went sour. If it wasn't for him saying he needed to know one of us was here to protect you, I would've followed 'em."

I can take care of myself! The fierce need to make the men in her life understand she didn't need their protection—particularly not when it endangered them—welled up with such force she choked on the resentment before she could say so. Another blessing.

"Thank you." Opal said the words so Pete could hear, but in her heart they went to God. The important thing was Pete stayed home when he could have been in danger. She'd swallow every ounce of pride she possessed in exchange for his safety. *But what a pass we've come to, when we're all so busy protecting each other we don't talk about it first.*

The familiar wash of regret pulled at her, almost making her miss Pete saying the Grogan men hadn't been on the farm.

"What do you mean Diggory and Larry weren't there?"

"We figure they must've been out hunting or something." Pete shrugged. "Course, now the problem is once they hear that Pa and Elroy went over and gave that warning, they might get furious

18

enough to make everything worse."

Cold swept from Opal's ears to her fingertips, making even her lips numb as she registered the danger. "Tell me they didn't speak to Lucinda!" Surely Pa knew better than to deliver bad news to Mrs. Grogan in the absence of her husband—any harsh words had to be spoken among men. "You know the Grogan men would take that as a threat to their women!"

"I dunno. She's Larry's ma and should keep him in line." Pete's sudden, mischievous grin dissolved when he saw the look on her face. "Naw, don't fret, Opal. Everyone knows this is a matter among men. They talked with Adam."

"Adam," she whispered his name. Her blood started moving again, warming her cheeks, making her lips tingle. It was a mark of how distressed she'd been that she could ever have forgotten about Adam Grogan.

Memories of murky darkness, crackling heat muffled by thick smoke, the acrid tinge of burnt wood creeping into her nose rose before her as if it were yesterday. Half-asleep from the morphine Dr. Reed had given her for her toothache, limbs heavy and eyes refusing to open, she'd never even registered Clara's attempts to pull her from the burning house two years ago. Even now, the recollections of smothering soot were hazy at best.

Until Adam. Even drugged by the doctor and half-choked by the thick blanket of smoke, Opal's awareness of Adam Grogan's deep voice calling her name had been clear as springwater on a sunny day. Not even the wearing of time had dimmed her memory of his cradling her against a solid chest as he swept her into strong arms she knew would carry her to safety.

"They talked with Adam," she repeated, relief leaving her knees weakened. "He'll talk with Larry, then. Adam will make it right."

"Yeah, Adam's always been the one with a level head." Pete rubbed the back of his neck. "If he weren't a Grogan, I'd even say I liked him."

"Me, too."

Pete raised a brow at her quick agreement.

"I mean, if he weren't a Grogan."

"Grogans don't stand for this kind of disrespect!" Larry's roar the next morning could've deafened an elephant. In Africa.

"We sure don't." Anger lined Pa's jaw, making Adam's gut churn.

But now wasn't the time to protest. Not until he heard Pa's line of thinking so he could reason him right back out of it.

"Specks coming onto our land..." Larry's words came fast and furious as he paced the small room he shared with Adam. "They got no right. If they think they can just push their way over where they don't belong and ain't wanted, they need to be taught a lesson."

"Agreed." Pa's outstretched arm brought Larry to a halt. "Any man who trespasses is asking for trouble."

"So what are we waitin' for?" Shifting his weight from one foot to the other, Larry glanced at Adam from the corner of his eye. "They've brought this on themselves. Let's take care of those Specks once and for all!"

"Thing of it is," Adam spoke slowly, careful to keep his voice thoughtful and free of force so as not to encroach on his father's position, "that the Specks have never come here before. Even today, they never raised their guns—just made it clear that it's best all around that we respect the boundaries."

"And that's what's troubling me." Pa swiped his hat across his brow. "I've known Murphy Speck my whole life. I don't like him, don't agree with the man, and wouldn't trust him as far as I could toss our heaviest draft horse. But he's never crossed our lines without cause. No matter how I try to avoid it, him bothering to come today means something stuck in his craw."

"And that something is me?" Disbelief, heavy and false, rang in his younger brother's voice, confirming Adam's suspicion that Larry had, indeed, breached boundaries on Speck land and brought this upon them.

"That's what they say." Adam struggled to keep his voice nonaccusatory. Setting up Larry's back any more than it already was would only worsen things. And it looked like his younger brother was bent on doing his crooked best to stir up more trouble than any of them could handle.

"Were you over there, son?" Pa's eyes narrowed. "Much as I can't abide the thought of Specks on

Grogan land, they're more than within their rights if they caught you."

If they caught him, not just if he was over there. Adam shut his eyes at his father's logic. To Pa, the problem didn't lie in breaking trust; it lay squarely in being found out. With that kind of creaking foundation, it wouldn't be long before the tenuous peace they'd built with the Specks came crumbling around their ears.

"Has anyone thought about what those no-good Specks are trying to do here?" Larry's demand conveniently neglected to provide an answer to the question at hand. "We all know Murphy's eldest is coming back here—failed at the mines, didn't he? So now he'll be wanting some good farmland close to home, and what's better than ours? They're laying the groundwork to get rid of us, and we shouldn't let them get one step closer!"

"Ben's coming back?" A flash of fear struck against the flint of his father's eyes. "With Ben home, they outnumber us."

"Hardly." Shaking his head, Adam tried to calm the storm. "Pete doesn't make much of a man yet. If anything, Ben just evens things up again."

"The odds are still better for us now." Larry kept on pressing. "And even a stupid Speck can count high enough to see it. That's why they didn't man up and do anything today."

"Makes sense."

"No, it doesn't." His disagreement came out too blunt, so Adam took another track. "It would make sense if you, Larry, and I had all been here. Instead, with just one, they would have been fools not to pick me off while they had no other opposition. If Diggory Speck wanted to end this feud once and for all, that would have been the strategy to use."

"No one ever said the Specks were smart." Larry's sneer didn't have Adam doubting anyone's intelligence but that of his brother.

"They're smart enough for that, or Pa wouldn't waste the effort worrying over what they might plan." When Pa's eyebrows went up, Adam knew he'd scored a point. "Grogans don't concern themselves with unworthy adversaries—especially not for generations."

"Adam's right." Pa plunked his hat back on his head. "You should know that, Larry. The Specks are just canny enough to be a threat."

"If you say so, Pa."

"I say so, all right. And, son?"

"Yeah?"

"*I'm* canny enough to know that you not answering about being on Speck lands means they were right." Pa's observation had Adam biting back a grin. "Which makes you the stupidest in the whole lot of us. Stay away from the Specks, son, or Murphy will have every right to make good on his threat. Trespassin's a shooting offense."

Adam started to breathe a prayer of gratitude that Pa wouldn't be deciding to saddle up with guns blazing anytime soon when Larry's mutter floated past him.

"Next time, I'll make sure they don't see me."

CHAPTER 3

I see you!" Opal swooped to the floor, nudging her face close to the baby's. "You're such a pretty girl, Matilda." She crooned to keep the ten-month-old from crawling away with the surprisingly quick speed she'd developed.

"Got her, did you?" Clara laughed when Opal, Matilda snug in her arms, settled onto the parlor sofa.

"For now." Opal ducked her head, pressing her cheek against the downy softness of the baby's hair. The gesture hid a sudden tug of sadness at the thought she wasn't anywhere close to having a child of her own. She breathed deep of Matilda's sweet, powdery scent. "You'll make me give her back, won't you?"

"Eventually, though I find most folks more than willing to return the loan without any urging when she needs changing." Leaning closer, Clara lowered her voice. "What I long for is conversation."

"You can converse with just about anyone." Snuggling the baby a bit tighter, Opal kept the accompanying thought to herself. *Someone to cuddle, now that's a different matter!*

"I know, but Saul is kept busy with his doctoring calls, and Josiah doesn't need me at the store these days. In any case, it seems all my time gets taken up keeping things in order around here." Clara cast a satisfied look around her newly rebuilt house. After the fire two years ago, the Reeds had recreated it as both a home and doctor's office for her husband. "That's part of why I'm always so glad to see you visit! I know Midge will be disappointed she missed it."

The mention of Midge, an irrepressible fifteen-year-old Saul had adopted just before coming to Buttonwood a few years ago, where he met his match in Clara, doused Opal's gloom. She'd held a particular fondness for Midge ever since the younger girl brought down her most prized possession—the old honeycomb-patterned quilt the women of the town had worked to restore in preparation for Midge's arrival—to comfort Opal during the treatment for her toothache.

When Clara realized the house had caught fire and that Opal, largely unconscious, couldn't leave under her own steam, she laid out Midge's quilt as a makeshift travois and dragged Opal toward the door. She owed her life to Midge's generosity and Clara's determination every bit as much as Adam Grogan's remarkable bravery.

"Where is Midge today?"

"At the Warren place, making candles." As she spoke, Clara wrinkled her nose and waggled her brows, eliciting a giggle from her little daughter. So the sudden seriousness of her next expression warned Opal the next thing her friend said would be important. "She and Alyssa are turning into quite the young women, and the boys in town are starting to notice."

"Pete stands straighter when they walk by." Opal didn't bother to repress a little snort. "And he's not yet sixteen!"

"But Midge is—and looks every bit as old as Alyssa, who boasts sixteen. It's something for us to keep an eye on." A burp cloth appeared as if out of thin air to be dabbed against Maddie's chin. "Thought I'd mention it while you were here, but what I really want to talk about. . ."

Opal tensed as her friend leaned back in a pose of relaxation, her pale eyes snapping with mischief. Clara looked far too pleased with herself for anyone else in the vicinity to be comfortable.

"Who's been chasing after you, Opal Speck? Shame on you for not telling me what was going on!"

"How did you know?" Somehow, she worked the words around the lump in her throat. Pete hadn't known Larry was chasing after her that day, and she wouldn't breathe a word to any soul, so there could only be one explanation. *How can I control the damage if Larry's spreading rumors?*

"Buttonwood doesn't rank as anything but a small town, Opal. Folks watch carefully and talk about what they see. You didn't expect to keep his interest a secret?"

"I hoped to." A snuffly wail penetrated her preoccupation, alerting Opal that she'd clutched baby Maddie too tightly.

"Nap time." Clara swept her daughter into her arms and bustled up the stairs, dispelling Opal's hopes that time would stop long enough for her to figure out a solution to the problem before her.

She returned to the parlor as swiftly as she'd left. "Opal?" Clara's brow furrowed as she sat down. "You don't look at all well. Saul should be back anytime now. We'll have him take a look at you."

"No thank you." *The doctor can't fix what's wrong. No one can.* Tears burned behind Opal's eyes, the first of many she'd feel before this all ended. She had no way out. Unless Larry was saying his intentions were honorable—then she'd have a choice: refuse, and spark the feud to slaughter her family, or marry Larry Grogan, tying herself to him for life.

It wasn't much of a choice, but she'd marry the lout before she let him destroy her family. If that was Larry's plan, she needed to find out. *Now.* "Why did he tell you, Clara?"

"He didn't say anything!" Her friend seemed taken aback, though whether it was the question or the desperation with which she asked it, Opal couldn't tell. "Like I said, there's plenty to see if you watch."

"So he hasn't said anything? It's just what you think you've seen?" Hope, tantalizing and intoxicating, made her head light. "Do you think anyone else noticed anything?"

"Observant as I am, it's possible I'm the only one to have marked his attention." Clara's brow furrowed. "I take it you don't want to encourage him, then?"

"Of course not! I want nothing to do with the man!" Opal twisted her hands in her lap. "And so long as you're the only one who suspects, we can stop it before it becomes a real problem."

"I never thought you'd feel this way." Her friend shook her head as though puzzling over something she'd never understand. "What did Brett Burn ever do to make you dislike him so?"

"Brett Burn!" Now Opal stared in confusion. "Who's talking about the blacksmith?"

"Me." Straightening her skirts, Clara leaned closer. "At least, I thought I was. Opal Speck, are you trying to tell me there are two men looking your way and you never breathed a word of it? Who's the objectionable one, then, if you're not talking about Brett?"

"Erm. . ." The way her head spun, Opal was starting to wonder whether maybe she shouldn't have Dr. Reed take a look at her after all. "That's not important, since the entire point is to ignore him." Outrage and obstinacy melded in her friend's face, calling for immediate diversion. "Now, what is it you were saying about Brett?" She injected a measure of wistfulness into her tone. "I hadn't noticed any partiality."

"Don't think I'm finished asking about the

mystery man, but you know I've always preferred to deal with possibilities instead of closed doors." Clara tucked her feet up under her and proceeded to recall all the times she'd—supposedly—seen the youngest of the Burn blacksmiths mooning over Opal.

"I don't have eyes in the back of my skull, so I'll have to take your word for it if he's sneaking glances during church." In spite of herself, Opal began to entertain the notion. "He never talks to me or walks me home or brings me tokens or anything to indicate he'd be interested in courting me, though."

"He asks about your beekeeping, Opal! And you ask about his work, too." Clara's list grew. "Maybe he's just waiting for a sign you'd be happy to accept his attentions."

"I ask about his work because he mends our tools and knows the latest advancements to help on the farm," Opal defended. "That's not talking; that's business."

"When your father and brothers talk with him, it's business." The correction came soft but firm. "And when he talks with you about your hives, that's not even a valid excuse. Those bee boxes of yours are made of wood!"

"There's such a thing as just being friendly."

"Even to a good-looking, hardworking bachelor the same age as you?" With romance on the brain, Clara drove her point home. "Don't you think you might make a good couple?"

"Never thought about it." Opal chewed on the inside of her lip and looked at her now-empty arms. *But I'm going to.*

"I can't think what happened to all my baking soda." Ma's fretting made Adam bolt his dinner.

"Done." He pushed back his plate. "I'll drop by the general store and pick some up for you, Ma."

"Thank you, son." Lucinda Grogan sent her eldest a fond smile. "But I can walk over there as well as anyone, and I know you've plenty to do in the fields."

But I used your baking soda on a sick cow and forgot to replace it. "I need to head into town anyway. Dusty's picked up a rock and bent one of his shoes something awful. One of the Burns will need to have a look at it."

"We'll go together." Ma beamed. "Willa can pick out whichever flour bags she likes best for her next dress."

Adam smothered a groan as his sister perked up. Who knew how long it would take the women if the trip involved more than staples? He'd planned on keeping a sharp eye on Larry for a good while yet, but that wouldn't be happening this afternoon.

It was worse than he thought. By the time Adam dropped the women off at Josiah Reed's General Store and headed toward Burn's Blacksmithing, he could've finished the entire trip alone twice over. With time to spare.

"Afternoon, Adam." Matthew Burn came up to greet him, his father and younger brother working at the forge.

"Good to see you, Matthew." Adam tilted his

head back toward the massive draft horse he was leading. "Dusty here ran into a rock this morning and bent his shoe. I was hoping one of you Burn men could take a look."

"Sure thing." Taking the lead from Adam's hand, Matthew led Dusty into the stable enclosure attached to the smithy. He patted the horse's shoulders, murmuring softly to soothe him. Even the most placid horse disliked the noise, heat, and smell of a smithy, so putting the large creatures at ease came as part and parcel of the job before a smart smith would go anywhere near a set of massive hooves.

Some folks held the opinion that three blacksmiths in one small—though growing—town ranked as excess if not downright foolishness. At least, that was the argument every Burn—and whatever townsman happened to be within hearing range—had ignored from almost every wagon train to pass through Buttonwood. No one blamed the pioneers for trying to secure a skilled blacksmith for their new homes, but Adam often had reason to be glad the Burns stayed in Buttonwood. There probably wasn't another town within a thousand miles where he could've gone to get Dusty taken care of that same afternoon—even if he lived there.

With Matthew fully engrossed inspecting Dusty's hooves—which he and Adam both agreed were due for a fresh shoeing anyway—not much chitchat went back and forth. That they held no penchant for gossip or babbling ranked as another reason Adam liked the Burn men. In a town as small as Buttonwood, most people made it their business to know everyone else's.

Ma sure does. Adam stifled the thought but didn't dispute the truth of it. If he walked over to the general store this minute, he'd find Ma talking up a storm at anyone who walked inside. Between Ma's surplus of talk over at the Reed store and Matthew's lack of it at the Burn smithy, Adam had plenty of time on his hands.

Too much time, for a man accustomed to seeing daylight hours as a commodity every bit as valuable as a good horse or plow. Spring days, when the earth smelled rich with sprouting green shoots and the sun shone brightly without the punishing heat of summer, called to the farmer in him. Back home, fields waited to be cleared, plowed, harrowed, and sown.

Unable to stay still, Adam wandered closer to the smithy to exchange greetings with Kevin, Matthew's father. The older blacksmith didn't hear him as he continued shaping red-hot iron. Metal on metal produced a rhythmic *clang*, the craftsman carefully bending what should have been impossible to his will.

If only forging a lasting peace with the Specks were so easy. The thought of Larry's escapade sparked a heat that had nothing to do with the smithy and everything to do with anger. *Pity you can't actually pound good sense into someone.* But Larry was too blind to see the danger he should keep away from.

A prickling at the back of his neck made Adam turn toward the entrance, where a woman stood backlit by the sun, her face hidden in shadow. It didn't matter. Wisps of soft hair teased away from her bonnet to catch the sun behind her and glints from the forge before her, giving her a burnished crown. Opal's fiery locks proclaimed her identity as surely as though she wore a sign saying, SPECK.

Adam's mouth went dry as she stepped into the shop, lissome and lively. With her pale yellow dress and red hair, she could have been a sunbeam sprung to life. As it had for years now, reminding himself of the danger she presented took more of an effort than Adam would like to admit.

Fire proved a worthy association for Opal, and not just because of her hair. How many times had Adam witnessed her fiercely protecting her family by trying to avoid violence? The warmth of her spirit reflected in the smile she gave readily to everyone else. Still he'd kept a distance, knowing he shouldn't notice her.

Until the day a real fire threatened to extinguish her life.

When Saul Reed raced for his house, yelling that Clara and Opal were inside the burning building, Adam didn't think twice. He didn't regret saving the girl he'd never managed to think of as his enemy, but the action still carried a heavy toll.

The feel of cradling her close as he swept Opal away from the house was seared into his memory like a brand. It served to reaffirm what he'd always suspected—Specks were trouble, but Opal was downright dangerous.

CHAPTER 4

Midge Collins drew in a deep breath for a friendly holler when she saw Opal walking down the street, only to swallow it when her friend ducked into the smithy, of all places.

Ah well. Polite young ladies don't raise their voices anyway. A rueful grin crossed her lips at the idea that Aunt Doreen's and Clara's tutelage might be rubbing off on her. Midge bore no intention of acting a stick-in-the-mud at the age of fifteen, no matter how she wanted to please the makeshift family she'd come to love.

Polite young ladies don't snoop either, she reminded herself as she slowed her pace, sidling up on the smithy. But in Midge's experience, informed women kept their eyes and ears open. She wasted no breath on gossiping, but *knowing*—now that was a different story.

Saul said knowledge made the difference between

helping and hindering, and Midge didn't respect anyone's opinion more than that of the doctor who'd saved her life just over two years before. As a matter of fact, she reckoned that God, if He existed like everyone in Buttonwood insisted He did, would understand Midge's constant status as lookout. After all, God could see and hear *everything*.

Not being so fortunate as that, Midge resorted to lingering in doorways when the need presented itself. Like when a friend who never stepped foot in the smithy marched in, wearing her favorite dress, the day after she met with Clara. Oh, it didn't take much to weasel things out of Clara, who'd confessed to watching Brett Burn's growing interest in Opal.

As though Midge hadn't noticed that *ages* ago. The one who bore watching, to her way of thinking, was that shifty Larry Grogan.

Casually peering around the door frame into the smithy, Midge spotted her friend's yellow dress, brightened by the forge's firelight, and squinted to get a better look. Sure as a sharpshooter never missed and told, Opal stood in deep conversation with Brett Burn.

Oh, she brandished a battered metal something-or-other, but if Clara's chat with Opal yesterday hadn't prompted this visit, Lucinda Grogan took tea with the queen of England every Thursday. This trip to the smithy didn't fall under the category of business, no matter if it involved some careful calculation.

Midge eased back, unwilling to be caught spying when there would be at least two other Burns around the place. Yet she lingered when she should've left—a sense she'd missed something, making her glance back into the smithy.

This time she ran her gaze over every nook and cranny until it caught on a subtle movement in the stable annex. *There. That's what I missed before.* Her smile came back full force as she took in the entire scene a second time, with the missing piece in place. Midge recognized the figure as Adam Grogan, and she followed his sight line to find out what he was gaping at.

Her eyes widened. *Oh, now* that's *interesting!*

"Ben!" Opal rushed down the church steps that Sunday, Pete and Elroy hard on her heels to greet their eldest brother. She pulled to a halt with the help of a big hug. "You're early!"

"Good to see you, sis." He tucked her to his side and pulled their brothers close. "You, too, Elroy." Ben made a show of tilting his head, overlong carroty curls spilling from under his hat as he peered at the youngest Speck. "This can't be little Pete?"

"Not so little anymore." Pete puffed up in protest, gaze sliding toward where Midge stood several yards away.

"I can see that."

"Four years makes a difference, son." Pa came up to them all with a smile broader than the sky above. "Glad to have you back home."

"Especially now." The lowered tone didn't stop Pete's whisper from carrying as more than one

Speck cast a quick glance toward the Grogans.

Or rather, where Larry and Willa stood. Opal didn't spot Lucinda or Adam nearby. Still, their fleeting looks constituted enough of a cue for Ben to follow suit.

He peered over, a frown darkening his face for the first time since Opal spied him. "That Larry Grogan stirring the pot again? We'll sort him out as needed, though I thought after his threshing accident he'd learned to settle down."

"So you *did* get my letters." Opal couldn't hold back the grumble. After all, it wouldn't have done him any serious harm to write back more often.

"Sporadically." Ben's apologetic smile turned appreciative as he continued to look toward Larry. "Who's the girl? Don't tell me old Larry's nabbed himself a pretty little wife while I was gone!"

Opal just about swallowed her tongue at the realization Ben's appreciation focused on none other than Willa Grogan. Willa had, now that she thought about it, blossomed during his absence. But in the after-church swell of greetings, folks had moved around just enough to confuse the rest of her family.

"Who? The blond?" Elroy shook his head. "Nah, that's Clara Reed—Dr. Reed's wife."

"Never bore any partiality toward blonds," Ben denied. "The brunette—looks sort of quiet but with a spark waiting to come out."

"That's Midge." Pete thrust his jaw forward. "Now, you may be my elder, but I've got an eye on that one. You can't just come waltzing in here and decide you're interested in her spark when I've been fired up about her for—"

"That's enough, Pete!" Opal stepped in before her brother worked himself into a lather over nothing. "Since when would you describe Midge as quiet anyway?"

"Well. . ." Loyalty warred with truth, and Pete settled for a shrug. "He don't know her."

"Yet." Ben dropped the word like a gauntlet, biting back an obvious grin as Pete tensed up again. "So why's she standing next to Larry?"

"Because you're not looking at Midge." Opal shot a pointed glance at Pete before laying a warning hand on Ben's arm. "The pretty brunette with the quiet air and the attachment to Larry? That's Willa Grogan."

"Willa!" Astonishment rang in four male Speck voices, setting off a chain reaction.

"She grew up nice," Ben mused amid Pa's spluttered warnings.

Elroy and Pete craned their necks and gaped as though seeing Willa for the first time in, well, about four years.

The whole tableau would have earned a roll of the eyes and a sigh from Opal at any other time, but as things stood, she swiftly separated herself from the Speck men. After the thunder of her family's joint exclamation, how could the Grogans not stir up a storm?

Sure enough, Larry's and Diggory's darkening expressions signaled trouble.

Lucinda, never one to smooth ruffled feathers,

bustled over to throw protective arms around her only daughter and glower at Ben.

Opal fixed her gaze on Adam—whose face mirrored the resignation in her own heart. "Sorry," she addressed her apology to him. "Ben didn't recognize your sister is all."

Diggory shouldered forward. "He shouldn't have been looking."

"Hold on." Ben held up his hands, palms out in the universal signal of avoiding trouble. "I meant no disrespect. It's been years, and my family needed to bring me up to speed on the new faces."

"I'm not new." Puzzled curiosity arched Willa's brows, making her eyes seem brighter than usual.

"No, Miss Grogan"—Ben swept off his hat and gave a little bow—"though I didn't recognize you alongside Mrs. Reed and some others. The years bring changes."

"So I see." Surely that wasn't *interest* tingeing Willa's agreement? A faint pink flushed her cheeks as she glanced at Ben in a way Opal would've pegged as admiration.

An admiration sure to invite adversity.

Opal bit her lip. Why, oh why couldn't Ben have noticed Amanda Dunstall? Or even Midge. As much as it would mean chaos with Pete, she'd rather deal with that than goading the Grogans!

Larry stepped in front of his sister. "Not enough changes for you to forget your place, Speck."

"My place is in Buttonwood, same as yours." Level and logical, Ben's words did nothing to soothe the situation.

"Maybe you should pick another place. I liked it better when you jaunted off for years."

"You would!" Pete's jaw pushed forward as he addressed Larry. "Ben's the better man, and you wouldn't want any comparisons."

"Don't insult Willa's brother." A swift dip of his hat accompanied Ben's words. "No need for insults. Every man stands on his own merit."

"True." His sister's agreement with his enemy pushed Larry's patience over the edge.

"You don't get to stand anywhere near her, Speck!"

"Strong words for a man who breaches boundaries, Grogan." Pa's eyes narrowed, making fear flash down Opal's spine. "Be careful who you insult."

"Some boundaries carry more weight than others." Adam's frown swept away the last of Opal's hope that further ugliness would be avoided. No matter he was right, and if his brother abided by that, they would all be fine.

"Ben's offered no offense," she reminded everyone. "Nor does he intend to."

"Keep it that way," Lucinda snapped, finding her voice when her husband showed up. "We don't want *any* offers from a Speck."

"But we'll make you one," Diggory added, quick to catch on to the problem. "Stay away from our women, and we won't try to claim anything of yours."

"Understood." Pa's jaw clenched so tight Opal couldn't see how the words got out. "And here's the last offer you'll get from the Specks, so listen and listen good. Keep your Grogan carcasses off our land, and we'll keep our bullets out of your hides. Otherwise, you'll be digging graves."

CHAPTER 5

She's dead." Larry gave voice to the obvious as Adam looked over Sadie's remains.

"Not surprising." He chose his response carefully. "She'd stayed with us longer than we could've hoped, and only stopped producing milk this spring. Not bad for an old gal." Adam patted the cow's side and stood up.

"Wasn't age that took her." Excitement colored his brother's voice now. "Look close—eyes clouded, froth at the mouth, and we both know she hadn't been eating or drinking again."

"Old cattle can get finicky." Noncommittal on the outside, Adam knew all too well what the signs most likely meant—especially given the sporadic losses they'd suffered the past two years.

"Someone poisoned her, and we both know who's to blame!" To a casual listener, Larry's accusation would ring with righteous outrage.

But Adam heard the current of satisfaction and even glee lurking beneath. He knew his brother's itch for trouble had grown to an all-out rash lately, and any pretext to attack the Specks wouldn't be overlooked.

"Assumptions won't get us anywhere." Holding up a hand when his brother tried to interrupt, Adam continued, "Sadie'd been on her last legs long before this, and there's nothing to be served by pointing fingers at our neighbors for what could be a natural death."

"It's not. You know it's not."

"You don't know anything."

Larry flushed, his scar a pale slash against the livid red of his rage. "I know this cow didn't die from old age, and I know you're trying to keep it quiet because you don't want *trouble*."

"Why do you want it so much you create it at every opportunity?" Adam thumbed his hat back. "Couldn't you focus on what's best for the family?"

"What makes you think I'm not? You stare down your nose because you won't grab a gun, but it's just fine to let enemies sneak onto our land, poison our cattle, and get away with it." The words came fast and furious. "Oh no. Big brother *Adam* will be content to wait until Benjamin Speck makes off with Willa or their old man finally settles the score with Pa for good before you get off your high horse and do something!"

"Or we can grab our guns and start a war over an old cow the Specks might not have touched, and be sure that those of us who survive will live with blood on our hands for the rest of our days." Adam jerked the rope off his saddle and flung the heavy coil at Larry's chest. "It's a short step off a steep cliff to go from a sick cow to accusing the Specks of plotting to kill us."

"True." Pa's entrance to the heated conversation took them both off guard, as Adam knew it was intended to. "Swipe the surprise off your faces, boys. An entire contingent could have snuck up while the pair of you went to war armed with nothing but hot air." He unrolled his butchering pack as he spoke. "Least you could've done was string up the carcass to make some use of the time."

"Yes sir." Larry knotted a noose around the cow's hind legs before flinging the free end of the coil over the sturdiest branch of the closest cottonwood. They joined together in hauling it upright and securing it.

No one spoke, but Adam sent up enough prayers to pepper heaven itself. *Please let Pa see reason, Lord. Don't let him seek revenge or make this feud fatal. . . .*

"So you heard Adam, but I was saying—"

"Heard your bit, too." Pa sucked his teeth as was his habit when thinking. "The thing of it is you're both wrong with a little right mixed in."

Adam held his peace—and his breath—until his father explained. It was too early to be relieved, and far too late not to be nervous about the situation.

"Which is the part I'm right about?" Larry cut straight to the crucial question, as he could be counted upon to do anytime it concerned him directly. "That the Specks poisoned our cattle?

That obviously it's the first move and the next will be worse? That we can't let them get away with it unpunished?"

About then he ran out of air, and in the pause for his next breath, Pa went ahead and answered.

"Sadie didn't die naturally, and the Specks most likely caused it." His first words brought a self-satisfied smirk to Larry's face before Pa kept on. "Assuming it's part of a grand plan to destroy our whole family would be getting ahead of ourselves, and going after any Speck without solid evidence is a plumb fool move."

Thank You, Lord. Adam felt a knot of tension ease from between his shoulder blades.

"Where's the part when Adam's wrong?" Petulance didn't suit a grown man, and Larry wore it worse than most.

"We can't let this go unanswered." Pa's answer returned the knot to Adam's back, bigger and meaner than ever. "After we butcher Sadie, tonight I'll leave her bones near the Speck place with a note."

"Next time it'll be one of theirs in return?" Glee didn't suit his brother any better as Larry volunteered to take care of things.

"That's right." Selecting a knife, Pa gave a sharp nod. A quick, clean cut to the cow's neck had the blood draining into the large bowl. "Grogans are too smart to start bloodshed." He wiped the blade on some long prairie grass as the stream slowed to a trickle. "But sure as shooting we know to finish it."

"Outnumbered again." Opal bit back a sigh and rolled up her sleeves as the men went out to work the fields, leaving her to face down the mountain of breakfast dishes. She started piling plates.

Sure, her brothers would tease her mercilessly if they heard her talking to the tableware, but they weren't around. Nobody was. *Which is the problem.* Opal scrubbed at the fragments of scrambled eggs with unwarranted vigor. *If I had someone to talk to, I wouldn't bother making the odd comment to the dishes!*

Nor the chickens while she scattered seed, or the cows when she milked every morning, or her bees when she went to the apiary. . . *All right. I'd probably still talk to my bees. But that's to be expected of any beekeeper. In fact,* Opal dried her biggest pan with a flourish, *I defy anyone to hear the welcoming hum of the hives and not want to be friendly in return!*

But maybe she'd make a point of not conversing with the cookery anymore, just to be on the safe side. Things hadn't been so hard before Pete grew old enough and big enough to help work the fields. Autumn brought the harvest, and winter snows imprisoned everyone equally, but it was spring and summer Opal came to dread. The warm months brought sunshine but stole all company and laughter. The only time she saw her family, the men bolted their food or headed for bed.

Opal returned the last dish into its place and pulled the second loaf of bread from the niche near the fireplace. The next slid in immediately afterward. Cooking for Pa, Elroy, and Pete took some doing, but with Ben home, there'd be no time to lose.

She started the stew meat, knowing dinnertime would come as swiftly as the blend of meat and vegetables simmered into a thick broth, and chopped potatoes, onions, and carrots to add in later. Opal readied the potatoes with a generous hand, as the supply held steady even after a hard winter. The carrots, by contrast, she sliced as thin as possible. Until her garden added to the larder, produce was precious.

The smell of warm yeast layered over the tinge of smoke, always managing to elude the chimney to linger in the dark confines of the soddy. No matter that Opal threw the door wide open and pushed back the curtains to their only window, light seemed swallowed by their dark earthen walls. Someday, perhaps, they'd whitewash them. . . .

For now, Opal removed the golden-brown loaf from her baking niche and popped in the final batch of bread with a smile. When this last round finished, she'd be out in the sunshine, free to visit her apiary.

Her broom made short work of sweeping the floor, still a necessary chore no matter the floor itself was hard-packed dirt. Loose dust got on—and in—absolutely everything, a constant battle from above and below when living in a soddy. Opal cast a glance at the ceiling, covered in pages torn from old catalogs she'd coaxed from Josiah Reed when his mercantile no longer needed them.

So long as the pages stayed tacked in place, dirt clods and insects didn't drop onto the table or beds. A few leafs looked to be working free of their moorings, spurring Opal to drag a chair beneath them, climb up, and affix them more firmly.

A woman needed an earthworm to fall in her hair only once in a lifetime, thank you very much. *Actually, I could have done without that even once. . . .*

Her musings ended when the bread finished. After a quick check on the progress of the stew, Opal stepped outside. Spring sunshine spilled onto fresh green grasses bright with new life.

Summer's glare heats the earth in golden browns, making the crops grow. Fire tinges autumn's rays, painting the plants for harvest. Winter nights swallow the daylight too soon, so it shines fierce, blinding white whenever it punches through the clouds. But spring. . .

"I always did like early sunshine best, Lord." She spoke the thought aloud, not bothering to stop and wonder whether it counted as prayer when she talked with God this way. It used to worry her, whether it wasn't respectful enough, but the Bible talked about even rocks crying out to Him. The Psalms, mostly David's thoughts and praises to God, was her favorite book of God's Word. Opal's words weren't washed in poetry like that king's of long ago, but she did her best to put her feelings into words.

"Spring sunbeams are the closest thing I can imagine to the breath of life. If I had to pick a color to represent hope, I'd pick the pale green of a new blade of grass in the soft light of a spring morning."

"So would I." The deep rumble of a man's voice jerked her to a halt.

"Larry?" She held her back ramrod straight against the note of fear her voice betrayed, refusing to turn and acknowledge him. *But it didn't sound like Larry. . . .*

"Adam." The muffled sound of booted steps on moist earth struck no fear in her heart. "I didn't mean to frighten you."

"You don't." Turning to face him, Opal could've kicked herself for the words. "I mean, you didn't."

"Ah." He came to a stop a respectable distance from her, one thumb hooked at the base of his suspenders. "Of course not."

Her pulse, which had slowed after the assurance Larry hadn't made good on his threats to come to the house, picked up its pace again at the half-smile on Adam's face. She frowned. "What are you doing here?" After the scene at the churchyard, the Grogans needed to stay as far away from her family as possible.

"You're not angry." His gaze seemed to take her measure, and Opal squashed the temptation to wonder whether she'd stacked up. "There's still time, then."

"For what?" Anxiety over his purpose, despite it being Adam and not Larry, began to gnaw the edges of her nerves. "And I'm not angry so much as dumbfounded that you'd be so foolish as to breach our boundary with the way things stand."

"Sometimes a little foolish behavior is the

smartest thing to do." His dark gaze met hers, drawing her into unspoken questions she couldn't answer.

"That doesn't make a lick of sense, Adam Grogan." She planted her hands on her hips. "And since you don't want to tell me what's going on, you can just scuttle back to your own farm. And stay there so none of my family feels obligated to make things any worse!"

"I'm sorry, Opal."

His apology was the first thing Adam had ever done to frighten her. Everyone knew Grogans didn't apologize.

Her eyes widened as he took a step closer and lowered his voice. "It's too late for that."

CHAPTER 6

It's too late for what, exactly?" Amazing how blue her eyes could look against the red of her hair—especially when she widened them like that.

It's too late for a lot of things. Adam blocked that line of thought before it could lead him anywhere worth regretting. He swiftly considered his options once again before arriving at the same conclusion.

When the wrath of the Specks hadn't descended upon them, Pa'd begun to stew about what devious schemes they must be hatching in retaliation for the cow skull and threat Larry left the night before. Larry's lack of concern, however, sparked a different suspicion in Adam—a suspicion confirmed when he'd run into Opal.

Larry didn't obey Pa last night and leave the "message" on the Speck doorstep. He'd done something worse, added an aspect yet to be discovered but sure to provoke fury the likes of which Pa never intended. And Pa'd slept in the room Adam usually shared with Larry to make sure Adam didn't follow Larry and interfere, ruining his initial plan.

So now Adam stared down a fork in the road likely to skewer him. Slink home without finding and fixing whatever Larry had done. . .or enlist Opal's help. That those blue eyes were wide with worry somehow made the choice easier. For as long as he'd been cooling Grogan tempers, Adam had known Opal did the same within the walls of the Speck farm.

"It's too late for me to go back now. There's something I have to do." He drew a deep breath and took a step of faith. "And I could use your help."

"How do we fix it?" Resignation added a grim set to her mouth, darkening the cornflower blue of her gaze and sending a surge of shame through Adam's chest.

We Grogans did that. She doesn't even know what the problem is this time. Just knows it needs to be fixed. And she's the one saddled with it because she's willing to keep a lid on her temper for the sake of her family.

Suddenly his irritation swung right back to the Specks for making Opal shoulder the heavy burden of peacekeeper. Didn't they know it was the man's job to protect, not the other way around? That half the task lay in keeping the weight of worry away from their women?

"Yesterday we found one of our milking cows dead, eyes cloudy, froth around her nose and mouth. Same as has been going on for the past couple of years."

"We aren't poisoning your cattle!" Fire leapt to life in her cheeks. "The Grogans aren't the only family affected by whatever's happening. We've lost three cows to the same thing!"

"Be that as it may—"

"There's no 'may be' about it, Adam Grogan." She flung an arm wide, pointing back toward his farm. "Take your accusations and your uncertainties back where you came from. I can't help you with imaginary issues."

Had he just credited her with keeping a lid on her temper? Adam shook his head and tried again. "Fine. Be that as it *is*," he stressed the word, only continuing after her grudging nod, "Pa believes otherwise."

"You want me to warn my family," Opal surmised. "Done."

"It can't be solved so easily this time." Adam let out a long breath. "Pa sent Larry with a warning of his own last night."

"What warning?" Every line of her body tensed.

"In spite of my best efforts, he sent my brother to put the skull in front of your house with a note inside."

"He'd dare breach the boundary again?" The angry red in her cheeks ebbed, drained by fear. "In bad blood?"

"When your family didn't respond, Pa decided you're all hatching a plot." One look at Opal's face right now would've convinced him otherwise, but Adam didn't have that luxury. "I figure Larry didn't follow orders exactly."

"They're going to kill each other." The realization robbed even her voice of its power, leaving nothing but a whisper.

"Not if I can find his message first." Adam reached a hand toward her shoulder to steady her, but she jerked back.

"Oh, we'll find it." Determination returned the strength to her words. "What do you think your brother planned?"

"Impossible to know for sure, but whatever he thinks would rile your family the most." Adam rubbed the back of his neck. "I thought maybe he'd put the skull in the barn, near your cattle, but it's not there."

"I would've found it when I did the milking," Opal agreed. "Perhaps he unearthed some sense and put it near your boundary line, where a warning would do good to someone about to trespass?"

"Checked there before I came over," he admitted. "Not that I held out any hope."

"Not near the house or the barn, nor the yard. I already slopped the hogs and gathered eggs, so I would've seen it."

"What would be the worst thing he could threaten?" Here's what kept tripping Adam up. The worst aspect of Pa's plan was to threaten the home— Opal's domain. By coming close to her, the move would have been unignorable. Because anyone with a lick of sense could see that Opal was—

Gone?

He watched for a moment as she hightailed it, hiking up her skirts enough to show trim ankles encased in her work boots as she practically flew over the ground. His reflexes kicked in a moment later, and he raced to catch up. Somewhere in the back of his mind he hoped none of the Speck men saw him chasing full tilt after Opal.

So why did he want nothing more than to catch her?

Please, no. Oh Lord, please. Opal prayed as she sprinted for her apiary. *Don't let Larry have done anything to my bees!*

She burst through the small grove of cottonwoods to the clearing housing her apiary and skidded to a halt. A swift scan showed nothing wrong. Rows of white frame hives, raised above the ground, stretched before her. No acrid tinge of smoke, no angry drone of outrage greeted her ears, no swarms blanketed the air above.

More importantly, though, was what she could hear. The happy hum of busy workers shimmered in the wind, the same welcome she'd received for years. *Mama's legacy is safe.*

"Bees?" Adam stood beside her, the only unfamiliar element in the tiny world she'd overseen since childhood. "I hadn't thought of Larry putting the message anywhere your brothers or father wouldn't find it first."

"Perhaps that's the point. He knows I wouldn't show them, and your Pa would grapple with the lack of response." She moved among the hives as she spoke, checking to ensure no damage had been done that she couldn't see from far away. Now that she'd calmed, she acknowledged the only thing Larry would've done to destroy the apiary—set it ablaze—would have been detected long ago. Larry didn't know enough about bees to do anything else.

And making the mistakes of his grandfather should be too foolhardy for the greatest of numskulls. But what better to reignite a generations-old feud than fire the rage of such memories?

"Then why bring it at all?" Frustration sounded in Adam's deep voice—far closer than she anticipated. He'd followed her among the hives.

He's not afraid of the bees. Opal kept her face turned so he wouldn't see her surprise. Since his grandfather died of a bee sting, the feud had started in earnest. *I thought all Grogans were leery of bees— yet another reason a coward like Larry wouldn't set fire to the hives. He wouldn't risk an angry swarm.* The thought comforted her.

"There." Opal spotted the off-white of the fresh skull, not yet bleached by the elements, resting by the hive closest to Grogan property. *Surprising, Larry came this close.*

"Larry's afraid of bees." Adam didn't bother to hide his astonishment as he picked up the thing. Beneath it lay a curled up strip of parchment.

Opal snatched it before he had a chance and didn't let him get out the protest she could see forming. "I need to know what it says so we can decide what to tell my family. Letting your father stew will just make things worse."

In large, easily legible script, the note read:

NEXT TIME WE LOSE A COW, WE TAKE A SPECK IN PAYMENT.

Opal choked back her rage, narrowing her eyes to make out the addition beneath it.

In underlined, slashing strokes, someone had added a second sentence.

And I got my eye on your only heifer!

She crushed the thin leather in her hand, vowing to burn it before any of her family ever laid eyes on it. Larry knew she'd never show it to them, all right.

"There's nothing I can say to apologize for this." Adam stood as though braced for her anger, hands behind his back. "I heard what Pa planned to write and never wanted you to see it."

"Thank you for warning me." Opal kept a death grip on the message. "I'll tell Pa about your cow and that your pa says the next death will be the end of any peace."

"Larry's trying to end it long before then." Adam peered at her, but for the first time Opal couldn't bring herself to meet his gaze. "I'm still not sure why he put it here."

"To show he wasn't afraid of anything...not even the bees?" The suggestion didn't sound convincing, but it was the best she could do at the moment. The knowledge of Larry's perfidy, the extent he'd go to in an effort to show her he'd accept no rejection, stole her wits. *If he'd put this message near the house and Pa saw it...* She thought she might be sick.

"Opal?" Did she hear concern in Adam's voice? "What is it?"

"Nothing." But she answered too quickly— Opal knew it as soon as his dark eyes narrowed.

He gave her a long, searching look she forced herself to meet even while she tried to slip the evil note into her pocket. "Oh no, you don't." Adam snagged her wrist, the sudden warmth spreading up her arm making her gasp.

The moment of hesitation cost her dearly as his other hand cupped her balled fist, coaxing her fingers open. She resisted, knowing she made no match for his strength but refusing to give an inch.

"What did he write?" He stood there, his hand grasping hers, not pulling or forcing anything, the warmth of his hold matching the concern on his features. "Larry added something to the message, didn't he?"

She felt herself give the barest hint of a nod before she could guard against him. Opal lifted her chin. "Not that it matters."

"Yes, it does." His already-square jaw hardened. "Give it to me."

"No." The order restored her as nothing else could, making her tug her wrist. To her surprise, she slid from his grasp easily.

Not stopping to consider the differences between Adam and his brother, Opal took the opportunity to shove the note deep into her apron pocket. "I think it's best if you go home now. Tell your father you made sure we'd gotten the message. I'll take care of the rest."

At his nod, she turned to make her way back to the house, where her cook fire could consume the evidence of this morning. *If only it could take away the memory.*

The sigh she bit back turned into a stifled scream as a strong arm snaked around her waist.

CHAPTER 7

I'll deal with the guilt later, Adam promised himself as he refused to let go. While Opal squawked and thrashed—managing to kick him in the shin and elbow him in the gut—he plucked the note from her apron pocket. He'd already started to let go by the time she smashed the back of her head into his chin, sending pain streaking up his jaw.

I deserved that, he reminded himself.

"You deserved that!" The echo sounded suspiciously feminine, an idea confirmed when Opal added, "Stop wincing those big brown eyes of yours and give that back!"

"Big brown eyes?" Affronted enough to speak in spite of his jaw, Adam hoisted the note out of her reach. He'd never been so glad of his height as now, when the little firebrand hopped and still missed her goal by a solid two inches. "What am I, a cow?"

"I can think of less flattering comparisons, if

you like." Her mutter wrangled a chuckle out of him as she abandoned the indignity of hopping and crossed her arms.

The chuckle died a swift death as he read Larry's addition to Pa's already awful statement. And reread it. Twice. "I'll kill him."

"Haven't there been enough death threats?" A glint of humor peeked behind the weariness underscoring Opal's words.

It only fueled his rage, making his stomach churn in a sour frenzy as he looked at the woman before him. This brave woman his brother threatened to kill. This woman who, by protecting her family, also protected Larry from the consequences of his actions.

The crunching pop of his knuckles told him he'd balled his hands into fists. "Only a coward threatens a woman." *And I wondered why Larry put it by the apiary. I should have known. If he breaks down Opal, scares her badly enough, he'll get the fight he wants.*

"Don't bait me, Grogan." Opal tilted her head. "We're both trying to avoid conflict, so don't make it easy to speak my mind about your brother."

"Who says there'd be conflict?" His growl did nothing to vent his ire. "Just about now we're probably a matched set."

"You can never be sure." Caution replaced humor. "But if you go against Larry, the blame lands right back on me."

"That's not..." Try as he might, he couldn't find a way to finish his denial.

"True?" She gave an exasperated huff as she

tried to finish his sentence. "You know they'll say I turned you against him. Or were you going to say 'fair'? What about this feud is fair? Or even sane?"

"I don't like it." Larry deserved the walloping of a lifetime, and Adam itched to deliver it.

"Huh." Opal raised a brow. "Not that anyone asked, or that it's for me to say, but I always figured you were the Grogan who put aside what he wanted for the good of the family."

Her assessment caught him off guard, leaving him silent for a long moment. "So that's what you think?" *And what does it mean to you, Opal Speck? That I'm a pushover or that I'm the better man?*

"Yep." She didn't give him another word on the subject.

"Maybe I think you're the same way."

"I should've known we'd come full circle." Opal rolled her eyes, but a small grin played around her lips. "So now that you've gotten back to your 'may be's,' you better get home."

"Yep." He didn't let his own smile free until she turned and started walking away. And still, he watched her go until she stopped and looked over her shoulder.

"And, Adam?"

"What, Opal?"

"Never come back." With that, she disappeared into the trees.

"Stay away from her." Adam's harsh growl raised the hairs on the back of Lucinda Grogan's neck.

THE BRIDE BACKFIRE

Who? She lifted her hand from the door but shuffled a few inches closer—the better to hear her sons' conversation. The glower on her eldest son's face when he'd stormed past the house moments earlier didn't bode well.

"Who?" Larry's slightly nasal tones seeped through the door frame. "And why should I?"

Don't antagonize your brother. Lucinda swallowed the admonishment. Her middle son sounded defensive, which meant Larry already had a fair idea what—no, make that who—Adam warned him against. *Not good. And it's a woman. The only way this could possibly get any worse would be if Adam named—*

"Opal Speck."

The terse syllables hammered at Lucinda's temples. *No, no, no. . .* She rested her forehead against the door, mind too full of dire possibilities to hold upright anymore. The drag of dismay cost her Larry's response, but years of raising him left her with more than headaches. Lucinda knew her son well enough to guess he'd denied or evaded the blunt confrontation.

"Don't try to sidestep this." Dark determination emphasized Adam's warning. Never before had he sounded so filled with scarcely contained rage.

Lucinda wondered whether Larry would be wise enough to realize it and drop whatever game he played this time. *Probably not.* Which meant she'd need to corner him once Adam finished.

"You've got us mixed up, Adam. *I'm* not the Grogan who avoids issues or ignores things. That's your domain."

Fool! Lucinda gritted her teeth. If it weren't for Adam's level head, she'd have lost her husband or the fool running his mouth right now a hundred times over.

"No Larry." Booted steps crossed the room. "*You're* the shame to our family name."

Her hand closed around the doorknob before Lucinda caught herself. No matter Larry's flaws, Adam hadn't earned the right to denounce him on behalf of the family. Especially not after she'd almost lost her middle son to that terrible accident two years ago. *Am I the only one who remembers how blessed we are to still have him?*

"Because I'd rather claim an angry bison than a coward who threatens a woman." Fury seethed through Adam's words, scalding away Lucinda's indignation.

Larry threatened Opal? The bite of shame galled her. *Well, she must have done something to provoke him! What did that vile little Speck gal do this time?*

"Cowards wait and do nothing. I'm a man of action."

"Leaving a death threat aimed at the only female in the Speck family? Making sure she'd be the one to find it, when she's alone? That's the action you're so proud of?" A muffled popping tattled of knuckles being cracked.

Adam's mistaken. Larry hates the Specks for his accident but wouldn't target Opal. Lucinda tried to swallow but found her mouth too dry. *I raised gentlemen! Please, Lord. Let me have that much.*

"I don't know what you're talking about." Fear turned Larry into the coward Adam called him.

"When nothing happened, I figured you didn't follow the plan. I went over there and ran into Opal. We found the message. If I hadn't read what you wrote on the bottom myself, I wouldn't have believed it."

"Then you know it only said I have my eye on her." The whine destroyed Lucinda's last hope.

"Don't even think about it. And know that the only reason you're still standing is she spoke up against me giving you the walloping you so richly deserve—didn't want things to get any worse."

"No need to get your nose out of joint, Adam. She's grown into a fine woman, and there's nothing wrong with me making a claim—" The sick thud of fist on flesh punctuated Larry's mutter before his groan filled the air.

Stomach churning, Lucinda couldn't be sure what sickened her more, that Larry lusted after Opal Speck, that her son would be so vulgar—even though it was just to bait Adam, she was certain—or that her sons were fighting each other.

"If I catch you so much as looking her way, I'll truss you up and deliver you to her pa myself."

Oh no you won't, Adam Neil Grogan! Lucinda took a shallow breath. *It won't come to that.* Because no matter how awful things were, one truth stood above everything else. . . .

Opal Speck is the one to blame, and she'll be the one to pay. I'll make sure of that!

"I won't allow it." Adam stared at the broken stretch of fence Larry should have mended last week, at the imprints in the softening spring earth, and resisted the urge to throw his hat on the ground.

After all he'd done to keep the peace this week, one wandering dairy cow could destroy them. When Willa confided to him that Marla didn't show up for milking, he assumed she'd gotten lost, maybe stuck in a mud hole. Instead, the oblivious animal ambled right into Speck territory!

Which left him precious few options, and not a single one of them any he'd jump at. Going after the beast constituted trespassing—right on the heels of threats flying thick.

Memories of the day the Speck men came on Grogan land pushed to the front of his memory. *Fences and family—best keep an eye on both of yours, isn't that what Speck warned?* Adam surveyed the ruined fence, fingered the threat still in his pocket, and knew he'd failed on both counts.

"Never come back." Opal's advice from the day before echoed in his thoughts, making the decision simple. Sure, she'd said to stay away, but losing Marla paved the way for Larry to accuse the Specks of thievery. Which made as good a pretext as any to come after Opal.

"I won't allow it," he repeated, following Marla's tracks until they petered out in the growing grass. An hour later, he'd searched every boundary line, forced to admit he needed to go deeper.

Another hour slipped away under the strain of fruitless searching while trying to find cover where none existed. Typically, Adam loved the rolling flatlands of the prairie, but today he'd trade his back teeth for a forest.

He'd have to check the homestead. The sun scaled the sky, inching toward noon—and dinnertime. Ma's sharp eyes wouldn't miss his absence, but more pressing stood the knowledge that the Speck men would soon converge near the place he suspected he'd find Marla.

Hours overdue for milking and feeding, she still hadn't gravitated toward home. Lately, it seemed the worst possibility proved reality, so he'd believe the contrary cow might have headed for the familiar sounds and scents of another barn. He could no longer avoid entering the hub of the Speck farm.

Adam moved stealthily closer to the barn until he pressed against its side. He edged to the corner and peered in the direction of the house, scanning for Specks on the horizon. The thought drew a grin until something moved by the well.

Opal. Stepping out of the house to fetch some water, she hadn't bothered with the bonnet usually shielding her from the sun. Now its rays played upon the burnished red of her hair, adding glints of gold with joyous abandon until she seemed a living flame. No wonder the sun thrilled to claim her.

"Drop the gun and keep quiet." A firm prod with the blunt end of a shotgun punctuated the hissed order. "Opal shouldn't be involved if Pa decides to kill you."

CHAPTER 8

A vague sense of unease, which Opal firmly told herself she should ignore, stalked her all morning long. No matter how many times she vowed Larry's threat the day before wouldn't affect her, she couldn't shake it. The hollowness in her stomach, the knot between her shoulder blades no amount of stretching could relieve, the heaviness of the air itself—none of it abandoned her until noon.

At that point panic wrapped around her, squeezing away any hollowness and leaving no room for pesky knots. Opal struggled against its tightening grip, searching for something, anything, to explain the inexplicable.

The men hadn't answered the dinner bell.

She rang it twice, racking her brain as she hurried toward the west field where Pa worked today, but no reason presented itself. Pa and her brothers never missed a meal. Pete grew so quick he couldn't spoon food into his face fast enough to fill out, so he most often beat her to the bell.

The only consolations she came up with were that God stayed with them, and that if anyone got hurt they'd have fetched her along with Dr. Reed. Cold comfort, considering the way things stood with the Grogans.

The thought added caution to her steps, making her duck behind the tall windrows of last season's corn waiting to be burnt. Only afterward could the next crop be planted free of any chance of the corn borer.

Clashing male voices revealed their location long before she spotted them. A swift glance showed five men at the far end of the field. *Wait. Five?* Opal crept closer. Pa, Ben, and Elroy stood in a semicircle facing Pete and... *Cursed Grogan stupidity!*

She didn't stop to consider whether her prayers for everyone's safety—even the trespasser's—nullified the previous thought. Keeping everybody in one piece mattered too much to get picky about how it got done. Then she caught a glimpse of the Grogan male's profile.

"Adam?" If anyone asked how she got from behind the windrow to the middle of the thick cluster of men, Opal wouldn't have been able to explain. One moment, she'd recognized the man Pete held a shotgun to, and the next, she stood beside him. Fast and foolish as that.

"Opal!" Five voices ranged in depth but matched in consternation made an alarmed chorus before orders came pouring in.

"Get away from him!" Pa wrapped his hand around her elbow and yanked her away.

"What do you think you're doing?" This from Elroy, who tried to step in front of her.

"Stop it!" She wriggled back to the front line by dint of sharp elbows and the tone she used to bully them into washing up before dinner. "Put your guns down and tell me what's going on this instant!"

"You shouldn't be here." Of all people, Adam held the least authority. Which made his statement all the more powerful.

"Even Grogan knows that you should go home, Opal." Ben's gaze bore a steely glint. "This is man's business."

"I'm a Speck. My family, my home, my business, too." She crossed her arms. "Have you taken leave of your senses, Pete? This is Adam, not Larry!"

"Oh, I know it." Pete's brows met in the middle, giving him the look of an angry buzzard. "I'm the one who caught him."

"What are you doing here, Adam?" *After I told you never to come back!* Opal kept the reminder to herself, knowing better than to bring up too many questions about their adventure the day before.

"We lost another cow. Looks like she got through a weak spot in our fence." Misery and resignation marched across his features. "Since we lost Sadie, we can't afford to let this one go."

"You hear that?" Ben burst in. "Lost another cow, he says. After their 'warning' from before. Search him, Pete."

Adam stood stock-still while her youngest brother

patted him down, grimacing when Pete reached into his coat pocket.

Pete drew something out, glanced down, and froze. Livid marks mottled his skin. His mouth moved, but no sound escaped as he passed his find to Pa.

The message. Opal couldn't even close her eyes against the horror of it, bound by some morbid need to watch her father's reaction to the words. She saw his eyes narrow, a muscle in his jaw twitch when he reached Larry's addition.

"Despite your trespassing and your family's threats, I'd been leaning toward something non-fatal." Her father gave a bark that could have been laughter but raised the hairs on the back of her neck. "More fool, me, to think any Grogan deserved to live."

"What's it say?" Elroy accepted it when Pa thrust it his way, reading aloud for Ben's benefit. " 'Next time we lose a cow, we take a Speck in payment. And I got my eye on your only heifer!' Our only. . ." Disbelief gave way to outrage. "Opal? You came after Opal?"

"No!" Adam shook his head. "I came to find the cow so we would avoid this."

"Then why were you by the house?" Pete's voice cracked. "I found you staring at her while she got water."

"Why would you be looking at me?" Stunned, Opal turned to Adam.

"Why does any man stare at a woman?" Elroy narrowed his eyes. "He liked what he saw."

71

"Don't be ridiculous." *As though a man like Adam would look twice at someone like me!* "This is your reason for brandishing shotguns at him? He probably was waiting for me to leave so he could find his cow."

"The man wasn't looking for a cow. He gawked at you like I'd look at Midge if nobody was watching." Red crept up Pete's ears, but he thrust out his jaw to make up for it. "Only I wouldn't look like I lost half my brains."

"Stop pretending to know what other people think, Pete." Opal refused to so much as glance at Adam for fear she'd get distracted wondering what ran through their prisoner's head. "Adam does not look at me like. . .that."

"Like a man?" Ben supplied. "He is one, ain't he?"

"No!" She realized her mistake when Adam gave a sort of growl, making Pete bash him in the skull and Pa push in front of her again.

Someday she'd wonder over his ability to take offense at something so paltry when he seemed indifferent to facing death, but for now she didn't have time to dwell on it. "Adam doesn't. . .I mean, he's"—she huffed as she shoved back into the thick of things—"a Grogan!"

"But still a man. Who ogled my daughter." Pa's tone brooked no argument. "And even though we only got half the message, he obviously planned what that note said."

"I'm sure there's another explanation." Opal swallowed.

"It's too late for excuses." Ben cocked his gun.

"He doesn't leave this property alive."

"But he has to!" Opal looked at the hardened expressions of the men she loved and knew her words fell on fallow ground. "It's murder!"

"Every man has a God-given right to protect his family," Pa informed her. "If Pete hadn't shown up early for dinner. . ." His left eye twitched. "Grogan set his course when he trespassed. He knew what he risked."

Adam stood utterly still, apparently accepting his fate.

Well, I don't accept it. Not Adam. She couldn't give up after all he'd done. "He saved my life two years ago. I owe him."

"You helped save Larry's." Elroy rejected her reasoning on behalf of the entire family, earning a glare that should have left him a pile of ash.

"Dr. Reed saved Larry, but Adam pulled me from that fire." She tried to appeal to their masculine integrity. "Consider it a debt of honor."

"Your honor—and safety—is exactly why I can't let him walk away." Pa wouldn't look at her. "There's nothing in the world that can save him now."

"You kill him, and the Grogans will come for us all." Opal threw herself to her knees before her father. "There'll be more death. Don't do this!"

"If we don't, they'll strike again." Elroy hauled her to her feet. "Run on home, Opal. You shouldn't see this."

"I'm not leaving until you listen to me!" Tears pricked her eyes. For Adam, the only Grogan man she'd call innocent. For her family, who'd turn themselves into killers. Over her. *I'm not worth it! How can I change their minds, Lord?*

And suddenly she saw the way to save Adam's life. . .if her strength held. Opal felt her tears burst free, washing away any ties to her past.

To save them, I have to betray us all.

Caught gaping like a schoolboy with a crush, Adam had no choice but to let himself be taken to the field where the remainder of the Speck men worked. Only then did he know the identity of his captor—Pete, the lanky boy he'd least concerned himself with.

"What on earth?" Murphy spotted them before his sons, though they followed hard on his heels. "I'd pegged you as the Grogan with half a brain, boy."

"Adam?" Elroy's eyes widened before he lowered his hat brim to hide his surprise. "I could've sworn we spoke with you about your brother trespassing and warned what would happen the next time."

"You did." His only chance lay in appeasing the men his family'd threatened the day before.

"Wait." Ben held up his gun. "Pete, where'd you find him?"

"Skulking behind the barn. I—"

"Adam?" Opal's cry interrupted whatever the youngest Speck meant to say as she rushed into the middle of everything.

Instead of taking advantage of the Specks' distraction to seize the nearest shotgun, Adam joined them in protesting her arrival. Some part of his mind registered that she wore a dress of pale green—the color of hope. It was then he began to wonder whether he had lost whatever sense God gave him.

If I lost it, Opal didn't find it, he fumed as Opal resisted her family's efforts to tuck her behind them and out of harm's way. *Doesn't she know Larry, for one, would've snatched her as a hostage right off the bat?* The woman needed a keeper.

He added his opinion to her family's bluster. "You shouldn't be here." It didn't take much to see she didn't see the value of the comment, but at least the other men backed him up. Adam wouldn't turn down any goodwill at this point.

Opal, of course, didn't budge. If anything, her indignation over his treatment grew. "This is Adam, not Larry!"

Nice to know she appreciates the difference.

His explanation as to why he'd ventured onto their land wasn't met with approval. Though, in light of the message Opal had passed along yesterday, he didn't expect it to be. Another troublesome cow seemed unbelievable.

"Search him." Ben's order made Adam's blood run cold.

Uncertain whether he'd need to show Larry's addendum to Pa at some point, he hadn't burnt the message. Hiding it hadn't seemed prudent, so the incriminating thing sat like a firecracker in his coat pocket. The moment Pete drew it out, Adam knew he might as well have been carrying around his own death warrant.

Opal's reaction told him the instant she recognized what her brother held. All color fled her face, eyes huge and dark against the ice-white of her skin. Her stricken gaze skipped over him to fix on her father's fury as he absorbed its meaning.

Lord, protect my family when this is over. Adam closed his eyes, knowing no words would save him. *Protect Opal from the bloodshed to come. Don't let her bear guilt for what's not her fault.*

Elroy read the blasted thing aloud, disbelieving even in his anger. "You came after Opal?"

"No!" Adam willed her to look at him, to never doubt he intended her any harm. "I came to find our cow so we could avoid all this."

Her slight nod took a weight from him he hadn't known existed. Then her fool of a brother burst out with the news he'd caught Adam staring at his sister.

Now he avoided Opal's glance as she asked why in favor of glowering at Pete. He had nothing left to lose, after all. *You couldn't have just shot me and left it at that?*

"Why does any man stare at a woman?" The disbelief had left Elroy's voice. "He likes what he sees."

"Don't be ridiculous." Opal's scoff sounded genuine.

Wait. Why would that be ridiculous? Adam opened his mouth and shut it again as she said something about his waiting for her to leave so he could find his cow. Not that he believed he'd be getting out of this one, but he wouldn't get in the way of her efforts.

Pete did a fine job of that, for him, as he accused

Adam of gawking—and looking brainless while doing it. Yep, the youngest Speck was starting to make dying at peace a real challenge.

Opal, for her part, still protested that Adam didn't look at her like a man looked at a woman, ending Ben's patience.

"He's a man, ain't he?"

"No!"

A growl burst from Adam's throat before he could stop it. Of all the blows that day, this hit the hardest. Worse even than the smash of the butt of Pete's shotgun against his skull in response to his outburst.

Disoriented, it took everything he had to remain on his feet. Feminine protests broke against male pride, and Adam knew it wouldn't be long before he met his Maker. The fog cleared to a vicious throbbing that must have affected his hearing. How else to explain what Opal was saying?

"What?" Four other men exploded with the question he would have asked if his vocal chords cooperated.

Tears poured down Opal's cheeks. She stared at him, imploring him to understand the impossible as she repeated, "You can't kill the man who's going to be the father of my child."

CHAPTER 9

She's overset—doesn't know what she's saying." Elroy grasped at straws to excuse her declaration.

"I know full well what I'm saying!" Opal also knew full well her face turned bright enough to rival a raspberry. Adam didn't say a word, which showed she'd been right about him catching on quickly. If he'd acted surprised, the jig would be up. Instead...

"You die now, Grogan." Pa shoved the barrel of his shotgun in Adam's gut. "Opal, you should've told me the day this filth laid a hand on you. Don't worry about a thing. We'll take care of everything."

"No!" Opal thrust herself between Pa and Adam, dislodging the gun. "How can you take care of it?"

"He took advantage of you, we take his life." Ben tried to pry her away, murder in his eyes. "It's not your fault he forced you."

"Adam would never force a woman!" Indignation

on his behalf filled her. "Apologize right now!"

"You—" Pa grappled before abandoning the words. "Willingly?" Disbelief mingled with hope, making Opal realize her father loved her so much he'd rather she betray him with his enemy's son than suffer what he feared.

A fresh wave of tears shook her. "I swear to you he never forced me." She couldn't stand to think what her brothers thought of her now. "Adam wouldn't hurt a woman."

"*That's* true." The emphasis Adam placed on the first word made Opal wince.

"We should still kill you"—Elroy practically shook with the force of his emotion—"for showing disrespect to our sister. Opal deserves better."

"Absolutely." Adam's swift agreement took the wind from her brother's sails for a moment, making Opal wonder.

Does he mean I deserve respect, or is he saying I deserve someone other than him because he doesn't want me—even if it spares his life? Sorrow swamped her at the idea.

"You're sure?" Pa stared at her midriff. "You're going to make him a father?"

"God willing." Opal prayed for forgiveness. She knew where this would lead—and that if she bore children, Adam would be their father. In the strictest sense, she hadn't told a lie. Deliberately misleading her father was more than enough to haunt her. "I'm so sorry, Pa."

"Too late for sorrys." Elroy's mutter sliced through her heart. "What are we gonna do now?"

"Ain't it obvious?" Pa didn't so much as glance at her. "Get the preacher."

"You can't be serious." Midge, realizing her mouth hung open, snapped it shut. Though, come to think of it, she'd never seen Peter Speck look so solemn.

"Pa sent me to fetch the preacher and a witness." He shoved his hands in his pockets, as though bracing for a blow.

"Opal said she's carrying Adam Grogan's babe, and your Pa's got a shotgun trained on him while you bring the preacher?" She wanted to be sure she had the facts right. "*Opal?*"

"You comin' or not?" The ferocity of his question convinced her as nothing else could. Pete nursed a crush on her, so Midge knew it would take a lot for him to bark at her.

"Let me get Clara and Saul." Something didn't add up here, and maybe her adoptive parents could sort it out before someone ended up dead. Or worse—married.

"No." His hand closed around her arm. "I'll hogtie you and drag you back with me before you get another soul involved. Only reason Grogan still breathes is so Opal won't be ruined. Got it?"

"Yep." Bumps prickled along her skin in spite of the warmth of the day. *When did Pete Speck get so forceful?* They walked in silence to the parson's house.

"Pa needs you, Parson Carter." Pete didn't offer any explanations, and Midge didn't add to what he said.

Honestly, what would she say? *Pete tells me Opal says she's carrying Adam Grogan's child and you're needed for a shotgun wedding. I know it sounds crazy, but the whole thing just might be real, because I've seen the way Adam looks at her when he thinks no one notices. If she had any other last name, I figure they'd already be hitched. . . .*

Actually, that'd probably do, in a pinch. But Parson Carter's wife might be around to overhear, and Pete had a point about Opal's reputation. So Midge kept her tongue between her teeth while the preacher brought out his Bible and they headed for the farm.

"What's this all about?" Parson Carter's share of courage didn't rank high under the best of circumstances. "Nothing to do with the Grogans, I hope?" He'd practically created a second career of avoiding the confrontations between the two families.

Midge, for one, could have mustered a heap more respect for him as a spiritual leader if he'd shown more—well, spirit! As it stood, she didn't see much to recommend his faith as having much practical use. Except that people listened to him because he was the pastor. *That would come in handy.*

Pete's grunt didn't reassure their companion any, but from the way he kept looking at her, Midge figured the parson took comfort from her presence. She even understood his line of thinking: If there was blood to be shed or wrongdoing to forgive, Pete wouldn't be bringing her along.

No one would come within ten acres of guessing

the truth behind their visit today. When news leaked out, folks would buzz around Buttonwood like vultures around a fallen bison. They'd pick the bones of the story until they had nothing left but sore beaks.

And for once, Lucinda Grogan wouldn't be in the thick of the gossip. Midge wondered how the old buzzard would like being on the rough end of things. The thought shouldn't make her smile, but it did. *I'll take my silver linings where I can find them!*

They reached the end of a windrow, and suddenly, Midge spotted Opal. She sat apart from everyone else—away from where her father held a gun on Adam. She didn't look up as they approached, but Midge could make out the trails from tears on her friend's face. Her smile vanished.

Ignoring the men, she hurried to Opal's side. Let the Specks explain things to the parson—she'd come for Opal. Midge sank to her knees, enfolding her friend in a hug before she spoke a single word. Not until Opal returned the embrace did she shift back enough to look at her. "So it's true?" Midge let no censure creep into her voice. Not a difficult thing, really, when she felt none.

"Oh Midge." More tears accompanied Opal's broken whisper. "I've made a terrible mistake!"

"Everybody makes mistakes."

"Not like this. Pa's disowning me. My brothers won't even look at me. They think—" Opal gave a hard swallow. "They all think I'm a hussy."

"Don't say that!" The very word brought back memories Midge couldn't afford. *Not now.* "Give them time to be angry. For now, Adam is the one who matters."

"He's a good man." A sniff, then a garbled, "Deserves better than to be forced into marrying me, but I don't see another way!"

"Hush!" Midge fought back the urge to go smack Adam Grogan. The fool hadn't made it clear he *wanted* to marry Opal? "He's a lucky man, and this is what's best for everybody involved."

"You're right." Opal accepted her handkerchief and mopped her face. The tip of her nose glowed a red rivaled only by her bloodshot eyes. "How do I look?"

"Erm. . ." Midge spotted some squirrel corn a few yards away. "You need a bouquet!" Ignoring the restless movements of the men, she made the short trip, plucked the fragrant flowers, and made an arrangement.

"It's lovely." Opal fingered the heart-shaped blossoms, pure white against the lacy green of the leaves Midge tucked in. "Thank you."

"All right." Midge tucked Opal's free hand into the crook of her arm and walked her over to where the men waited. "The bride is ready."

"Is the groom?" Parson Carter fiddled with his collar.

"He better be." Mr. Speck hefted his shotgun high.

"Then maybe you oughta untie him." The wedding would be memorable, but Midge tried to soften it a little. She hoped Opal didn't notice that Adam looked about as miserable as a man possibly could.

Without a word, Pete flicked open his pocket-knife and did the honors before stepping back. Midge put Opal's hand in Adam's freed ones and joined Pete at a distance.

In what had to be the quickest wedding on earth, the preacher hurried through the part where he asked if anyone had a reason why the couple shouldn't be joined in matrimony. All the same, it seemed ages before he finished.

But, finally, they heard the words, "Then I pronounce you man and wife. What God has put together, let no man"—the preacher paused to glower at the Specks until they lowered their shotguns—"tear asunder."

For a moment, all was silence and peace while everyone let loose the breaths they'd been holding. Midge just started to think they might all make it through this when the groom opened his mouth and spoke for the first time since pledging, "I do."

Determination lit Adam's gaze as he pulled Opal close, ignoring the Specks. "Don't I get to kiss my bride?"

CHAPTER 10

Adam heard various shouts as he swept Opal into his arms but didn't care. If they shot him, they shot him. He was done standing around waiting for them to do it.

He'd gotten called out for gaping at Opal. Accepted that Larry's note would get him killed. Withstood Opal announcing to her family he wasn't a man, gotten bashed in the noggin for taking exception to the same, and not called her out on her grand deception to pass off another man's bastard as his.

He'd held her hand, looked into blue eyes awash with tears, seen the pathetic clump of flowers she gripped as though they could save her from being his bride. All told, it was more than enough to make a man reckless.

She didn't resist as he pulled her close. Her eyes widened when he lowered his head to hers, pressed his mouth against lips swollen from crying. Opal went still before melting against him, warm and soft and everything a woman should be.

Everything she's already been to another man.

He ended it, withdrawing so abruptly she almost lost her balance. The bewilderment and wonder on her features could have fooled him into thinking he'd given Opal her first kiss, but given the circumstances, Adam knew better.

Who? The question sank its teeth into him the moment he realized what she'd done and didn't let go as Parson Carter took Midge back to town. *Whose child does Opal carry? Whose child will I raise as my own?*

Because that, of course, was what he'd do. Their hasty marriage couldn't be annulled without physical evidence of nonconsummation. And if he denounced her as a liar, his family would seek vengeance. Their families would battle until blood flowed on both sides.

No, he'd continue the pretense she'd begun. Opal must have seen today as a God-given opportunity, knowing he'd take her as his wife in exchange for his life.

"I always figured you were the Grogan who put aside what he wanted for the good of the family." Oh yes. She'd known he'd marry her and keep her secret, too.

But why hadn't she wed her lover? Adam would find out everything from the woman he'd spend his life with. *She'll learn the meaning of what it is to honor her husband straightaway. There will be no lies between us.*

They didn't exchange a word as everyone walked to the Speck soddy. He waited outside while Opal went in to gather her things. It took only moments for his new wife to emerge with a satchel holding her worldly goods.

"I don't know when I'll be back." Her words sounded dry, as though she'd exhausted all her crying.

"You won't be." The first words Adam spoke to his bride, and they made her shudder.

"He's right." Her father jerked a thumb toward him. "You're a Grogan now. You belong with them."

"Pa!" Opal reeled back at his words as though she'd been slapped. "You're my family!"

"Not anymore." He didn't look at her as he walked into the house. "Don't forget to move your apiary. No one here will tend it for you. Consider it and all that goes with it your dowry."

Sobs wracked her as she grabbed each of her brothers for a hug when they walked past. "I love you all more than you know."

Each gave her a fierce embrace in return.

"Good-bye, Opal." Ben shut the door behind him, and it was done.

She turned and walked in the direction of the Grogan boundary, making it out of sight of the house before she collapsed. Huddled on the ground, clasping her knees to her chest, with her bag and cloak strewn beside her, Opal made the very picture of desolation.

Adam hunkered down beside her to wait it out. He extended a hand to pat her shoulder, but her flinch made him end the contact immediately. "You were right when you said I wouldn't hurt a woman, Opal."

"I know." Her answer came out muffled. "But you could do worse."

"Your secret is safe with me."

"Promise?" She peered up at him, wary and hopeful. "Pa might forgive me someday if he never knows I lied." Opal's face fell again at the reminder of what she'd done.

"Whatever your reasons, it saved my life."

She gave him an odd look. "My reasons should be fairly easy to understand."

"Pretty much." Since she showed no signs of getting up, he went ahead and sat down beside her. "Why don't you tell me everything."

"Like what?" Opal gaped at him now. "You were there."

"Let's start with the basics." He reached over and enfolded one cold hand in his. "Who's the real father?"

There was a roughness to his hands as he clasped hers, a capable strength Opal found so reassuring it took a moment for the full meaning of his question to take hold.

"The real father?" Repeating the words squeezed no sense from them, unless. . .

A shiver shook her as Opal considered the possibilities. Surely Adam didn't believe her to be with child in truth? Her new husband couldn't think so lowly of her!

"Yes." His steady gaze told her that's precisely what he thought.

"No!" Opal could scarcely gasp the denial as her breakfast clawed its way up the back of her throat. "I wouldn't. . ." She swallowed hard, searching for an explanation and finding none.

"You will." Determination underscored his order. "I need the name of the man whose child I'll be raising."

Dear Lord, how can I convince my new husband I haven't made him a cuckold even before our wedding night?

Wedding night. The very thought drove every other concern from her mind. *I'm a married woman. A wife. Tonight. . .*

Her alarm must have shown in her expression, because Adam's softened. "Whoever he is, it doesn't change things. You don't have to be afraid."

"I know!" *Because I'm not carrying any babe!* Opal realized her hands were tearing clumps of grass from the ground and stopped. How best to tell him?

"No matter your answer, I won't seek to have the marriage annulled."

"Annulled!" The word loomed larger than life, an undeniable threat. If Adam dissolved their marriage, nothing would stop her family from seeking vengeance. "You can't!"

"I know." A muscle in the left side of his jaw twitched. "Without proof of nonconsummation, it's not an option. I understood that when I married you, Opal."

"But you considered it." Her face grew hot enough it must match her hair. "If you had proof?" *If I tell you the truth, will you discard me? Destroy everything I worked for today?*

"I try to consider everything." He smudged away her tears with his thumb.

"Everything?" A huff of laughter escaped before she could hold it back. *You didn't consider the truth—that I'm untouched. That no man before you so much as kissed me!*

"And everyone." He shifted, laying the warmth of his palm against her stomach. "This child will bear no stigma, Opal."

Tears did nothing to cool her shame as she met the gaze of her husband. "You mean it, don't you?" Wonder at his selflessness stole her sorrow for a moment. "You'd take a child you didn't sire into your home, into your life, and stand as father?"

"Yes." He shifted away, doubts rushing to fill the space he'd taken. "I don't like lying, Opal. But I don't see another way to avoid bloodshed. If my family knows I'm not the father, there'll be no stopping them."

"They won't." She wouldn't allow it.

"But I know, Opal." Adam rubbed the back of his neck, staring at his boots. "And for my own peace, I need a name."

"Please don't ask this of me." She closed her eyes. *I can't tell him the truth, but the lies have to end. As things stand, they're piled higher than a windrow.*

"Our wedding was a farce." He clasped her hand in his once more. "Our marriage needn't be."

"I'll be a good wife to you, Adam." The words spilled over from her heart. He deserved so much more than having to settle for lies and a woman he didn't want. *I'll try to make up for it.*

She couldn't ask him to understand. *After tonight, I won't have to. He'll know there is no child. Adam will know I betrayed my family to spare his life. . .and that I betrayed his trust by not telling him the truth.*

"Tell me his name."

Opal swallowed. "I can't."

"Yes, you can." A rumble of anger edged his voice. "You're choosing not to tell me. Not to trust me."

"If I only had myself to think of things would be different." *But I won't risk my family.*

"I know you've more to think of than yourself." His agreement took her by surprise. "Now you have a husband. A husband who's already promised to claim your child as his own."

"Thank you for that."

"Don't thank me." He shook his head. "I don't have much of a choice. But I want to know. . .who is the true father?"

"Ask me tomorrow." She shied away from the question, from another lie.

"Why tomorrow?" Suspicion darkened his gaze. "Why wait?"

"Because. . ." This time her blush had little to do with shame and everything to do with embarrassment. "I know you're a man of honor. You won't even consider setting me aside once we. . ." She couldn't finish the sentence.

"Once we've faced my family?" He let out a

deep breath. "I already told you his name won't change things between us."

"Then not having a name won't change things between us." She dug her nails through the dirt she'd exposed by uprooting the prairie grass. "Ask me tomorrow, if you still want an answer."

"Of course I'll want an answer. One day won't change anything!"

"Yes, it will." Opal dug deeper. "One day can change everything. Force your family to accept me, avoid a feud, and make ours a marriage in truth."

"You talk in circles. Unless. . ." He stopped pacing to stand before her. "You don't mean a day, at all. You mean tonight."

Her voice abandoned her, leaving Opal with nothing to give but a tiny nod.

"That's what you were saying about my honor." His form blocked the sunlight, casting his features in shadow, but Opal could see the hardening of his jaw. "That I wouldn't seek an annulment after our wedding night."

"Yes." Her whisper scarcely tickled her own ears, but it seemed he heard it. *When you won't be able to get an annulment. When I won't be a maid anymore, but a wife. When my family is safe.*

"Then I'll ask you tomorrow, Opal Grogan." His use of her new last name pierced her heart. "But tonight won't make any difference."

"What?"

"Until you're my wife in trust," Adam reached down to grab her satchel once more as he spoke, "you won't be my wife in truth."

CHAPTER 11

W here is he?" Lucinda twisted a rag in her hands and peered out the window. "Adam's never missed dinner!"

"Maybe he went into town for something and stopped by the Dunstalls' café?" Her daughter's suggestion failed to calm her concerns. "Adam will be fine."

"You're sure he wasn't in the fields?" She turned to her husband and second eldest. "Nowhere on the farm?"

"We checked." Larry's shrug only made his mother worry more. "All we found was that gate needs fixing in the southeast pasture."

"Weren't you supposed to take care of that earlier this week?" Her husband squinted at Larry. "Why does it still need mending?"

"Well"—Larry's gaze shifted away from his father, alerting Lucinda her middle son was doing some fast thinking—"with things the way they've been with the Specks, going near the boundary doesn't seem a good idea."

Since when have you been so preoccupied with what is or isn't a good idea? Lucinda covered her anxiety by fussing with the faded curtains. "Seems to me that's exactly why you'd be keeping that fence in good order."

"Aw, Ma. . ."

But Lucinda wasn't listening to Larry anymore. Her attention focused on two shapes coming closer. "Adam!" *But who else?* She couldn't shake a feeling of doom, despite the surge of relief. "Here he comes!"

"See?" Willa's smile shone through her voice. "Adam wouldn't give us any cause to worry."

"No?" The word came out as a croak, dry and rough as she hurried to the door and rushed out to meet her son. And Opal Speck. Lucinda's years hadn't touched her eyesight, and she hadn't missed the satchel her son carried.

"Adam!" She gave him a swift hug. "Where have you been?" Lucinda's gaze flitted on Opal. "We were worried."

That she blamed Opal as the cause for that worry carried through. It was plain enough in the way the girl didn't move a muscle that Opal was standing on her pride. *As though a girl like that has anything to be proud of.* Lucinda felt the corners of her mouth tighten. *Coming between my sons. . .* The thought brought her attention back to Adam.

"I have some news." Discomfort showed in the line of his shoulders, the telltale way he rubbed his jaw.

"What's *she* doin' here?" Excitement filled Dave's voice. More importantly, the presence of her youngest child alerted them to the arrival of everyone else.

Lucinda looked at the tableaux as though viewing it from a far distance. Willa came to stand beside her, as she always did. A good daughter. Larry stopped just beyond Diggory. . .until her husband's hooded glare and less subtle jab made him fall in line. Dave scampered right up in front of everybody, eyes bright with interest and expectation as he stared at Adam.

Adam. Her eldest. The one who kept them all together.

The one who even now stood beside a Speck.

He opened his mouth, and Lucinda had a wild urge to slap her palm across it and hold back the words to come. With a mother's intuition, she knew as certain as sunrise and as dark as the depths of a moonless night that her family would be changed forever by what Adam had to say.

"You all know Opal." He reached for the upstart's hand, drawing her forward as though presenting someone of importance.

"Yeah!" Dave practically shouted the agreement while the rest of them managed grudging nods. "But what's a Speck doin' here?"

"That's what I need to explain." Adam's gaze sought hers, and Lucinda's hands caught on Dave's shoulders for support as the scene grew smaller, dimmer. "Opal's not a Speck anymore. She's my wife."

Blackness descended, a fuzzy blanket promising to block reality. Lucinda swayed into its softness.

"No!" Larry's bellow dragged her back from the darkness. "It can't be!" It wasn't the outrage in his shout but an underlying anguish that tore into her mother's heart anew.

"It is." Opal's whisper, a pale apology, floated around them for a heartbeat.

"When?" Diggory didn't bother denying Adam's statement. Instead, her husband wanted to know the details. As though his answer could somehow salvage everything.

"Today."

"Then it's not too late! Dave, fetch Parson Carter straight away!" Hope glimmered once more as Lucinda laid out her plan. "You'll get an annulment."

"No. . ." Opal's moan, so desolate and plaintive, would have moved any woman to feel for the girl. At least, it might have if the girl hadn't reached out to clutch Adam's sleeve.

"Don't you touch my son!" Lucinda knocked her hand away.

"Ma!" Willa's gasp didn't spear her half so much as Adam's frown.

He reached for Opal's hand and tucked it in the crook of his arm. "Annulment isn't an option."

"I don't believe it!" Larry's denial came so fierce and furious it took everyone aback. "You wouldn't."

Anyone would think his words were directed at his older brother, but Lucinda noticed Larry's gaze hadn't moved from Opal. The intensity of his stare unnerved her. *What hold does this girl have over my sons? Lord, protect my family!*

"She'll lie, then." Lucinda glowered at Opal.

"She'll say an annulment is possible."

"I can't." If the girl went any paler, she'd turn transparent. "I can't lie that an annulment is possible."

"You will." Larry all but hissed the order. "You'll do it so we don't seek revenge on your family for trapping Adam. I know you'll do it."

"No, she won't." Adam set his jaw. "Opal is with child."

And with that, the darkness won.

"Ma!" Adam barely caught her before she hit the dirt. He scooped her up, noticing for the first time how thin the skin of her face looked. *She's getting older.*

Guilt hit him like a load of rocks. *This will almost be too much for her. But, Lord, what else am I to do? Tell her Opal is my wife and carrying my child? Or tell her the truth, and watch the feud erupt and Pa and Larry get themselves killed? That would be harder on Ma than anything.*

He carried her inside, laying her on the worn sofa before he realized only Dave had followed him. Shouts rang outside.

"Whose is it?" Pa's yell carried best. . .followed by the unmistakable sound of flesh striking flesh.

Adam raced outside in time to see Pa cup his cheek and step forward, fury in his face. "Stop!" He planted himself between his father and his wife, who'd obviously slapped the older man for his insult.

"How dare you!" Opal's outrage almost fooled

Adam, who knew the truth. "I'm not the type of woman to bed one man and pass off his child as Adam's!" She moved forward, casting a pain- and accusation-filled glance his way. "That you'd ever even consider such a thing. . . . You should be ashamed of yourself."

I never would have thought it, Adam agreed. *But here we stand.* His eyes narrowed. She had no right to strike his father, no matter the foulness of his insult, when the offense proved just.

"Wipe that look off your face, son." Pa obviously interpreted Adam's disgust as being aimed squarely at himself.

"You don't talk like that to my wife." He struggled against the urge to defend Opal and the knowledge she didn't deserve it. But he couldn't let his father know that. "Ever."

"Had to ask." After working his jaw side to side, Pa let loose a begrudging shrug. "I won't make that mistake twice."

"Thank you." Opal's regal nod acknowledged the closest thing to an apology Adam had ever heard come from his Pa.

Maybe she knows what she's doing, to convince everyone. The thought didn't make him rest any easier. *How am I to live with a wife who lies so well?*

"I still can't believe it." His brother's bewilderment didn't spark offense as he stared at them. If anything, Larry sounded. . .sad?

"Believe it." He couldn't have anyone doubting his wife or his marriage. "Opal and the child are mine."

THE BRIDE BACKFIRE

Despite the situation, there was something. . . primal. . .about saying that aloud. Something *right*. It was the same sense of calm he'd had when he'd agreed to marry her in the first place.

This, then, must be from God. A peace that passes understanding. *Because I sure don't understand, Lord.*

"Are you sure?" Now his brother was pushing it, his hoarse query making Opal bristle anew.

"Yes." Adam laid a hand on her arm, feeling some of her tension ebb. "Opal wouldn't tell me another man's child is mine." His words skated the fine edge of truth, when that was exactly what she'd told her father. His peace fled in the face of her grateful smile, a smile pretty enough to make his mouth go dry.

"Not that." Larry peered at Opal, searching out her secrets. "I mean are you sure she's expecting at all?"

"Yes!" His mother's cry made them all look to the house. There she stood, clinging to the doorway as if unable to stand without its support. "It wouldn't be the first time a hussy lied to trap a decent man!"

Opal tensed again, her fingers digging into his wrist, sparking an anger whose power almost overwhelmed him. For the first time, he realized what his wife faced—what Opal knew awaited her when she reached his home.

Far from trap him, Opal's actions spared his life. Sure, she'd turned the situation into a means of saving her own reputation, but she hadn't set out to sacrifice his freedom. Of course she was with

99

child. Otherwise why would she put herself in such a terrible position?

"Opal never sought to trap me." His words came out so low they could have passed for a growl. "Never been more sure of anything in my life."

"I take it her family knows?" Pa got back to the matter at hand. "You haven't run off with her so we'll have a herd of angry Specks on our doorstep?"

"They know." Opal bit her lip but said no more.

"They're the ones who fetched the preacher, aren't they?" Ma all but shrieked the words. "Did they force you to marry her, Adam? Shotgun weddings aren't valid!"

"Yes they are." Pa rounded on her. "If a man got our Willa in the family way and thought twice about doing the honorable thing, it'd be valid enough."

"*Willa's* a good woman."

"So is Opal." Adam knew the truth of it, despite their situation. "And make no mistake, it was my choice to marry her."

CHAPTER 12

His choice? Opal listened to Adam defend her and wanted to weep. *What choice did he have, Lord? Marriage to me or death?* She looked at the expressions painting Grogan faces.

Anxiety darkened Willa's pretty eyes. Curiosity, avid and eager, kept young Dave's head swiveling back and forth so he wouldn't miss anything. Pride bent to resignation as Diggory acknowledged his son's decision by reaching for her satchel. Larry's fury came off so palpable, Opal wouldn't look at him.

But it was the defeat lining Lucinda's shoulders as she clutched the door frame that most closely mirrored Opal's heart. Set apart, reaching for strength wherever she could find it, grasping at any hope this could be made right. . .

Oh how I wish it could be so. But how can you make things right when you're not the person you thought you were?

Opal balled her fist against the sting of her palm—a fading reminder that she'd struck another person in anger. It didn't matter that Diggory Grogan offered the ultimate insult. That he accused her of sleeping with multiple men before marriage, lying about it, and then passing off an unborn child as belonging to the wrong man in order to trap him into an unwanted marriage. Words paled compared to actions. After so many years of telling her father and brothers that physical violence didn't solve anything, she'd lashed out the first time she found herself alone in her anger.

Hypocrite.

The knowledge stung more than her hand ever could. And the more she thought about it, the more she could add to the list of people who'd believed the worst of her.

After all, Diggory wasn't the first. He certainly didn't rank as the most important, and she should have foreseen the assumptions his family would jump to. Especially when Adam thought much the same thing. The only difference was how much a hussy he thought her. Somehow, that didn't make them any less hurtful.

Even her own family now believed she'd betrayed her raising, their good name, and her family loyalty for fleshly weakness. *The look in Pa's eyes when he said I wasn't a Speck anymore...* Another surge of sadness threatened to overwhelm her.

"Opal." Adam stood before her, hand extended.

Not knowing what else to do, she took hold and followed him into the Grogan home for the first time. Oh, she'd been on their homestead before for harvesting, threshing, work bees, and the like to exchange a helping hand.

She stilled at the thought. *Threshing. If I hadn't been here for Larry's accident, I wouldn't have fetched the ice. He wouldn't have thought I harbored secret feelings for him and skulked on our land to act on the supposed attraction.* Her stomach heaved as she followed the progression. *If he hadn't crossed the boundary, Pa and my brothers wouldn't have been so up in arms when Adam came looking for his milk cow. If I'd never stepped foot on Grogan land... If I...*

She stopped cold, bringing Adam up short. *Oh Lord. I thought I was saving Adam. But really, this entire mess is my fault!*

She lurched away from him for a few steps, turning her back to lose the contents of her stomach in a patch of wild grass. Opal gagged on her realizations until she had nothing left but the hollowness of despair.

"Here." A man's kerchief appeared before her, a warm hand patting her back as though to comfort her. Adam had stayed. His kindness proved the breaking point.

Despite her resolve not to let the Grogans see her cry, Opal felt tears pour free. She stayed bent over for an extra moment, mopping her face clean, trying to gather her composure.

"Well Larry, I guess now we know Adam's not been hoodwinked. The gal's pregnant, all right." Diggory's laughter stiffened her spine, giving her the strength nothing else could have. If he weren't such an abysmal, callous excuse for a man, she would almost have been grateful.

As it was, Opal straightened up, tucked the soiled kerchief in her apron pocket, and summoned a sickly smile. They'd never know she grinned at the irony of how her sickness over the deception was interpreted as proof of its veracity.

"We've put your things in Willa's room," Adam told her just outside the house after everyone else had gone inside.

"Willa's room?" She looked up in consternation. *How am I to make an annulment impossible if we sleep separately?*

"Willa's room," he repeated the words with a determined gleam, and Opal knew he'd meant what he said earlier. "Until I can build us a home of our own, I'll stay with Larry in the barn. It's for the best."

"Don't leave me." She hated to beg. Hated that she needed him for more than fulfilling her plans. But the thought of being alone in the Grogan household turned her stomach afresh. If nothing else, she counted Adam as her ally.

"When the time is right, we'll have a house." His gaze held a deeper meaning than the words he spoke so lightly. "A real marriage."

"When the time is right. . ." She tested the words, certain he meant *When you tell me the name of the father whose child you carry.*

"I'm glad we understand each other."

"Oh, I understand." She had a husband. Now what she needed was a plan.

Think, Midge. Think! She rolled over, snuggled into her quilt, and waited for inspiration to strike. A deep breath to calm her racing thoughts didn't do much. Stretching and wriggling her toes, her never-fail plotting method left her without any brilliant insights either.

This is one of those times when everybody else I know would pray. Maybe I should give it a try.

She wiggled her toes some more.

Maybe not.

After all, praying hadn't helped her parents make it past their bouts with influenza when she was little. Praying hadn't helped her sister survive. . . .

No. Not going to think about that.

Midge stopped wiggling her toes. The point was God either hadn't heard or hadn't cared, because prayer hadn't helped her when she needed it most.

Saul had.

Which was the only idea for helping Opal that she kept coming back to—telling Saul and Clara. Oh, Midge knew Opal's reputation was at risk, but she knew firsthand that her makeshift family wouldn't turn their backs on a woman just because of her circumstances.

They were some of those Christians who actually practiced what they all preached and loved folks for who they were—warts and all. Didn't they keep telling her that the beauty of Jesus was that He gave His grace to everyone who accepted it, even though nobody deserved it?

Well, Midge knew she deserved it less than most. She wasn't worthy like Saul and Clara. And Opal, who'd always been so kind and tried so hard to keep her family from fighting with the Grogans, she deserved better than Midge, too. That was probably why Midge's prayers didn't do much, come to think of it.

She burrowed deeper under the covers. *I saw how Adam looked at Opal that day at the smithy.* She tried to marshal her thoughts, sniff out the facts. *I know he saved her from the fire, and any woman would find that romantic. . . . She's so pretty, with her bright hair and blue eyes, it's no wonder he stares. And Adam Grogan's a fine-looking man, even if he is older. Real tall, with lots of dark hair and kindness in his face. Haven't I heard Alyssa say so often enough?*

She didn't spare a thought for her friend, who had a crush on Adam. All Alyssa need do was crook a finger and half the boys in Buttonwood would come running. The other half, Midge allowed herself a small smile, would do the same for her. But none of them could help Opal if she were in trouble.

Opal and Adam might be a good match, but there's something havey-cavey about the whole thing. Opal's not the type to consort with a man. I thought maybe she'd given in to the man she loved because they were separated by family hostilities, but now I know different.

Midge had seen Opal's expression after Adam's kiss. That wasn't the look of a woman who'd been bussed by a longtime lover. Not by a long shot.

106

There'd been no knowing in her reaction. . .just surprise. And enough hesitant excitement to re-assure Midge that the marriage still might work.

All hopes aside, though, knowing that Opal wasn't carrying Adam's child changed everything. It didn't take much to figure out that she'd lied. But why? Because she'd wanted to marry him? Things between the two families were wound tighter than ever, so what had Adam been doing on Speck land in the first place if he and Opal weren't seeing each other?

There were too many questions, not enough answers, and one troubling certainty—whatever caused the wedding yesterday would cause a lot more trouble before this was over. And Opal would be the one to pay for it.

Until she knew more, she couldn't tell anyone. But still, Midge had to do *something*.

CHAPTER 13

W hat?" Adam felt the reverberation from how hard Larry slammed their door through the wall where he hung his hat.

"You heard me, Adam." His brother circled him. "How could you do it?"

"Opal carrying a child out of wedlock never figured into any of my plans." He chose his words carefully—as he had all day. As he'd have to for a long while.

"That's not what I meant."

"You know better than to question why I married her, Larry." Sinking down onto his bed did nothing to ease the weight from his shoulders. "It had to be done." *Just not for the reason everyone thinks.*

"That's not what I meant either." Larry shouted this time but must have realized his voice would carry, because he lowered it. "Why *her*?"

"It doesn't matter that her last name used to be Speck." Adam addressed the only other possible cause for Larry's outrage. "Opal's a special woman. God-fearing, kind, smart, pretty—"

"I know that, blast it!"

"Watch your mouth, Lawrence Grogan. There's no cause for cussing."

"Yes there is." A muscle worked in his brother's jaw. "She was *mine*, Adam."

"No." Bile seared the back of his throat. *Can Larry be the father of Opal's child? My own* brother, *Lord?*

"Yes." He hissed the word. "She was for me, and you took her. You knew it, and you took her anyway!"

"I didn't know." Adam pushed his hair back. *Didn't I?* A memory fell into place. The day he'd gone looking for the cow skull and startled Opal, hadn't she called Larry's name before she turned around? "This is why you kept crossing the boundary? To see Opal?"

"You read the note." Larry loomed over him. "Knew I claimed her."

"Fool!" On his feet now, Adam looked down on his younger brother by a good two inches. "And if you caught a bullet for your sneaking and started a war? You put us all at risk for an infatuation?"

"And you did any different?" Larry threw back his shoulders. "Don't pretend to be righteous now, Adam."

Red hazed his vision as the pieces fell into place. Larry, determined to cross Speck lines. Larry, eager to start a fight over any little thing as a pretext to go over there. Larry, adding the damning extra line to Pa's threat. Larry, so preoccupied with Opal he didn't mend the fence he should have. His brother's selfishness paved every step of the journey leading to this impossible situation.

Dear God, what if Larry is the father? What am I to do then? How is it Your will that I'm wed to this woman?

"How did you do it, Adam?" Larry's hands fisted, the most prominent vein in his forehead springing to life. "How did you get to her?" A heartbeat of silence then, "If you forced her, I'll kill you."

"I didn't force her." Even through his anger, Adam could see Larry's sincerity.

"Didn't think so." He lowered himself onto his bunk. "So what was it? What made her choose *you?*"

The crimson halo around everything eased away at his brother's disconsolate look. Larry hadn't been with Opal. *My brother isn't the father.*

For a split second, Adam considered sharing a part of the truth—that between Larry's note and Adam's trespassing in search of the missing milk cow, Opal's interference had saved his life. Just as quickly, he rejected the idea. But how to soothe Larry's pride without making things worse? "I saved her life." *And now she's saved mine, but we're far from even.* Adam's jaw tightened. *She owes me a name, for starters.*

"You used that against her?" Larry's head came up like that of an enraged bull. "Held it up as a debt?" The shove, when it came, didn't surprise

Adam. "As though she owed herself to you?"

"No." Adam hadn't toppled from the push, but he planted his feet. "There's just a bond that's formed when something like that happens." *Like the way I never forgot how it felt to hold her, even for a few minutes.* "It's not something I can make you understand."

"You don't have to." Larry pointed at his scar. "Opal helped save my life. It's part of what lies between us."

"Part?" A chill crept up the back of his neck.

"Yes." A fervid gleam entered his brother's eye. "Opal and I were destined to be together."

"You *were* together?" There was a sharp note to his question, but Adam had to ask.

Larry's bark of laughter did nothing to ease his mind. A long silence stretched between them, Larry obviously turning over his answer in his head. A hint of triumph rimmed his response. "What do you think?"

I'd rather be anywhere but here, Lord. Opal swallowed back a lump of grief and scooted closer to the edge of the bed, trying not to disturb Willa.

No. That's not true. I want to be home, Father. I want to be in my own bed, listening to the snores of my family. Pete's nasal whistle, Pa's snorts, Elroy's gusty breaths, and Ben's rusty rumble used to keep me awake. Now I can't sleep without them.

The Grogan house was too quiet. Willa, normally a quiet girl, didn't make so much as a peep while she slept. The luxury of having an honest-to-goodness room for just the two of them, not just a corner of the soddy curtained off, only emphasized how alone Opal was.

Only silence filled this home...and it seemed to be waiting for something. The weight of expectation pressed upon her chest until Opal could barely squeeze out a breath. Stillness screamed for truth, and she had to keep that locked inside. Because the facts would unleash the conflict she'd fought to suppress for so long.

If I tell Adam there's no child, he'll seek that annulment. He never wanted me as his wife. Strange how a dull pain spread through her at the thought, an odd accompaniment to the fear that followed. *Pa will take umbrage at the insult to me and determine to carry out the sentence he proclaimed against Adam earlier today. Guns will fire before tempers cool. Even if we all make it through the aftermath alive, Pa will never understand, never forgive me for betraying the family and lying to him to save Adam.*

Obviously, that wasn't an option. She tapped her fingers against the cornhusk mattress, eking some small comfort from the familiar rustle. *If I get up now, slip away back home, and confess to Pa, he'll be so angry.* A muffled sob escaped her. *That I lied to save Adam—that I'd go so far to marry him. He'd see it as putting myself in danger. Then he'd go after Adam for agreeing to it. Even if I explained that the note was Larry's, it wouldn't help. The feud would still start up, and I couldn't protect them.*

No matter how she looked at it, there was no

solution. Her mind churned, her mouth went dry as though to make up for all the moisture her tears spent, and still, not even the temporary solace of sleep offered escape.

The blue-tinged light of early morning seeped around the door frame to find her still awake. Her lips stuck together, and surely some great desert had emptied itself in her eyes to make them so raw. She angled out of bed—already hanging so close to the edge she would've had nowhere but air to roll—and stumbled to the washstand.

A woven rug covered the floor, the chilled softness of its bumpy texture a familiar tickle to her toes. The splintering snap when the thin layer of ice on the wash water gave way seemed overly loud to Opal, but the cold wetness of it quenched her thirst and rinsed the grit from her eyes.

"Good morning, Opal." Willa peered over the edge of the blankets.

"Morning, Willa." She simply couldn't bring herself to call it "good." "Hope I didn't disturb you last night."

"Not at all." Her new sister-in-law swung her legs over the side of the bed. "Though it is strange…"

"Yes it is." Opal didn't ask what the other woman referred to. The sudden marriage? Having her here at all? That Adam chose not to sleep with her? With so many options, and none of them flattering, it served no purpose to speculate.

The two women dressed in silence, preparing for the day ahead.

As much as it's possible to prepare. Opal couldn't

113

quite stifle a sigh at the thought but tried to distract herself by making the bed.

"I wish I could tell you today will be easier." Willa fluffed her pillow and hugged it to her chest, ruining her efforts.

"Easy is as easy does, my mother used to say." *Though I've never seen it done.*

"Do you think anyone manages to do that?" She cocked her head to the side. "Make everything easy?"

"No." For the first time in what felt like years, Opal felt the stirrings of a smile. "It wouldn't be fair to the rest of us."

"True!" Willa's giggle faded all too quickly. "Though"—she paused as she reached the door. "seems to me there's a lot of things that aren't fair."

Don't I know it. The knowledge doused her rising spirits as Opal followed her sister-in-law to the barn, where cows waited. She had to sweet-talk them, take it slow so they'd get used to her, but it wasn't long before she settled into the ages-old rhythm of milking.

With each squirt into the bucket, a regret tugged at Opal's heart. *It isn't fair to my family that I've abandoned them.* The harsh, metallic ring of milk in an empty pail. *Who'll take on my chores?* One insistent, streaming spray after another as she worked faster. *Who'll make sure they're fed enough. . . and what they eat is worth eating?* Finally, the stifled splash signaling a full bucket. *Who'll take care of Pa and my brothers now that I'm not there?*

After she and Willa toted the fresh milk to the Grogan springhouse, they set about gathering eggs.

"We haven't gotten around to the spring cleaning yet," Willa said by way of apology for the smell around the coop. "They've only just begun laying again, so we haven't turned them loose in the farmyard yet. But we'll leave the coop open when we leave. Today's good enough." Willa sidestepped a cock who'd taken exception to their presence. "Watch out for Jackson—he's a flogger."

"I can't abide a flogging rooster." Opal kept her distance. "Whenever we came across one, he ended up in a pot."

"Or a frying pan." Willa offered one of her shy smiles. "I love fried chicken. But around here, we find use for floggers."

"What other use can there possibly be for foul-tempered fowl?" Something troubled Opal's memory, but she couldn't quite draw it out. Hadn't she heard the Grogans used chickens—

"To chase cows up a hill when they've got the bloat." There was a forced lightness to Willa's tone.

"I see." Opal didn't say another word. Sick cows were a sore topic. Besides, it seemed as though they were headed back to the house.

Lord, help me. I've always liked Willa, but facing another day with the rest of the Grogans— A thought interrupted her, mid-prayer. *Only it's not a day, is it, Lord? With Adam determined to leave me in the house until I spill my secrets, I'll be facing Lucinda and Larry for weeks, even months. . . .*

And suddenly, Opal's stomach couldn't help but give the Grogans more "proof" of her delicate condition.

CHAPTER 14

If that girl takes sick in my vegetable garden, she'll regret it." Lucinda knew no one heard her mutter, but it made her feel a little better to say it anyway.

Who wanted to hear the sounds of someone emptying her stomach of a morning—or anytime. No matter if the girl was carrying or not.

I didn't toss my turnips over any of my babies. Just went to show those Specks weren't made of the same stuff as she—and her children—could claim. *And if I were of a mind to be generous, I'd even say I understood why Opal would want Adam. My son would make any woman a fine husband.*

Pity she wasn't in the mood for generosity. She hadn't raised a fine boy like Adam to be wasted on the likes of Opal Speck. *And it's not too late.*

All she needed was to get rid of the girl, and her spawn, before they did any more harm. She brushed away a shiver of unease at the thought of the baby.

Despite her weak stomach and Adam's confidence, I'm not convinced she even carries a babe. Her paring knife moved more quickly, a flashing menace in the morning sun. *Even if there is a child, there's no way to vouchsafe it belongs to Adam. You can't trust a hussy.* She'd make short work of the upstart, just the same as she did these potatoes.

Because she had a plan. For the first time in over twenty years, Lucinda hadn't minded her husband's snores. His wheezy grunts hadn't interfered with her sleep one bit.

No, she'd been wide awake, going over ways to make the Speck girl so miserable she'd hightail it before all was lost. If Parson Carter kept his word—and the man saw the wisdom of not crossing the Grogans, though Lucinda would be paying him a visit that morning as a reminder—they had until Sunday before all of Buttonwood would hear of this disaster.

Which meant she had five days to fix things and keep Adam from being ruined. Keep it contained, erase it from existence, make things right. Five days.

Opal would be long gone by then. Of course, running back to her family would be out of the question. *It's not far enough. If she stays close, Adam will go after her. And Larry. . .* Well, Lucinda had enough to deal with already before speculating on what went through her middle son's head. He fancied Opal, too. That much was obvious. How far he'd go and what it would mean for the family—those were paths she didn't want to tread.

Difficulties I won't have to handle if I get rid of the girl. And it shouldn't be too hard, either!

After a fitful night full of false starts and impossibilities, the solution presented itself early this morning. With her mother gone so young, Opal had been the only woman of the house for most of her life. And Lucinda had seen firsthand the chit's boldness, the way she tried to make decisions for her family, how she talked back to the Grogans. Hadn't she even dared to strike Diggory the day before?

At the very thought, Lucinda's hand slipped, the knife nicking the fleshy part of her palm.

Now look what the brat made me do! A ribbon of red spooled around her wrist before she staunched the flow with a clean rag.

No matter. Lucinda could handle the hard things in life, but Opal. . .she'd given orders for so long, she wouldn't be able to manage when someone else took over. Oh no, the girl didn't have a meek bone in her body. She wouldn't like it one bit when she didn't have her hands on the reins.

But on the Grogan farm, Lucinda ruled. At least. . .in every way that would matter to Opal.

A slow smile spread across her face as she set the first batch of potatoes in the skillet, hearing the hungry crackle of hot grease. It was one of the little things she enjoyed—the sound of doing something right. Every woman learned, sooner or later, that the little things mattered a great deal.

Lucinda looked up as her daughter and the interloper walked through the door.

It was time to teach Opal Speck just how much those little things could add up.

The next morning's wash water splashed on his face as cold as the reality he awoke to. Adam had always thought mornings were the best part of day, when the world stretched its legs to see what it could accomplish before the sun sank low.

He fought the impulse to sit this one out. Today would be a gamut the likes of which few men deserved to face. As a matter of fact, he'd be hard pressed to come up with the name of even one man meriting a shotgun wedding to his enemy's daughter who carried another child that may or may not belong to his very own brother.

Though Adam didn't see fit to question God's judgment about the necessity of all this, he took exception to the idea he might be that one deserving male.

Which didn't mean the barn would muck itself or the cattle feed kindly appear in the troughs. The lump in his brother's bunk told him Larry wasn't going to do it.

Obviously he was taking Opal's marriage hard—much harder than Adam could have foreseen. It would be so easy to shake him awake, demand an answer to the question Larry wouldn't answer last night. *Could you be the father?*

As he stared down at the sleeping form of his brother, rage surged through him. "Get up." No response. "I said, *get up*." He reached out, grabbed hold of Larry's shoulders, and shook. Hard.

"No."

"Tell me how far things went with you and Opal." He hadn't stopped shaking his brother. "Tell me if there's a possibility you're the father of my child."

My child. The words struck a chord, sounded so right that when his brother shook his head, Adam lifted him from the bed by the front of his drawers. *He's threatening everything, and he may just be doing it out of spite.* "Do you have any claim to her?" Dread ripped the words from his throat.

"Yes." Larry shoved his hands away. "More claim than you. I wanted her first."

I doubt it. He'd always noticed Opal, and it had only gotten worse since he carried her from the flames that threatened to take her life. But these were thoughts he'd squashed, things he'd never said, because they'd only do harm. *Not anymore. I won't keep quiet. She's mine now.* "I doubt it." The words seemed to transfer his animosity to Larry.

"Believe it." If his brother were a dog, Adam would have said he bared his teeth. "Opal always looked pretty, but after she helped save my life, I realized what truly lay between us."

"A feud?" Adam considered himself too good a man to put down his brother by pointing out Opal's own worthiness would lay between her and Larry ever being anything.

"Destiny." All but vaulting from the bed, Larry shoved his face too close. "We belong together."

"Parson Carter might say different."

"But would Opal?" The sneer cut down Adam's triumph. "Did you ask her? Did she really have a choice about marrying you?"

"Yes." *More of a choice than I did, that's for sure.*

"You lie!" Flicks of spittle flecked from his mouth. "Opal only married you to avoid a feud! She did what was necessary."

"That's—" *possible. More than possible.* The realization stopped him midsentence. *Why didn't I consider that she lied about the baby being mine to save my life and spare her family from Pa's vengeance?* Instead, he'd assumed she didn't want to marry the father or was unable to. The idea she'd fornicated with a married man sat ill, but Adam far preferred it to this option. Had Opal wed him both to stop the feud and because she'd been unable to wed the father of her child, all right. . .because that father was Larry?

"I went after her first."

Larry's shove caught him off-balance in more ways than one, but Adam held his ground. "I saved her life."

"So she could spend it with me." He moved in for another shove. "You aren't God. You can't give and take away what's mine!"

"Is the child yours?" Adam knocked his brother's hands away. "Tell me now or lose your chance."

"How can any man know he's the father of any child with absolute certainty?"

"Opal wouldn't play a man false!" His defense of her erupted before he considered the ramifications. If only Larry wouldn't catch on. . .

"Then why do you ask if I could be the father?" A crafty gleam lit his brother's gaze, but more disturbing was the wild hope behind it. "You say she wouldn't play a man false. . .then you'd know you're the father if you'd claimed her."

"You're not the father." Adam knew it in the way Larry evaded the questions. Assurance settled over him like a blanket.

"No, Adam"—he rocked back on his heels—"*you* aren't. Opal wouldn't play a man false, it's true. And you wanting to know what lies between us shows there's nothing between the two of you. Release her."

"She's my wife." Adam spoke slowly, letting the words drop like stones. "We'll raise our child together, make no mistake."

"No!" The howl pierced his ears. "It's not too late to let her go." Larry's hands scrabbled at Adam's collar. "Give her back to me. She doesn't belong with you, and no matter what you say, you know it. You can't fool me!"

"I don't have to." Adam turned and headed for the door. "You're fooling yourself if you think I'd set aside my wife." *Not without anything less than absolute proof you sired the babe in her belly. And you want her so badly, you would have told me immediately if that were the case.*

His step lighter, he headed for the barn. But by the time he arrived, not even the familiar scents of animals and hay could lift his spirits.

Larry didn't say he wasn't or couldn't be the father. He said no man could know for sure. . .which would be true if he thought Opal and I were together, as well. He recalled the fervent gleam of hope in his brother's gaze when he noticed Adam's slip. *The triumph in his voice when he announced I wasn't the father. . . Can I really be sure it's not because he just learned the woman he loves hadn't betrayed him?*

And if that's so, can I keep them apart?

CHAPTER 15

W hat are you doing here?" Opal could scarcely keep the question in until she and Midge were out of sight of the house.

"Who would believe me if I told them you greeted me at the Grogan farm, and *you* asked me what *I'm* doing here?" Her friend's grin all but demanded an answering smile. "Anyone in Buttonwood would tell me the world's gone mad and taken us along for the jaunt!"

"I'll not complain that our jaunt takes me away from Lucinda." Opal's voice lowered despite the distance they'd covered. "But what did you tell Clara and Saul about where you were headed, and why?"

Does the whole town know of my hasty wedding? Parson Carter promised not to breathe a word, instead allowing the "happy couple" to announce the "glad news" at a time of their choosing, but better plans had failed.

"We need more honey for the store, so I hurried up and volunteered to visit you." Midge winked broadly, with the complete lack of ladylike decorum that Pete swore made her so appealing.

"Can't abide a woman who puts on airs." Opal's heart clenched at the memory of her younger brother in happier days. Pete probably stayed at home now, saddled with the lion's share of her chores.

"Of course, Clara wanted to come along, but little Maddie's fussy over teething, and I reminded her she'd had a nice long visit with you earlier this week when I was at the Warrens'. So it's my turn." The laughter faded from her face. "She didn't need to know the other part—that she wouldn't find you if she headed to the Speck farm. I know you're not telling folks yet about. . .everything."

A hard swallow and a nod were all Opal could offer her friend, whose gaze held a shrewdness that made her uncomfortable. Midge had never been a typical young girl, and Opal couldn't shrug away the feeling she saw more than she should even now.

"Which is, of course, why I've come."

Because I haven't told you everything? Opal bit her lip. There was no chance she could confide in Midge the full, sorry truth about what she'd done. Her chest ached at her own betrayal. *I can't tell her what Adam thinks I've done either.* Pain streaked upward, intensifying the ache. *Or what the Grogans think of me.* The heat of anger burned away some of her remorse.

The sight and sounds of her apiary further dispelled some of the gloom that had settled around

KELLY EILEEN HAKE

her heart since the day before. No matter how much it seemed the world had come crashing down about her ears, her bees disproved her self-centered fancy.

All around them, thousands of striped workers went about their business. Springtime meant a flurry of comb making and scouting, each colony focusing on the home containing its entire existence. Each hive a self-contained, well-run world unto itself.

In those small worlds, so tight knit and busy, everyone had a role to play. Tasks to perform. A purpose among all their relations.

Oh God. The now-familiar thickness of impending tears clogged her throat. The memory of her father denying her, refusing to acknowledge her as part of their family sloughed at her soul. *"Not anymore."* Two words robbed her of her home, leaving her nothing and no one to call hers.

Oh God. Opal couldn't seem to get past the pained cry to the Father she knew hadn't abandoned her. The only one she could still claim. *Oh God. . .* Nothing more came. No way to express the need within her save the simple supplication of calling His name, a constant cry within her heart.

I can't ask Him to take it all away, undo my mistakes. There are so many. Too many. . .

She should have held back after Larry's accident—mentioned the ice to Clara and left it alone. Instead, she'd jumped at the chance to help Dr. Reed. Now look where her foolish hopes that their families could lay aside old differences under new kindnesses had gotten her!

Maybe she could have told Elroy about Larry's

increasing attentions, have her brother put a bug in Grogan's ear and keep him away. But she'd been too afraid of sparking the feud.

At the very least, she shouldn't have let Adam keep the threat she'd found in this very apiary. A chill of guilt stole over her as she remembered the moment Pete drew the thrice-cursed thing from Adam's pocket. Resignation dimmed his handsome features. He'd known in that instant, just as she had, that he may as well have been carrying his own death decree.

Why, oh why didn't I insist on burning it immediately? Without that final piece of damning "evidence" against him, Adam might have suffered nothing more than bruises and bluster at the hands of her family for his trespassing. Instead, the die was cast.

Because she'd do anything to protect her family—even marry Adam. And her family would do anything to protect her. *Even if it meant letting me do it.*

If the scenario weren't so dire, the irony would have made her laugh. Even for someone as practiced at finding the bright spot in any situation as Opal, the search turned up nothing to make her smile. The thought flitted across her mind that she'd managed to keep her family safe, but too many threats loomed over that accomplishment like a Sword of Damocles for her to take any comfort in it.

Though Adam didn't know it, he could still annul the marriage. Lucinda, for all her silence this morning, hadn't accepted the wedding yet—her lack of chatter spoke of schemes to instill foreboding. No, the victory she'd won yesterday—if Opal could call losing her family, her freedom, and the respect of everyone she'd ever met in one fell swoop any sort of victory—constituted a minor skirmish.

She looked over her shoulder, knowing she wouldn't see the Grogan farm, nor any of her new in-laws, but unable to quell the impulse. Opal held back a sigh at the thought of battles and ambushes she'd face for years to come.

Oh God—she finally found the words she needed—*give me strength to make it through this war!*

Midge waited. She didn't mind letting Opal sort through her thoughts while they stood surrounded by the energy of the hives. Their restlessness matched something inside her, made her feel like she didn't have to move so much when other critters were so busy.

Normally, though, she wasn't very good at waiting. Anyone who ever met her could tell in a blink that patience wasn't her strongest virtue.

Come to think of it, she wasn't all too sure she showed particular strength in any of the virtues. *No, that can't be right. I'm a good person. There's got to be one. . . .*

Patience got chucked from the list right away, but there were a heap of others to pick from, weren't there? Like peace. Peace definitely ranked as a virtue. *Nope. Sitting still chafes me something awful.*

She crossed peace off the possibilities.

Wasn't mercy on there, too? Midge wrinkled her nose. To her way of thinking, justice trumped mercy any day. People lied, cheated, hurt others all the time and got away with it. They deserved to be *punished.* But she didn't remember justice being on the list. As a matter of fact, she couldn't quite recall what the other virtues were supposed to be.

Sure hope memory isn't one of them. I ought to ask Aunt Doreen about it later. I'm running out of options. Funny how that gave her a sinking feeling. *Me not having any virtues fits in with that whole idea I had about my prayers not being good enough.*

But what's the use in being good enough if I can't be me anymore? Saul and Clara kept trying to lead her to God, but something deep inside Midge balked. Because when it came down to it, if she let Jesus in, it sounded like there wouldn't be any room left for Midge. *And it's been real hard making sure I got this far.*

She started pacing. This was why she didn't like staying still—left a body too much room to think about things that didn't do anyone any good. *Seems to me that "not giving up" ought to be on that list of virtues.* She perked up at the thought. *Maybe that's the problem! I'm going by someone else's list. I ought to make my own—just fill in some important things those folks long ago forgot.*

Who knew? Maybe if it was on a list, it would matter more. And then she'd be closer to being good enough. . . .

"Oh Midge!" Opal's voice jerked her away from

the trap of her thoughts. "I didn't mean to ignore you. Here you've been so quiet. . ."

"We both had a lot on our minds." She shrugged away the discomfort. "You more'n me, that's for sure."

Now that Opal was ready to talk, she wouldn't let a minute go to waste. "Lucinda has it in for me." Opal settled on the safest topic. "She stayed almost completely silent all morning."

"That's scary." Midge couldn't help but agree. Lucinda Grogan simply didn't do quiet. "You've got trouble on your hands if she's thinking that hard. She's bound to turn up something you don't want her to."

"What do you mean" The quick-fire response told her Opal hid more than one secret.

"We both know your new mama-in-law has a nose for unpleasant tidbits and a habit for sharing them." They strolled through the rows of hives, the whitewashed boxes gleaming in spring sunshine. "You marrying Adam will bring out the worst in her."

"There's nothing she can do about it." The declaration lacked strength.

"Depends on what she finds." Time to put away the kid gloves and work the truth out of Opal. "Folks give away a lot without saying a word, without ever meaning to or knowing they've done it. And Lucinda will be looking."

"What do you think she'll find?" The scoff showed bravado, but her friend's fear seeped through.

"Cut line, Opal." Midge grabbed her hand and

plunked down in an inviting spot. "Lucinda will have you under her thumb, watching you squirm until you give up something she can use. And we both know it's only a matter of time, because you're too good and too honest to keep up a pretense for very long."

"Pretense?"

"If you're going to dodge reality, do it with someone else, Opal. I know you better, and I know you don't have the time to waste trying to fool me."

"What do you think you know?" Apprehension settled like a death mask across her friend's features.

"You're not going to make Adam a father, for one thing." No sense sugarcoating it.

"Midge Collins, if you even think about suggesting that I'm about to bear the child of another man, you can march yourself straight back to town and...and..." Tears burbled out the rest of whatever Opal tried to say.

"So that's what Lucinda's been on you about, eh?" Midge slung an arm around her friend's shoulders and let out a satisfying snort. "Featherbrain."

"Then you don't think—"

"There's a better chance baby Maddie could sing opera. I should've seen it coming that the Grogans would accuse you of something like that the instant they heard you've a little one on the way."

"Don't care." Opal let loose a long mumble into her handkerchief that sounded oddly like "Schack dig he four sane it."

Which, of course, made absolutely no sense. But when Midge told Opal so, her friend lifted her head with a stubborn glower to declare—quite clearly this time—

"He deserved it!"

"Who des—" And suddenly it fell into place. "You smacked Diggory for saying it!" Midge tried to choke back her laughter but just ended up choking. When she got her wind back, she managed, "Good for you!"

"I shouldn't have struck him." Now that she'd finished defending her actions, Opal looked properly penitent. "He's my elder, and when we're angry, we're supposed to turn the other cheek."

"Oh good." Midge leaned back and grinned. "I hope he did that, then. That way you could get him again!"

~~~⌘~~~

"She's got spunk," Pa grunted, raking the dried stalks of last year's corn into windrows. "I'll give your new wife that much."

"Don't I know it." Adam searched for a way to shift the conversation to the topic most on his mind while his father seemed inclined to be amiable and Larry worked clear on the other side of the field.

A devilish grin creased his face. "And you nabbing her has got to be giving old Murphy absolute fits. That's not to be discounted. Especially when the dupe can't do a thing about it!"

"That's not why I married her." He pushed prickly, dried out husks of plants into more orderly piles, trying to organize his thoughts.

"Naw." Pa whipped his hat off and fanned his

face with it. "You married her because you found yourself on the wrong end of a shotgun."

"That's not what I meant." *But it's truer than you can ever imagine.*

"Doesn't matter what you meant. Things happen when a man lets a pretty face overrule his common sense." He slapped his hat back on. "I'm sure you didn't mean to get her in the family way either."

Adam held his peace on that one. The truth—that he absolutely was *not* responsible for Opal's predicament—would only get his family hopping mad. Ugly accusations would be flung, honor defended, shots fired. . .and lives lost.

"Didn't think you had it in you, son." Pa resumed raking. "Takes gumption to go after something like that. I'd wondered if Larry's sneaking hadn't been headed that direction, but never so much as suspected you'd be the fox in the Speck henhouse."

"You thought Larry might be after Opal, and you didn't stop it?" Splinters dug into his palms from where he gripped the handle of his rake, but Adam ignored them. "You'd let him prey on a vulnerable woman just because of her last name?"

"Give your brother some credit. The Grogan men have always had a way with the ladies." Pa straightened. "Glad to see it didn't pass you by, that's all."

"Oh yeah." He covered his irritation by moving to a new row. "I'm a real charmer." *Can't even get my own wife to tell me the name of her baby's father.*

"Must've been more charming than your brother. He's had his nose out of joint since you brought her back."

But what if I didn't? What if Larry got to her first, and I just stumbled into a wedding? His mouth went so dry, he drained his canteen. It didn't help.

"Of course, that spunk of hers is going to cause problems. She and your ma are going to butt heads like two old goats."

"My thoughts exactly." Adam seized the opportunity. "Ma and Opal will be at each other's throats as long as they live under the same roof."

"We'll manage." Pa gave the refuse a particularly vicious jab. "Somehow."

"I'll need to build us a home. Wood's too scarce, so it'll be a soddy or dugout. The question is where?"

"Your inheritance, you mean?" Pa propped himself up on his rake. "As the oldest, you're supposed to inherit the house. But I'm a long way from kicking the bucket, so you'll need a place to set up for your own."

"Yes. I was thinking the southeast meadow. Make a dugout from that knoll. It'd be the quickest way." Adam laid out his plan. "I wouldn't neglect my responsibilities on the farm."

"Never thought you would." Pa fingered his beard, an avaricious light entering his gaze. "You think we could get the delta land out of Murphy as Opal's dowry?"

"Her apiary is her dowry." He could scarcely get the words out fast enough. The land that birthed the feud would have no part in his marriage. "It's part of why I said the southeast meadow—the far end of it would be a good place to move her bees. The conditions seem about the same."

"Bees?" Pa's swarthy skin lost some of its sun-fed color. "She's bringing her bees to our farm?"

"Yep." Adam appealed to the one thing he knew outweighed Pa's hesitation over the insects—his practicality. "The hives and honey they produce are valuable—good income even when crops fail. And real beeswax candles are a luxury out here, too."

"Once you're situated, just keep them—and your wife—as far from the homestead as possible."

CHAPTER 16

"M idge!" Opal gasped at the audacity of such a statement, but a smile snuck toward the corners of her mouth.

"Ah, there it is." Midge pointed, completely unrepentant. "The hint of a smile. That's what I hoped for!"

"Trickster." Her reprimand held no heat. "I should tell you that's no excuse for being so outrageous, but since it worked that would make me a hypocrite."

Hypocrite. The reminder stole away what little merriment Midge brought. *Liar. And so many other things I never would have wanted.*

"I know you're going to feel bad about giving Mr. Grogan what for," her friend's voice called back her attention, "but he had no right—and no cause— to accuse you of tricking his son into marriage with another man's child."

"Didn't he?" *I did trick him. And Adam knows full well I'm not carrying his child. So do I have just cause for my indignation?* "I mean, he doesn't know me." She tacked on this last to deflect Midge's curious glance.

"That's not what you meant."

"Oh?"

"No." Midge shifted, resting back on her knees to look her in the eye. "You meant that Diggory hit closer to the truth than he knew, because you aren't carrying Adam's child."

"How can you say that?" Something tore inside her at her friend's casual dismissal. "I thought you said they were featherbrains for believing that!"

"Listen better. I said they're featherbrains for thinking you might be carrying another man's child." A pause. "Not that they were knocked in the noggins for thinking you didn't have Adam's."

"Oh." The astuteness of Midge's assessment stunned her into silence for a precious moment before she rallied. "Well, that's what they think!"

"Forget what they think. You're trying to distract me from what I know." The younger girl settled back on her heels and crossed her arms. "And doing a poor job of it."

"What makes you think I'm not carrying Adam's babe?" Anger pulsed through Opal. "If you didn't believe it, why didn't you object at the wedding?"

"I didn't know until after, what with the pair of you all set to say 'I do.'" Midge shrugged. "Besides, there was the small matter of four Speck shotguns trained on Adam's head and other vitals. I figured you made up the whole thing to save his life."

"It wasn't fair of me to expect you to try and stop it." Opal rubbed a hand over her eyes, not sure whether to be glad someone saw her good intentions for what they were or be even more sorrowful it hadn't been Adam. "Wait. What do you mean you didn't know until after?"

"The kiss."

"It's normal for a groom to kiss his bride." Opal ignored the heat in her cheeks, focusing instead on the prickle of the prairie grass poking against her skirts. She shifted, trying to evade the discomfort.

"Nothing about that wedding came within an acre of normal. And there you go again, blushing just like yesterday. You looked so flustered at having his arms around you, I'd say it's a minor miracle no one else figured out that you two couldn't be lovers."

"What?" *Adam didn't notice my innocence. Why would anyone else?*

"You're my friend, and you're in trouble." Midge narrowed her eyes. "So stop beating around the bush and admit you're as pure as fresh cream butter."

"Midge!"

"All right, all right." Her friend held up her hands, palms out. "At least you were at your wedding yesterday, even if you're a fully married woman now."

"Stop it." Opal looked away. *Adam didn't want me because he thinks I'm used. And he knows I lied to him, even though he doesn't know which lie.* "Just stop it."

"If you and Adam both agree to say the same

thing"—Midge let loose a whoosh of breath Opal couldn't miss—"it's not too late to have this thing annulled. People twist the truth all the time for worse reasons. Even if last night—"

"No!" Opal's head snapped back to her friend so fast she heard a faint popping sound. "If we annul the marriage, our families will kill each other. Pa won't take the slur to my honor, and the Grogans will be up in arms over my lying about Adam's character. It's too late to make things right."

Not even Midge had anything to say to that. An uncharacteristic silence fell between them, Opal pondering the impossible situation once more and coming up with nothing new.

"So what's Adam say about this whole mess?"

"Don't ask."

"Too late. I asked." Midge's eyes narrowed. "I'll even ask again, if you make me."

"Adam. . ." Opal couldn't really find the words. *How does a woman tastefully say that her husband thinks she's hoodwinked him into raising another man's illegitimate offspring?* She gave up. "Adam wants me to tell him who the father really is."

"What?" Midge sprang to her feet. "But Opal, this changes *everything!*"

Silence, Midge felt fairly certain, didn't register on that roster of virtues. Good thing, too, because when she got excited, her mind started going a mile a minute. It only seemed natural that her mouth tried its best to keep up.

Like now.

"Of all the addlepated mistakes!" Trampling the earth between the rows of hives set loose an ominous hum, so she forced herself to slow down. "But there's your solution. All you have to do is tell Adam that you made the whole thing up to save his life, and you'll have the makings of a fine marriage. Most women would jump at the chance to have a grateful husband!"

"I can't." The muffled tones of her friend's voice made Midge turn around to see Opal's legs drawn to her chest, her forehead resting on her knees. "Adam took me as his bride, but he hasn't made me his wife."

"Obviously." Midge flopped down next to her friend. "Otherwise there wouldn't be a snowman's chance on a sunny day he'd still think you carried any man's child."

Her friend's ears, the only part of her visible, turned scarlet.

Midge knew from past observation the color stained Opal's cheeks as well. Another option occurred to her. "Opal, when I said before that you and Adam could get an annulment if you just said the same thing, it's true. You wouldn't even have to tell a falsehood." The rush of possibility carried her away again. "If you're unhappy about this whole thing, I'll never breathe a word. You can prove that the marriage wasn't consummated, and Parson Carter will dissolve it. And you know that for as nice as he is, his liver's whiter than a lily. He won't cross your family or the Grogans. It can be like that wedding never even happened, if that's what you want!"

"No!" When Opal yanked on her wrist, Midge realized she'd started heading toward town. "It won't happen like that. The Grogans will challenge Pa for slandering Adam's good name on my say-so. Not to mention threatening to kill him. The whole thing will backfire."

"And it hasn't already?" Midge shook loose. "You're stuck over there with no one to help you. I always thought Adam was the Grogan with enough brain between his ears to make a respectable rattle, but with him foolish enough to think you're expecting, I'm revising my opinion."

"So long as Pa and my brothers stay alive, I can live with the Grogans." Determination glinted in Opal's blue eyes. "It's more than worth the trade."

"Do you think they'd agree?"

"Pa, Ben, Elroy, and Pete will never find out." The barest breath of a pause. "And I don't care whether most of the Grogans would agree. Adam's alive, and I'll be as good a wife to him as I can— even though he doesn't want me."

"Don't be so sure." Memories of Adam cradling Opal to his chest for a beat too long after carrying her from the fire surged to the front of Midge's mind. "He saved you once, too."

"Because he's a good man." Sadness covered her friend's face like a thick blanket. "He deserves better."

"Good gravy and grits, it must be something catching!" She waved a hand before Opal's eyes as though to test her focus. "One day at the Grogan farm and your wits went dull."

"Stop it." The chide couldn't mask a quick grin.

"There is no better than you, Opal. Adam's a lucky man. He'll figure it out sooner or later, but the sooner the better."

"Any way to help hasten the realization? I'm out of ideas." Her friend gave a gusty sigh. "Though considering my ideas so far, that may be a blessing."

"You'll balk at it."

"After yesterday, you'd be surprised."

"All right." Midge tilted her head so she could see Opal's reaction. "Even if you're not going to go to Parson Carter, why don't you tell Adam the truth about your. . .er, status? My guess is he'll be real glad to hear it, and maybe you two could have a long and happy marriage. . . ."

Midge's voice trailed off as Opal shook her head faster and harder until her bonnet went flying right off. "Impossible!" she gasped. "I can't tell Adam I've never been with a man!"

"Don't get missish on me now." A thump on her friend's back stopped her gasping and started up some spluttering. "It can't be harder to tell your husband you're a good woman than to have him thinking you're some sort of Jezebel."

Midge went quiet after that. Memories of her own past cut off her words like a knife to the throat. Luckily, Opal'd found her ability to speak again.

"I don't mean because it would be awkward!" Her face, a pinkish scarlet, clashed terribly with the fiery wisps of hair dancing around her face.

"Even if it would be the most embarrassing thing on earth—and I'm sure it would—I'd get through it if I thought it would make things better. But if I tell Adam I'm still pure, he'll be the one to call for Parson Carter quicker than I can blink!"

"No he won't. He married you and didn't tell his family that the child he thinks you're carrying isn't his. He won't start the bloodbath for the opposite reason."

"You'd think so." Opal buried her face in her sodden hanky. "But he told me on the way to meet his family he'd already considered an annulment, but it wasn't possible without proof."

"So you can't tell him you have proof."

"Never."

At least, that's what Midge assumed Opal meant. Things went pretty watery again. Well then, an indelicate question couldn't make things any worse. "Do you know when he plans to take his wedding night?"

"Yes." A mighty sniff and a few bleary blinks, then Opal got to the crux of the problem. "Adam says he won't make it a real marriage until after I trust him enough to tell him the name of the father."

Well that's a fine mess.

"And you can't make up a name, because it was winter and there was no one around but the people in town." She turned the problem around in her head. "So you can't tell him the truth, and you can't make up a lie. . . ."

"I'm stuck, all right." Opal patted her apron pockets for another hanky, accepting the one Midge passed her. "And it's only a matter of time before Lucinda, for one, realizes I'm not showing."

"Hmm." Midge flipped the problem over and looked underneath for any hidden solutions. There, in the shadows of her past—the knowledge no proper young lady should have—lurked the germ of an idea. "Opal?" She considered how best to suggest the unthinkable.

"What?" A miserable, wet *honk* punctuated the question.

"You only have one option left."

"There's another option?" Opal's eyes widened. "If it's not annulment and it's not slandering the name of an innocent townsman, I'll do whatever I have to do."

Oh, how easily the innocent are led astray. . .but that's exactly what we'll be counting on.

"Neither of those." Midge took a deep breath and summoned a confident smile. "You're just going to seduce your husband."

CHAPTER 17

There you are!" Lucinda pounced the moment Opal returned from her outing with that uppity Midge Collins. "Should've known you planned to waste half the morning yapping away with your friend when there's work to be done." A broad gesture encompassed her spotless home.

She took pride in her housekeeping, as any good wife and mother ought to, but it didn't serve her plans to flaunt the fact to her new daughter-in-law. A dull pain flared in her midsection, a rejection of Opal's new role.

No matter. She won't be here for long.

"I'll be happy to lend a hand wherever needed." The upstart even managed to say it with a straight face.

Lucinda tucked away the proof of the girl's prowess at lying. "Happy to help, eh?" She drew out the word "happy," as though testing it and finding it false. Which, of course, she did.

"I thought I'd show Opal around today, Ma." Willa's hasty offer earned her a scowl. "Show her where we keep things, how the machines work since there are bound to be differences."

"Perhaps some other time, dear." She casually walked behind the girls and made a show of looking out the open door. "It's such a fine day. Don't you think it's a fine day, Opal? You've seen enough of it to be certain."

"Very fine." At least the girl knew enough not to argue.

"Well, with a beautiful day and three women working, I'd think it's a perfect time to begin spring cleaning!" She sprang the trap shut with military precision. "Just think how much you'll learn about this household, Opal." With an effort, she kept her smile from being too wolfish.

Oh, you'll learn. You'll learn to rue the day you looked twice at my son. You'll learn that I can make your back ache and your eyes tear and your hands bleed before I'm through. But most of all, you'll learn that there isn't a place in Buttonwood far enough from this farm—that it's best to leave the Nebraska Territory altogether.

"Spring cleaning?" Apprehension laced her daughter's brow. "What did you have in mind, Ma?"

"Whatever needs to be done, I'll see to it." Opal's stiff neck brought her that much closer to being broken.

"Everything calls for a washing, of course." Lucinda started small. "The rugs beaten, the bedding and quilts laundered, the mattresses restuffed, and the stove needs a thorough scrubbing."

"Where do you want to start?" The girl's words could have been deferential had they come from another woman. Instead, they sounded a challenge.

"I've dinner going, so the stove will keep until tomorrow." She kept her tone light, trying not to let any triumph creep in. "And, of course, it's too late to begin laundry. Might be a good time to see about stuffing the mattresses."

"With both of us working, we can finish today," Willa offered.

No, no, no. Willa's not supposed to spend time with the girl. This isn't an opportunity to make nice or help her be comfortable. She's supposed to be hot and burdened with the dry, itchy work. "Willa, I'd thought perhaps you could see to—"

"Showing her where we keep the dried husks in the barn?" Willa already headed out the door. "This way, Opal."

Lucinda held her peace as they left. Even with Willa's help, Opal would have to work through the morning and the entire afternoon to see the job done.

Then, tomorrow, Lucinda could begin making the small comments about restless sleep, tossing and turning. About cricks in her back and neck and hard stalks poking her through the mattress—jabs that shouldn't happen if the job were done right. Unless, of course, Opal had meant for it to?

Because working the girl into exhaustion wasn't enough to bring the type of misery Lucinda intended. For that type of despair, she'd need to take away Adam's support of his new bride. Which suited her just fine.

Lucinda shoved away a twinge of guilt.

It's not bearing false witness. I'm just speeding things up so Adam realizes the type of girl he's chained to in time to make a difference. If she stayed, he'd find out that it's all true. He'd just find out too late.

Opal didn't like whiners. Complaining didn't make work any easier, quicker, or more pleasant. It might be good for letting off steam, but the only other thing it accomplished was to make a body seem lazy, weak, petty, snobby, or spoiled. In short, all the things Grogans were raised to believe Specks succumbed to. She'd rather wear shoes two sizes too small than complain. In fact, she point-blank refused to do it.

Aloud, at least.

Within the confines of her own mind, however, she allowed herself to acknowledge her suspicions that Lucinda thought up the day's activity as a punishment for daring to marry Adam. Opal slept on one of these mattresses just the night before and saw no urgent need for restuffing.

I didn't actually sleep, her innate sense of fairness pointed out. *But that didn't matter. It could have been a bed made for a queen and I wouldn't have slept last night!*

The edge of the mattress she and Willa lugged outside late this morning had struck her as perfectly comfortable the night before. Together they managed to heft it in a bulky fold over the Grogans' sturdy wash line. It sagged toward the ground, lumpy as the corn husks inside slowly shifted toward the earth.

"Just a minute." Willa darted toward the barn and came back moments later carrying a horse blanket, which she spread underneath. "This'll make it easier to carry the old out to the compost heap."

"Right." Opal already started cutting through the threads stitching shut the reinforced cotton. In no time they were scooping armfuls of the crinkly old bedding onto the horse blanket.

It took a couple of trips to the compost heap before they'd emptied it completely. Then they turned the entire thing inside out and took turns beating the empty covering until dust and debris danced in the air. By that time, bits of the dried material tickled her throat, scratched her arms, and clung to her dress, but it couldn't be avoided.

Opal didn't hold with vanity but knew full well that she presented a poor picture the moment Lucinda chose to ring the dinner bell. In addition to the dried bits of plant, she'd taken the last shift with the rug beater, so moisture from the heat of the work dotted her brow and made errant locks of her hair stick to her temples.

Willa, having rested for a few moments and even washed up at the well, looked a far sight better as the men came in from the fields. If it weren't so completely absurd, Opal would suspect Lucinda waited until she looked her worst to summon Adam—to show him what a horror he'd married. *You're just going to seduce your husband.* Midge's brilliant solution of that morning echoed in her mind. As though it hadn't seemed a ridiculous suggestion before.

"I better go see if Ma needs any help." Willa hurried to the house.

Opal put her frustrations into the last few whacks of the rug beater until she was satisfied that the mattress cover, at least, classified as clean. She raised her arm to swipe back a few hairs with the back of her hand.

The Grogan men trouped behind her to the well, the sounds of water splashing intensifying the tickle in Opal's throat. She hesitated to follow, instead hanging back until they'd all gone inside. Then she made hasty work of rinsing her arms and face, patting them dry with her slightly scratchy apron front before rolling down her sleeves and heading for the house.

It took a moment for her eyes to adjust to the dark interior of the house after the bright noon sun. When she could see, Opal paused. Diggory sat at the head of the table, Lucinda, Willa, and Dave to his left, Adam to his right. But Larry sat on Adam's other side, leaving the foot of the table the only open space.

The clear message as to her low status in the eyes of the family carried the extra unpleasant touch of sticking her beside Larry. But more than anything, the fact Adam supported the arrangement left her adrift.

"Looks like she's stopped dawdling." Dave, the young boy who'd spent a lazy morning fishing, greeted her arrival with a scowl that would have made Lucinda proud.

It must have. She wore one to make a matching set. "Now that you've graced us with your presence, take a seat. I'll tell you we won't wait dinner on you again. If you expect to enjoy the bounty of my husband's table, remember that we don't tolerate laziness on *this* farm."

Opal didn't feel the itch of tiny pieces of corn husk in her mouth anymore. Instead, the insistent clawing of hot words tore at her throat. She swallowed them.

"Ma! Opal finished beating that mattress while I came in to help set the table." Willa's unexpected defense soothed her just enough to make speech possible.

"I'll remember." She forced a smile and moved toward Adam. "I know how hard *my* husband works on *our* behalf."

"Larry," Adam all but barked his brother's name, "why have you still not moved?" His words sent hope piercing through her.

"Because he is my son." Diggory's bushy brows now lowered. "And his place at my table won't be usurped. That gal is not a Grogan, and her place is at the foot of this family. She should just be thankful it's not beneath it!"

"You speak of my wife." Adam rose to his feet. "Her place is by my side." Without another word, he plunked *himself* at the foot of the table.

Opal's eyes went wide.

"Adam!" Lucinda all but shrieked. "What foolishness is this?"

"The foolishness of a family who cares more for past grudges than current commitments." For the first time, as Adam set his jaw and glared around the table, Opal acknowledged his resemblance to the rest of his kin. "If you deny my wife her place, you deny me mine. Larry, move up."

Silence stalked every person at the table, from Dave's unhinged jaw to Diggory's too-tight one. But no one made a move.

"Now!" The sudden explosion of Adam's order made Larry jump.

He didn't move much to the side—but it was enough. Opal slipped onto the bench, hanging off it really but seated next to the man who'd made her his priority.

My husband. The thought humbled her. *Perhaps . . .just perhaps, this could work, after all.*

"Don't think I've forgotten," Adam's murmur, so low no one else at the table even heard it, caught her off guard, "that yesterday you told me to ask tomorrow. I'll be expecting my answer."

Though it seemed years ago instead of just the day before, Opal knew he meant to ask her the name of the father. Again.

She stifled a sigh and passed the biscuits.

Then again, maybe not.

CHAPTER 18

Another morning dawned, making Adam a man with a marriage almost two days old—not long by any standards. The measure grew shorter when one considered they slept in different beds. In different buildings. He fought back a wince.

Lord, You know full well why I had to make that decision. Not only would Ma raise hue and cry if I booted Larry from the barn and installed Opal with me, it'd be akin to a fasting man surrounding himself with his favorite foods. Leaving the temptation untouched, the hunger unfulfilled, would be next to impossible.

Besides, Adam never intended his wife—no matter how convoluted that story came to be—would live in a barn annex. Shotgun wedding didn't mean slapdash home, and he'd already laid the groundwork for their own place by talking with Pa yesterday. Now, all he needed to do was get Opal to trust him enough that they could move forward with this marriage.

At the moment, he got on with the morning chores. Larry's turn to do the mucking meant he moved forward with the feeding—the far better rotation. He grabbed two big, tightly woven baskets and headed to the silage pit behind the barn. The fragrant corn fodder, chopped up and left to ferment, made a moist and heavy feed the cows loved.

The rich scent of it mixed the sour tang of buttermilk—though none went into making silage—with the sweetness of corn. Adam figured he liked the smell as much as the cows did. But filling the baskets and emptying a hefty measure in the manger before each stanchion left a man with time to think.

And Adam's thoughts were full of his new wife. He'd watched her with Larry the day before enough to be certain Opal didn't return his brother's interest. If anything, she kept as far away as possible. That meant there wasn't any real impediment to the marriage. Sure, his family didn't accept her, but that would take time. *Time, I have.*

Daisy followed him eagerly to the watering tank, the great horse lowering her head to take deep drafts. Water splashed down her long throat, fascinating Adam as it always had.

God's imagination knows no bounds. So the unthinkable to us—that Opal and I should be man and wife—may well be as practical and beautiful as anything else in this world. How am I to know? After all, they'd only been married for two days. Not long enough to make the marriage real, but long enough for Adam to learn a few very important things he hadn't suspected about Opal Speck—make that Opal *Grogan*. He liked the sound of that.

Her temper rivaled any in her family. She just kept better control of it. Opal hadn't come to this farm and set up a sulk, either. She pitched in and, despite the situation, didn't complain. But, other than the revelation she didn't harbor a secret love for his brother, Adam's most important discovery was that his intriguing little wife had a determined streak that could out-stubborn a mule. And she'd focused it on avoiding him.

Oh, he had no questions as to why she kept as far away from him as possible. She'd begun that little dance just after dinner the day before, following his reminder that they were due a certain conversation. Which went to show that forewarned definitely made an intelligent woman forearmed.

How else to explain how Opal, who'd scarcely set foot on Grogan property aside from community events in years past, developed such a staggering specialty in slinking around unseen? Her newfound ability made his father nervous. Adam would have found it amusing if it weren't so aggravating.

Which, come to think of it, pretty much sums up Opal. Too bad—it's her turn for a little aggravation!

He'd known Opal would be along to help Willa with the morning milking. And now she couldn't hie off or pretend she hadn't heard him call. A slow grin spread across his face when she spotted him and shot a quick look toward the door.

"Mornin', Opal." He banged shut the lid on the oat bin and finished with feeding the horses. "I want a word."

"Oh?" She snatched a three-legged stool and milk pail, making a beeline for the nearest cow. She set them both down, working them into the layers of hay and settling herself on the stool in less time than Adam would have thought possible, given her skirts. "What about?"

"A *private* word." He put a staying hand on her shoulder before she began milking the beast and would have good reason not to stop.

"Willa and I need to do the milking." Her feigned innocence would have put suspicion in the softest heart. "I take my responsibilities seriously, Adam."

"Your first responsibility lies with your husband."

"Go ahead, Opal." Willa's voice came from the next cow, where she sat milking. "I've milked these cows by myself for years."

"But"—his wife's anxiety came across as true—"I don't want your mother to say I'm shirking."

"Then stop dragging your heels." He shoved back a twinge of guilt over how Ma had been treating her. There'd be an adjustment period until he had their dugout set up. "Come on." Adam slid his hand beneath her elbow and braced her until she stood, reluctantly walking with him into the crisp chill of the morning.

He led her a good distance from the barn, making sure no one would overhear their conversation. Every step chafed at him, wearing his patience a little thinner, until he turned to her. He didn't bother wasting a word, just raised a brow, waiting. Now that he'd gotten her alone, she'd have to spit out the truth.

She didn't spit out anything. As a matter of fact, Opal didn't even look at him. Her gaze traced rolling patterns in the clouds, her breath came in nervous little hums he almost found endearing. But not a word crossed her lips.

"Opal. . ." He spoke her name slow and low. It was half invitation to tell him what he wanted to know, half warning if she didn't.

"Yes Adam?" She blinked, her smile too bright.

"I suggest you start talking, wife."

"Wife. . ." The term seemed to galvanize her. "Yes, husband. We've much to discuss."

At last.

"I've several concerns, Adam." Pain clouded her gaze. "I've no right to ask, but I—" A hard swallow cut off her words, like she choked back strong emotion.

It struck him, suddenly, how fragile she was. Despite her facade of strength, his bride found herself in enemy territory, torn away from everyone she loved, and had given herself—in the eyes of God and man—into his power. Was it any wonder she feared his reaction when she told him the name of her child's father? What the consequences could be?

"Ask." He laid a hand on her shoulder. "What most troubles you?" Adam waited to hear of her worry that he'd set her aside when she made her revelation. Or her fear that his parents would make the rest of her life miserable, perhaps.

"My family needs me." She fingered the pin she always wore near her heart. "They think I betrayed them. . . ." A tear splashed onto the back of her hand.

"You're not asking to go back?" Something lurched inside him. *She's leaving me.*

"Could I?" Hope, pure and beautiful, shone in her eyes, lightening the blue. "Just some days. I wouldn't neglect my duties here. But Pa and Ben and Elroy and Pete don't have any women—only me. If I could have a baking day, help tend a garden, maybe a little washing. . ." The words poured forth like an overflowing stream, the flood of her heart.

Her concern isn't for her at all. Adam couldn't answer for a moment. Couldn't even listen to the rest of it as she continued. *It's for her family.*

"Only two days out of six. Or even just the afternoons. . ." She didn't stop to draw a breath the whole time she talked. Just stared up at him like he had the power to make her dreams come true.

And what small dreams they were—to do double the work.

"Yes." What other answer could he possibly give? "I'll talk to Ma about which days would be best."

"Thank you." Gratitude lit her face, making her beautiful. "Oh Adam." She bit her lip. "Thank you."

"Pa's agreed to let you have the meadow bordering Speck lands for your apiary." He couldn't resist the urge to add to her joy. "Let me know about moving it."

"Soon." She fingered her brooch once more. "The meadow is a good place for them—no blockages for the scouts."

"Good." Now that she seemed so much happier—like she didn't dread talking to him—Adam suddenly realized how much he wanted her to want to be around him. But still... "Opal, you know I have to ask. You promised you'd tell me who the father is."

The change in her expression came on so sudden, it was like watching a spring storm roll in across a clear sky. "I can't tell you."

"You wouldn't break your word." He refused to believe it. "Tell me."

"I'm not breaking my word." She closed her eyes. When she opened them, pain darkened them once again. "I said I'd tell you if you asked tomorrow." She drew a deep breath and squared her shoulders. "That meant yesterday."

Opal didn't even try to hold her head high after she left Adam and returned to the barn. Sure... she'd expressly avoided him after dinner the day before to avoid breaking her word. Never mind she'd assumed he would never have cause to ask the question again. He'd shunned their marriage bed and so still didn't know the dismal truth.

The only thing I've created are half-lies. Opal considered them for a moment. Naming Adam as the man who *would be* the father of her child. Saying she *couldn't* give him a name. Telling him he absolutely *can't* get an annulment. Then telling the

Grogans she couldn't *lie* about nonconsummation.

Every single statement skirting truth's edge but dipping into deception because Opal knew how it would be interpreted. She sighed as she helped Willa carry the fresh milk to the springhouse. They lowered the pails into the cool, slow-flowing springwater until only the top third stayed above the surface.

That's how I feel. Sinking so deep, I can barely keep my head above the water, Lord. I'm so busy watching my words, my faults rise higher and higher until they'll wash away what I love. I try to change the things that need changing but make so many mistakes! And what can I do but wade through them? Even if it takes me deeper still. . .

"Do you want to gather the eggs or go fry the bacon for breakfast?" Willa had the grace to wait for Opal's response before heading to the house, despite the obvious choice.

"I'd be more than happy to gather the eggs and feed the chickens." Better to face a few hen pecks than Lucinda's beak! "The corn sheller doesn't need two people."

So they split ways, her sister-in-law moving homeward and Opal grabbing a basket. She searched the raised lean-to, originally a toolshed, which the Grogans converted to a winter coop first. As it had the day before, the stench of the accumulated winter droppings below made her wrinkle her nose. The coop needed a thorough spring cleaning. Otherwise the daily task of gathering would become something to dread.

She briefly considered offering to take on the

unpleasant chore but discarded the idea. Lucinda would probably take offense, seeing it as an implied insult or Opal trying to tell her what needed to be done. If she did the work without asking, her mother-in-law would assume Opal was acting snooty and making decisions about the farm.

After a long, cold jail sentence, most of the hens happily roamed the farmyard, testing their freedom, investigating the offerings of springtime as plants and insects poked from the ground. Only a few kept to the coop, moody clucks who took exception to her search and showed their displeasure with sharp pecks and indignant squawks. Later more hens would return to the nests, when laying truly began.

Today, Opal left without much to show for the experience but a few scrapes on the backs of her hands and satisfaction in a thorough job. *Now for the real task of hunting eggs.* The sun showed more of its strength as morning aged, brightening the farmyard for her exploration. Left to search around fence posts, beside walls, and beneath mangers, she became familiar with favorite spots of the Grogan chickens. More importantly, she became more familiar with the farm.

She even discovered a well-hidden nest tucked under the corner of the corncrib, with no fewer than four eggs nestled beneath the outraged young biddy guarding them. She puffed up to look twice her size, but Opal won the day, carrying her find to the kitchen.

Considering she'd harvested twice as many eggs

as she and Willa managed the previous morning, she felt pretty good about the work. Neither Willa nor Lucinda heard her enter over the sizzle of bacon frying in the skillet, so Opal simply set the basket on the table.

"How are the chickens?" Lucinda somehow managed to make it sound as though her hens would suffer under Opal's care.

"Well enough, though. . ." She let her words trail off, as though hesitant to say more.

"Though?" An imperious brow hiked toward the older woman's hairline.

"Now that the hens roam free, it might be a good time to have one of the men collect the winter waste." Opal wrinkled her nose for effect. "Not that I envy them, but I know they'll be fertilizing the fields about now."

"True." The speculative gleam in Lucinda's eye before she turned back to the stove told Opal her gambit worked.

I'll be cleaning out that coop before the week is out. Opal shook her head at Lucinda's predictability as she made her way back to the barn.

The Grogans used a different model corn sheller than she'd always operated, but it worked on the same principle. This Rufus Porter design featured a hand crank that looked a lot like a spinning wheel laid on its side and belted to a box where you pushed in the corn up top. Stripped cobs came out the bottom, and the kernels spewed out the side into whatever bag or basket awaited them.

Opal hauled over a bunch of corn, stuffed it into

the top, and started turning the wheel. Same as with any machine she'd ever used, starting the thing made for the roughest work. Before long she whirled that wheel for all she was worth, excepting a few stops and starts to put in other loads. It took awhile before she filled the feed basket, but she didn't mind.

The sound of the sheller, the rhythm of the work, the sight of corn kernels piling high were the closest she'd come to home in two days. When Opal finished, she balanced the basket on one hip and headed in the general direction of the coop.

"Chick, chick, chick," she called, clicking the roof of her mouth to catch their attention. When she spotted the first feathers, Opal began the continual process of reaching into the basket, filling her palm with corn, and scattering it along the ground. Hens came rushing around fences and from under hay-stacks, their thin legs at odds with their top-heavy bodies. Anticipation made them race toward her, causing the slightly hitched stride Opal found so familiar and oddly comforting.

She flung more and more handfuls in wider circles, birds following her like so many eager puppies nipping at her heels. Only instead, they darted their necks down to snatch a morsel of food with their beaks before tilting back their heads to swallow it whole.

The roosters managed to behave as though she bestowed the food upon their harem at their express command, strutting like glossy overseers. From time to time, they'd find a particularly appealing kernel and let loose an imperial "tut, tut, tut," until a group of hens came rushing over to fight for it.

By the time she'd finished, her heart didn't feel so heavy. The simple chores reminded her that a greater design guided everything, making farmyards and animals and shelling corn the same wherever one went. It was vastly reassuring to find the familiar when surrounded by so much strangeness.

God ordered the world. It wasn't her place to change it, and fighting her circumstances wouldn't do anything but give her grief. Instead, she'd work here, help out back home, and do what she needed to maintain the balance. Because that was a different thing entirely from changing, and peace was worth maintaining.

Opal watched as Adam wiped his feet before entering the house then moved to follow him.

Whatever it takes.

CHAPTER 19

Midge sucked in a breath as she jabbed another finger with her needle. With a glance around, she saw Clara rocking Maddie, listening as Saul read from the Reed family Bible. The Bible where even Midge's name pranced across the genealogy page, despite her not being related by blood.

As that blood, tainted by the past Saul saved her from, welled into a droplet, Midge stuck the injured finger in her mouth. Of all the folks in Buttonwood, only Saul and Clara knew the truth about where she came from.

The first honest, truly honest, people I ever met, and I made liars out of them without even meaning to.

Over two years, and they hadn't breathed a word that Saul hadn't found Midge on the streets of Baltimore. She'd found him while trolling the streets.

But not in time to save her sister. No. By the time Midge brought him back to their alley, Nancy's blood had left her body. *And Nancy left me.*

Midge looked down at the diluted smear around her pricked fingertip and squeezed it until it welled dark red again. She stared at it for a long time. The more of it that gathered, the longer it sat, the darker it became until the red seemed closer to black.

This is who I am. I don't belong with the Reeds any more than Opal belongs with the Grogans. The only difference is I'm lucky. And since I don't deserve my good fortune, and Opal deserves better than her misfortune, I have to figure out a way to help her.

She sniffed, trying to dislodge the lump in her throat. It didn't do much good. But suddenly, something Saul was reading caught her ear.

"Wait a minute!" She sat up straighter. "Can you go back a bit? Reread that last part?"

"Of course." Surprise lined Saul's face, and Midge knew Clara's expression would be the same if she cared to look.

But for now, her attention stayed riveted on her adopted father as he read from Galatians.

" 'But the fruit of the Spirit is love, joy, peace, longsuffering, gentleness, goodness, faith, meekness, temperance: against such there is no law.' "

Saul made as though to go on, but Midge cleared her throat to stop him. It would have been disrespectful to outright interrupt a reading of the Holy Book—asking for him to reread part didn't count—but she had a question. They were always encouraging her to ask questions about God and the Bible, so for once she aimed to take them up on some answers!

"Yes Midge?" Excitement gleamed in Clara's green eyes, making them almost catlike.

"Is 'fruit of the Spirit' another way to say virtue? I mean, I thought there were only seven virtues, but there are two extras tacked on."

"Fruit of the Spirit are traits of good character. You can call them virtues. We all fall short but keep trying." Clara's explanation didn't quite answer what Midge was looking for.

"I think she's referring to the classical virtues." Saul's expression grew thoughtful. "They are both lists of goals for behavior, but they are different. The fruit of the Spirit are spiritual values, Midge. Classical virtues have more practical applications."

Well, that's good. I'm not peaceful, long-suffering, gentle, good, meek, temperate, or someone who shares this faith! Love has to be earned and joy's hard to come by, so those don't overflow from me either.

Midge decided to can the fruit. *Practical sounds more my style.*

"Then what are the classical virtues?" She crossed her fingers behind her skirts. Sure, she knew Saul and Clara wouldn't like the old superstition, but she couldn't help hoping she scored better marks on the next list.

"Faith, hope, and charity are the first three." Clara's comment didn't make Midge feel much better.

Well, I do have hope. . . .

"That sounds a lot alike to me." And her saying so sounded like a grumble, but she wasn't pretending to be long-suffering, after all.

"Temperance makes both lists, too. It's the other three virtues that sets them apart." Saul pinched the bridge of his nose, the way he always did when he was thinking.

"Oh?" Midge inched toward the edge of her chair.

"Prudence, justice, and fortitude." He sounded triumphant that he'd remembered.

"Prudence means wisdom, right?" Midge decided that being able to keep her head in a tough time counted, so she gave herself a checkmark for that when Clara and Saul nodded. And hadn't she just thought the other day that she had a strong sense of justice? This was more like it! "What's fortitude?"

"It's—"

"Wait!" Clara hushed Saul before he could make things easy by just telling her. That was the hitch about Clara having taught her to read and write—she kept wanting to make Midge think and learn. "What does it sound like?"

"*Fort* and *attitude* put together, so like someone who acts like they can't be brought down." It sounded silly to Midge, and she got a crazy image of someone wearing a little wooden fort and walking around as though nothing could hurt him.

"That's actually very good." Saul's brows went up over his spectacles. "Fortitude is another word for perseverance—a way of saying it's someone who doesn't give up, even when things seem impossible."

Well, what do you know? Midge popped to her feet and went to give each of them a hug. She would've tickled baby Maddie but didn't want to wake her up.

"What's this for?" Clara's smile seemed a touch confused.

"Not much." *I got a solid four out of seven.* Midge scampered up the stairs with a lot of planning to do but decided to let her family know why she seemed so happy. "It just turns out I'm a virtuous woman, that's all!"

But I've still got a few tricks up my sleeves. . . .

"Adam?" The feminine voice called loud to carry into the field and reach him.

Adam pushed on, the steel tip of the plow he guided breaking thick earth behind Daisy's powerful pull. His wife may have avoided him two days ago, but he hadn't yet found the temperance to hold another conversation with her since the morning before.

His grip tightened on the worn handles as he remembered the way she oh-so-casually walked away from her promise to reveal the identity of her child's father. Literally turned her back to him and walked away as though she owed him no explanations simply because the sun had set and risen.

And I let her do it. Adam pushed harder, and Daisy picked up her pace. *I let her walk away because I was afraid of my own anger. Of what I'd say. Of how I'd make things so awful for her here that she'd run away and the feud would descend upon my family after all. Biding my time is the best choice.*

"Adam?" The voice sounded closer now, slightly out of breath.

"I'll speak with you when I'm good and ready." He bit out the words without so much as looking over his shoulder. "Not before."

"Well, I'm ready now." Now that her breath caught up with her, the woman didn't sound familiar. "And I hope you weren't planning to talk to Opal that way."

"Who are you to tell me how to speak to my wife?" His shoulders stiffened, but he kept plowing forward.

Maybe you need *someone to tell you how to talk to your wife.* A small, too-logical part of him made the suggestion, but he squashed it. He'd been more than reasonable.

"Someone who knows you should at least look a body in the eye to have a civil conversation." Midge Collins bustled into view, walking backward so she could face him. "But maybe I overestimated your ability to *have* a civil conversation."

"Whoa," Adam called the big draft horse to a halt and stared at his unwelcome visitor.

With her arms folded across her chest and freckles marching across her nose, Midge Collins looked determined to have her say. What she had any say in escaped him at the moment, but Adam knew he'd be hearing about it.

"I'm not in a civil mood." He stalked past her to unhitch Daisy from the plow, leading her across that field and the next toward the nearest stream.

The sound of Midge's footsteps tracked him. "You don't belong here."

"It's God's green earth, so I figure I belong as much as anyone." A defiant note crept into her voice. "And I need to talk to you."

"You know it's not proper to be alone with a man." *Think, girl. Days past you were at my wedding, the penalty for me supposedly fornicating with a young woman!* He'd always found irony laughable in the past, but this went beyond what anyone could term humorous.

"That's all right." She stopped right beside him as they reached the water's edge. "I'm not planning on a proper conversation."

"What?"

"Go ahead and smile." She tugged at her bonnet brim. "You look like you don't know if you want to grin or try for a quick escape. I'm pretty fast, so my advice is you let out a smile. It'll make you feel better—civil, even. Then hear me out."

"Miss Collins, you have my full attention." Adam kept a lid on his grin anyway. *Not planning a proper conversation. Ha!*

"I'm glad you're not feeling civil. It means I don't have to shilly-shally around things, talking about the weather or," her voice took on a clipped, oh-so-proper enunciation, "how pleased I was to attend your wedding." She dropped the pretense. "Sometimes civility can be silly."

"There's a difference between chitchat and civility."

"Not for women."

Silence wound around them while they considered that.

"I think you may be onto something." The thought made him grin.

"You'd be surprised what I catch on to." She reached out to stroke Daisy's mane. "Now, Adam, fact of the matter is, I did attend your wedding because Opal's my friend."

"Don't be so sure." A sudden memory of his bride-to-be's youngest brother ratting him out revived old anger. *He gawked like I'd look at Midge if I thought no one was watching.* Seemed far too coincidental that the witness Pete "happened" to run across was none other than the girl before him. But Adam wouldn't stoop so low as to say so.

"Well, Pete asked me because he likes me." Her matter-of-fact answer gave him all the satisfaction of having taken his revenge on Pete, with none of the guilt. "I went because I care about Opal."

"You two are that close?" Adam trod carefully. *Could Midge tell him the name of any men hanging around with Opal?* If he worked it right, maybe she'd never know what he was angling for. . . .

"Close enough to know that she'll make you a good wife. Then again, I'm not close to you, but I didn't try to interfere with the wedding because I thought you'd make her a good husband." She cast him a shrewd glance. "I caught you gaping at her from the Burns' stable annex while she talked with Brett, you know."

"I don't gape." He bristled at the idea he'd been caught staring at Opal. *Twice. In one week. By two different people.* He stopped bristling.

"Pete said he caught you so easy because you were busy gawking at her on the farm. Do you like that better?" She shrugged. "It doesn't matter. I just figured you were smart enough to realize what a special woman she is and scooped her up."

"She's special, all right." *And driving me mad with her secrets. Mad enough not to trust myself around her.*

"I shouldn't have swallowed the story so fast."

"Story?" It took effort not to shift or make any movements to give away his unease.

Midge, true to her word, still caught on. "You just went still as a statue and twice as stony."

"What story?" *What do you think you know?*

"Now that's the question, isn't it?" She cocked her head to the side. "Some stories, folks carry around until they wear out then patch them up with new material to trot around again. But the most interesting tales are made up out of whole cloth. Like this one."

"I'm not here to amuse you." He didn't pretend he didn't understand her direction.

"Never said I was amused by it." Midge's gaze pinned him with the finality of truth. "You never touched Opal before your wedding day, and we both know it."

"Don't make assumptions."

"There's advice you should take to heart." She hadn't blinked in too long. "But anyone who knew Opal, or who cared more about her than their own pride that day to look, could see it on her face that you'd never kissed her before."

Adam remembered the feel of Opal in his arms, the soft look of wonder on her face when he drew back, his initial impression after their embrace. *Midge offers a better explanation than Opal'd never been kissed at all, considering the situation.*

"No need to admit it. You swept her away with that risky move—one that almost had the Speck boys have you leave with a bullet as a souvenir, by the by."

Swept her away, eh? He felt. . .taller. . .at the idea.

"You went still again," Midge's observation broke through his thoughts, "but I'll discount it since that grin takes away the stony look."

"Is that why you came?" He wiped the grin from his face. "To tell me you believe I wasn't her lover?" *And still aren't, but that will change as soon as she coughs up the name of the child's father.*

"That and to see your reaction." Midge started tromping back up the short embankment. "Judging by that grin you aren't sporting anymore, seems I won't need to deliver my warning."

"I trust you'll keep your suspicions to yourself?" Adam wouldn't verify them but didn't want her blabbing.

"Of course." She stopped. "And I'd like to help Opal with her apiary. I know it'll need to be moved, and I'm interested in learning about the bees, if that's all right."

"All right." Not that he'd deny a simple request when she kept such a dangerous secret, but Adam couldn't shake the feeling Midge had another motive for wanting to be around Opal.

"Thanks." Suddenly, without all the spunk and vinegar, she seemed what she'd been all along—a young girl trying to look out for her friend. "No warning, but. . .Adam?"

"Yes Midge?" He couldn't help but think Opal had chosen a good ally.

"Be good to her. She deserves better than you know."

CHAPTER 20

Waiting made time seem to unwind still more slowly on the Grogan farm. Opal knew she'd angered Adam and didn't want to push him about the times she could go over to her family's farm. If she asked after the stunt she'd pulled at the end of their last conversation, he might change his mind altogether. So she cooled her heels and took whatever task Lucinda shoveled out.

Her new mother-in-law seemed determined to account for every moment of Opal's day, as though in retribution for her very presence on the farm. Little did she know that the constant tasks keeping her busy were also what kept Opal sane.

Even so, she found it hard to hide her smile when Lucinda requested that Opal clean out the "winter accumulation" in the chicken coop. *Lucinda can't know I maneuvered this.* But, Opal reminded herself, no matter how she'd be glad the next time she gathered eggs, today would be far from pleasant.

Armed with her oldest apron, a broom, a scrub brush, thick gloves, a bucket of water, and an empty bucket for disposing of the waste, Opal marched up to the converted lean-to and shooed away the chickens. A cursory check turned up a single egg since she'd looked before breakfast. She set it aside and got to work.

Loading up the old nests, well worn after winter, into malleable bundles wouldn't have been unpleasant if it weren't for the pungent stench and accompanying ammonia fumes almost overpowering the now-empty coop. Opal toted the nests to the compost heap, gulping in the fresh air between. She judged the compost to be the less offensive of the two places.

When she returned to the coop, she stood as near the entrance as possible to wield her broom. She whisked out the old straw, dotted with the distinctive grayish-white of chicken waste, sodden and long overdue for replacing. Opal swallowed back her gags to haul bucketful after bucketful back to the compost heap until she couldn't tell which smelled worse.

Back into the corners, along the shelves, in the crevices of the wood, not a stick of straw escaped the purging. By the time she'd removed everything offensive, she felt distinctly lightheaded. *I breathed in too much of that ammonia,* she decided, turning over the now-empty waste bucket and sitting outside in the shade for a moment. She breathed deeply of the fresh air, letting her head lean against the wall of the coop and her eyes drift shut until the world stopped twirling.

"Enjoying the shade, are you?" Diggory's gruff tone dripped contempt. "Good to see my son married such a *hardworking* woman."

"He did." The criticism stung—both at its injustice and at the core truth she wasn't the woman for Adam. She stood up to face him but moved too quickly. The ground swayed.

"Whoa." Diggory reached out to clamp his hands on her shoulders, keeping her at arm's length but supporting her nonetheless. "Easy there."

When the ground stopped swaying, Opal realized it hadn't been the ground at all. She blushed. "The coop needed cleaning, and I got a little dizzy."

"You stay too long in there and the ammonia will do that to you." He hesitantly removed one hand, as though seeing if she'd topple over. When she remained upright, he drew back the other. "Especially in your condition."

The blush grew hotter and, if experience had taught her anything, brighter. "It's nothing, really."

"You were right to take a minute." His voice stayed gruff, but now it held no censure. "I can have Dave finish carting out the old bedding and straw. Plenty of other things for you to do."

"It's already finished." She reached for her water bucket. "I'm ready to start washing it down."

"Good." With that, he left her with her scrub brush. . .and her thoughts.

Opal sucked in a deep breath before ducking into the coop. She stayed close to the entrance, letting the place air out before she ventured to the confines of the dark corners. The top roosts felt the rough swipes of her brush first as she worked her way back then down. Periodic stops to empty filthy water and fetch fresh kept her head from spinning.

Coming this far, and having Diggory see her struggle, Opal refused to leave a single nook not scrubbed. She couldn't poke a broom back and sweep out debris anymore. Only the deepest, darkest, bottommost corners of the lean-to presented her with difficulty. Getting back into the very corners for a thorough scrubbing necessitated lying flat on her stomach and reaching beneath the lowest roost.

She'd just finished the final one when she heard the heavy thud of men's boots race up to the coop. Opal didn't have time to wriggle out and stand up before he came inside and witnessed her indignity.

"Opal!"

Adam's shout gave her such a start she banged her head on the roost. "What?" Scooching backward so she could rise up on her hands and knees to rub the back of her head, Opal eyed her irate husband.

Whatever it is, it can't be good.

"I know I told that girl we wouldn't wait dinner on her." Ma sniffed and wielded her ladle. "Diggory, why don't you go on ahead and say the blessing?"

"Because I'm going to check on the gal." Pa stood up. "She close to fell over earlier, cleaning out that coop in her—"

The rest of his father's words were lost as Adam

vaulted off of his seat and out the door, hitting the ground running and not stopping until he reached the coop. No sign of Opal anywhere around.

He stooped a considerable way to get inside but didn't see more than the outlines of empty roosting shelves after the brightness of outdoors. Adam squinted and made out a figure lying prone on the ground.

"Opal!" It came out as a howl as he hunkered down to help her. His chest constricted so tight, it was little wonder she'd had a hard time catching her breath in the confines of the coop.

Thunk. The lowest roost shook as Opal backed out from beneath it, a scrub brush in her hand and a frown on her face. She scooted back until she could kneel then reached up to rub what would probably be a sizable lump on the back of her noggin.

"What?"

"You didn't come to dinner." *And I thought you might be passed out in here.* Now that he looked around, he saw that the coop hadn't been this clean since they converted the lean-to from its original purpose as a toolshed. Possibly even before that. In fact, the only part of the whole place anything less than pristine was Opal herself.

She'd shucked her bonnet at some point—a practical decision since there wasn't an over-abundance of light in the place. Now the finest pieces of her hair wisped straight up around her face, decorated with the odd bit of straw. A smudge graced her left cheek. Her apron boasted more shades than a painter's palette. Those skirts she shook out stayed rumpled despite her efforts, and her brows almost touched in the middle while she scowled at him for invading her domain. No bows and lace could ever compare.

He leaned in for a quick peck but found his way blocked by a scrub brush.

"What do you think you're doing?" She scrambled to her feet.

How can any woman look that appealing and not expect to get herself kissed? He wanted a chance to sweep her away again.

"Seeing if you're all right." *True. You weren't passed out. Now I'd like a closer inspection.* He took a half-step forward.

She practically backed out of the lean-to. "Just didn't hear the bell from under there." She waved the brush, bristles out, in the direction of the corner. "I'm fine."

"Pa said you felt dizzy earlier." Another half-step brought him the proximity he wanted.

She seemed to realize that backing up would be a mistake. For one thing, she'd fall out of the raised coop. "Only for a moment. It passed." She spoke quickly, making him think his nearness made her nervous.

Good.

"Kind of him to be concerned, though." Opal blinked those blue eyes of hers at him and added, "Nice of you, too."

"I wasn't being nice." A slight shift brought him even closer. "I was being your husband." He leaned closer, his eyes fixed on her mouth.

"Good of you!" This time, she stepped out the

door and down the step. "Now that I know they're keeping dinner for me, I won't make the family wait any longer!" With that, she hustled toward the well, ostensibly to wash up.

But Adam knew the truth of it.

His wife had flown the coop.

CHAPTER 21

All through dinner, Opal battled a heightened awareness of Adam's closeness. His knee bumped hers beneath the table. His fingers brushed hers when she passed the salt. His smile reached out to her over their bowls.

Ridiculous. Smiles do not reach anything. And of course his knee bumps mine. The closer I scoot to Adam, the farther I am from Larry!

But no matter how she tried to apply logic and reason, her heart still beat in erratic excitement because her husband came to the chicken coop to check on her.

No. He thought I might be ill, and he ran to my side. Genuine concern made him bellow so loud when he saw me on the ground like that. Even the indignity of her activity paled in comparison to the significance of his actions. She snuck a peek at him from the corner of her eyes, only to have to ask for a roll when he caught her looking.

Then that look in his eye when he kept getting closer. Almost a predatory gleam, like he was moving in for. . .a kiss? She barely managed to suppress a scoff, knowing it would draw undue attention at the table. Opal'd caught a glimpse of herself in the water before she washed up. Hair sticking straight out as though making a run for it, a smudge on her cheek, and an old, stained apron hardly made the image of an irresistible woman.

But what if he *had* wanted to kiss her? What then? Could it mean. . .

Opal dropped her spoon.

Can it mean he's ready to make this marriage real? She ducked her head and focused intently on fishing her spoon out of her soup then drying it on her napkin. Maybe if she took long enough, her blush would go away.

I've surely done enough turning red to last a lifetime by now. But the thought didn't give her any hope she'd be spared further blushes. If anything, considering what lay ahead, she'd experience them more frequently.

"I like when you blush." Adam's warm breath tickled her neck, his voice a low whisper as he caught her napkin from sliding off her lap. "Makes me want to know what you're thinking." He leaned back, expression as casual as though he hadn't said a word.

Only Larry seemed to have noticed anything as, of course, warmth suffused Opal's face. Adam's brother looked from her to her husband then back, eyes narrowing as she all but scooted off the bench to move farther away from his gaze.

Adam's knee bumped hers again. Or maybe hers bumped Adam's. Really, who could tell? Opal, for one, occupied herself trying to think of chill streams, winter snows, breezy shade—anything that might cool the heat in her cheeks.

Anything that kept her from thinking about whether or not her husband wanted to kiss her. And if he did, if he wanted other things, too. And how if he wanted those other things, maybe Midge's suggestion that she lure Adam into the marriage bed to avoid an annulment would be easier than she'd thought.

Unless I get so flustered just by him standing within a foot of me that I run away like a scared rabbit! She sighed into her soup and realized every last Grogan was staring.

"Mmm, delicious!" She gave another sigh. *I am a ninny.*

"Thank you." Lucinda looked as though she'd searched the compliment for any hidden barbs and come up empty-handed.

"We'll teach you the recipe," Willa offered. "It was Grandma's."

The gesture of acceptance touched Opal. "I'd be honored."

"Don't be. My ma's recipe ain't goin' to no Speck." Diggory shoved his bowl away. "And don't you glower at me, boy. You may have married her, but you aren't living together as man and wife. She hasn't proved herself a Grogan."

"Yet." Larry's fierce utterance took them all aback, but Opal doubted he took note of his family's shock. He didn't so much as glance at anyone but her.

Memories of his advances came flooding back. Larry's hand imprisoning her wrist in the meadow. Larry following her toward the house until Pete saw him and told Pa. Larry's threat on the note that doomed Adam.

His gaze pinned her now, even as his actions had trapped his brother and left her with no options.

Your fault. She thrust her hands beneath the table so he couldn't see how rage made them shake. *This is all your fault, and you dare look at me and all but announce you're not finished?* "How dare you?" She raised her head to look him in the eye.

"Don't take that tone, missy." Lucinda's snap held no sting this time. "My son just stood up for you. He thinks you're not hopeless."

"We can make her a Grogan." The intensity in Larry's gaze sickened her. Whatever the man planned, she didn't want any part of it. Never had.

"You won't make me anything," she vowed. "Adam married me as I am." *He just doesn't know precisely what that means.*

"That's right." Adam's arm came around her shoulders, and she leaned into him, grateful for his solid strength. "Opal has nothing more to prove to me."

Because the only thing I have to prove is that I can live on this farm and not tear Larry limb from limb, and Adam already understands that. She closed her eyes. *Understands me.*

It was then she realized her husband was still speaking.

"Opal already *is* a Grogan."

"No she isn't!" For a split second, Lucinda feared the words boiling in her heart burst from her own lips, but everyone at the table turned to her youngest son.

"Dave!" Willa gave her head a swift shake.

My own daughter, taken in by that Speck tramp. Lucinda bit the inside of her cheek. Speaking against Opal now would only drive Adam further away from the family and closer to the source of all their discontent.

Time is running out. I've only two days until the Sabbath—until Parson Carter tells all of Buttonwood that Adam's shackled to this troublemaker for the rest of his born days. The metallic taste of blood filled her mouth.

"Opal is my wife." Adam spoke slowly, as though every person at the table wasn't painfully aware of the facts, with his arm slung around the hussy. "She carries the next Grogan."

No blushes from his bride this time, Lucinda noted. *The girl's gone red as an apple over anything and everything, but one mention of the child and her face goes pale.*

"The child doesn't change me," the chit remarked. "When I'm not expecting, I'll still be Adam's wife."

I knew it! The Jezebel carries no grandbaby of

mine! Otherwise, she'd seize on her claim to Adam with both hands and not let go.

"Adam's wife or not, we'll make a Grogan of you." Larry hadn't stopped watching the girl beside him since the conversation began.

His overt, inappropriate fascination made for another mark against the woman whose very presence—no, *existence*—was tearing her family apart.

"Make no mistake, brother." Adam's arm tightened around her shoulders. "Opal is my wife."

"For now." Her middle son either didn't realize or didn't care what he provoked. "Even should you set her aside, she can't go back to the Specks."

Now there's a thought. Lucinda's mind whirled. *Perhaps Adam is convinced the child belongs to him, and he's waiting to claim it? It stands to reason. My son would never abandon his own.*

"I will never set her aside." Adam's declaration shook her.

"No shouting at the table!" She sent him a sharp glance. *You'll set her aside when she reveals her true nature.* "I won't have you fighting with your brothers over nothing."

"I am *not* nothing." Where the girl found the gall to speak stumped Lucinda. Opal looked up at Adam in a nauseating display. "Thank you for defending my honor. I'm proud to be your wife, and though I claim the name Grogan, the Specks are my kin. That can't be changed, and I wouldn't want it to be."

"You speak well of them under my roof?" A vein

pulsed in Diggory's forehead. "After we've taken you in?"

"My husband brought me to his home." Unbelievably, the girl kept speaking! "And I'd be a poor daughter and sister to speak ill of my family."

"They are no longer your family." A fanatical light came from Larry's grin.

Lucinda saw where this was heading and couldn't let it go a step further. "Neither are we."

"Yes we are, Ma." Adam rose to his feet. "You will accept Opal as my wife or force me to make a choice. The Bible is clear to whom I must cleave."

"No." Her breaths came shallow, and she had to grip the table to stand up. "It's not about us accepting her when she still plays Speck games, causing division among us!"

God forgive me for the exaggeration I must use now. Adam won't see the subtler ways a woman sows conflict within a home, so I have to give him something more concrete.

"What have I done?" Opal played right into her hands.

"As if you don't know." Lucinda suppressed any sign of victory. "Did you think I wouldn't realize the reason for my aches and pains these last two nights? That I'd attribute it to old age and your secret wouldn't be found out? That the Grogans are so foolish we wouldn't notice such a blatant stunt?"

"I don't understand." Her bewilderment came across beautifully—all the better to convince Adam what a liar he'd married.

"My mattress, Opal." Lucinda bit the injured

part of her cheek again, letting tears well up. "What will I find if I open the seams?"

"This is nonsense, Ma." Adam's voice held the heat of anger.

"What are you implying?" The ice of winter, a direct contrast to her son, crept into the girl's tone.

"I want the truth, Opal. From your own lips. Confess now and we'll hear no more of it." She moved to slide her arm through Adam's. "For my son's sake, we'll start afresh."

"Cornhusks." Willa sounded confused. "Opal and I put cornhusks in the mattresses, same as always."

"Did seem lumpier than usual." Diggory shrugged. "But not much to fuss about."

"You'd sleep standing up if you had to," Lucinda pointed out to her husband. "Others of us are more sensitive. But, Willa, were you with Opal the whole time?"

She asked knowing the answer full well. After all, hadn't she called her daughter away, asking for help moving the settee so she could sweep behind it? Then asking her to stay for the moment it took for the cleaning, so she could help put it back in place?

"Aside from helping you with the settee." Willa slid a sideways glance toward Opal. "But I'm sure Opal wouldn't do anything wrong."

"This is your last chance. Have the integrity to tell us why you wanted to hurt me." Lucinda bit her lip as though anxious. "Be honest."

"I did nothing."

"So be it." She raised her head high and swept toward the alcove where her and Diggory's bed rested behind a thick curtain. She pulled out the sewing scissors she wore on a chain at her waist and bent to snip the seams along the bottom edge of the mattress. Lucinda guided Adam toward the opening. "Reach inside, son. Let's see what you find."

And she waited as, one by one, he pulled forth the stones she'd slipped inside earlier that very morning. Small enough not to be noticeable when carrying the mattress but large enough to cause discomfort when caught in the rope supports beneath the mattress, where she'd been careful to tuck them.

The gasps around him turned to glares, but Lucinda hardly paid them mind. Her focus was all for her oldest son.

He has to be shown. . . .

Chapter 22

The first stone could have been an accident. Easily. The second possibly, if less likely. But by the time his hand rustled through the husks to close around a third rock, they might as well have taken up residence in Adam's stomach.

How could she? He groped for an explanation even as he searched out two more of the offending objects, placing them in a neat pile beside his parents' bed. When he found no more within his reach, Adam stood, walked to the head of the bed, and withdrew his pocketknife.

Swift slices made short work of the tight seam, but Adam didn't kneel to finish the job.

"Opal." For the first time, he looked at his wife.

"Adam." All color had fled her cheeks, leaving her hair a brilliant flame of defiance as she raised her chin.

No need to ask whether or not she'd done it.

She made no more protestations of innocence. Only insolence flashed in those blue eyes. Anyone walking through the door of the soddy at that moment would swear she had cause for righteous anger. The kind that swept over Adam as he saw his mother surreptitiously rubbing her lower back.

Sure, Ma hadn't been the most welcoming person in the whole world, but that was to be expected.

Ma's smart enough to suspect I didn't run around with Opal Speck and that the shotgun wedding was a farce. Stands to reason she'd be wary of the woman she thinks tricked me into marriage. He looked at Opal's rigid stance, a slim line soon to swell with another man's child. *Especially since it's true.*

"Come here." Adam stared at his wife. The same woman he'd wanted to kiss earlier that day.

Opal drew closer, not challenging his authority. She stood at the head of the bed, shoulders tense as she ignored Pa's fulminating glower, Larry's calculating air, Willa's betrayed expression, and Dave's angry fidgeting.

"You find the rest." He stepped back and gestured for her to finish the job.

She sank to her knees, spine straight as could be, stiffened by a pride the likes of which Adam never saw before. He waited as she groped around, making the dry bedding rasp and shift until she pulled out first one stone then another. Opal plunged her arm into the mattress again, reached until it swallowed her shoulder, and then gave up. "Seems like there aren't any more." Her voice took on a flat quality he hadn't heard before.

"You'd know." Pa kicked one of the rocks, making it fly and hit her skirts before it bounced off. "Planting these to make my wife miserable, after all she does."

"Rotten thing to do." Willa's admonition took everyone by surprise, since she rarely spoke against anyone.

"Isn't it, though?" Opal agreed with his sister but looked at his mother as though in challenge.

"Why didn't you just confess?" Adam wanted to know. "Ma gave you the opportunity."

"I couldn't." Her tone kept that lifeless luster he found so disturbing. "She knew that."

"Suspected as much." Ma sounded more triumphant than sorrowful. "That she wouldn't give an inch. Hoped I wouldn't risk looking like a fool if my suspicions were wrong, didn't she?"

"I don't like it." Larry looked from Ma to Opal and back again. "Don't like it one bit, Ma."

"How could you wish that on anyone?" Adam still couldn't reconcile such a petty act with the woman who'd helped keep peace for so long.

"Didn't." Her gaze stayed fixed on the wall.

"No need to wish when you can make it happen, eh, girlie?" Pa bent over to pick up one of the rocks. "Handy for a stoning. That's what they would've done to a woman like you in biblical times. Not pure on her wedding night—"

"Pa!" Adam clamped a hand around his father's wrist, making him drop the stone. "There'll be no talk of that."

"She must be punished, Adam." Pa wrenched his hand away. "I know she's with child, but you'll have to think of something."

"I already have." He knew what would hurt her most. "Opal, there are seven stones. One stone for each day makes that a full week you won't go to help out on the Speck farm. Aside from church the next two Sundays, you won't see your father or brothers."

"No!" She swung from the wall to fix on him, eyes wide and pleading. "Please, Adam! Don't do this!"

"I didn't." He forced himself to see past her tears to the hard heart behind them. "You brought it on yourself."

"Why?" But she wasn't looking at him. Opal stared at Ma. Her shoulders never drooped, but the one whispered word belied her pose. "Why?"

Ma's gaze went colder than Adam had ever seen. "Because he has to learn. I won't have my son shackled to a liar." Her voice lowered almost to a hiss. "Adam needs to know what you *really* are."

"Buzzard!" Midge's indignation went a long way toward soothing Opal's own roiling temper. "I wish she *had* slept on rocks. Old besom probably waited until that morning to plant the things, though. Ooooh, I'd like to get my hands on that Lucinda and make her fess up."

"She won't." Opal poured a measure of water in the pie tin beneath yet another hive. "If you waved a loaded shotgun her direction and told her to spill the truth or else, she'd take the bullet."

"Idea has merit." Her friend plunked a few pebbles into the tin. "At least if you won't get vindication, you get a little vengeance."

"And then I'd be known as the woman who smuggled rocks into mattresses and shot her mother-in-law."

"Folk heroes have been made from less." Midge's grin faded. "Still burns my biscuits that Adam didn't think twice before condemning you."

"I shouldn't blame him for believing Lucinda." Opal recited what she'd been telling herself for the past two days. "She's his mama, she put on a very convincing performance, and the evidence was indisputable. Rocks came out of the mattress. Who would believe she put them there just to make me look bad? I shouldn't blame him."

"Just because you think you shouldn't doesn't mean you don't." Her friend took a sip of water. "I would."

"I do." *It shouldn't feel good to admit that.* "It's not fair that I should expect him to trust me over his mother and his own eyes, but I'm angry at him all the same."

"Justice is a virtue, you know." Midge sounded particularly pleased to tell her so. "Wanting some doesn't make you a bad person. In fact, I'd be worried if you didn't."

"Maybe if I'd yelled and flung accusations at Lucinda, he would've thought twice." Opal confessed the other part that still festered. "Instead, I got so mad I shook. Barely managed to choke out a single word once I realized what she'd done."

"If you'd started hollering, they'd have thought you went daft. Now, there's a thought." She came to such a sudden halt, Opal almost bumped into her. "Maybe Lucinda wants to drive you crazy so they can have you put away."

"Even after two years you still think like a city girl sometimes. They don't have any of those places in the middle of the prairie even if I did start raving. Her plan seems to be more along the lines of making Adam set me aside. Or maybe making me so miserable I head for the hills. She'll learn it won't work."

"Glad to hear it." Midge squinted. "I can understand why the bees need water, but why do we put pebbles in the tins?"

"So the bees can have a place to drink without drowning." *Pity life doesn't always come with a pebble to give you better footing. Just stones planted by devious mothers-in-law.*

"And Lucinda said something about showing Adam what you really are? What do you think she means?"

"A liar." Opal's mouth went dry. "She made up the rocks in the mattress, but I think she knows I'm not carrying Adam's baby. Lucinda just doesn't know how to prove it."

"She won't have to wait long." Midge stuck her finger in the stream of honey Opal poured into a tin and took a taste. "Mmm. Everyone will know when you don't start showing."

"By then, the marriage has to be real." Opal

dribbled in a little wine and placed the tin under the first of twenty hives, next to the water. "Or Adam will get that annulment."

Midge sprinkled salt on the mixture. "What's this stuff for?"

"After winter, hive supplies run low and most of the workers are busy building combs instead of making honey. So if there's an apiary, sometimes bees will raid other hives to steal food." Opal set down the next tin and moved on. "This way keeps them the most productive. I don't do it for long. . . and not every day."

"They go on raids?" Her friend looked at the hive before her with new respect. "Viking bees!"

Opal laughed for the first time since she'd cleaned out the chicken coop. "Viking bees. . .I like that."

"Yeah, but you've got someone even more ruthless to worry about. I figure you've got a month before your secret's out. A little less with Lucinda so suspicious."

"Less than a month." Opal froze for a second. "I only have a couple weeks to convince Adam to become my husband?"

"No. He's already your husband." Midge nudged her out of the way so she could sprinkle the salt. "You just have to convince him to act like it."

CHAPTER 23

T omorrow everyone will find out about the marriage." Opal sounded like she didn't know whether to be afraid or horrified.

Neither. "Good! It's the perfect time to start laying the groundwork." Midge could see that Opal needed some encouragement. "With you two being introduced as husband and wife, it's only natural for you to be looking up at him all admiring, always touching him, whispering to him. . .things that will catch his attention."

"I'm beginning to see why Pete's so obsessed with you."

"Don't be silly." She pshawed. "I don't need to do anything to catch your brother's attention."

"Right. People will think I've anticipated my vows and the marriage was necessary." Opal gave a big sigh. "Which is what the parson thinks, and my husband thinks, and both our families think, so

I suppose it shouldn't matter."

"But it does." The very idea of everyone in Buttonwood finding out where she *really* came from made Midge's stomach turn, and the thought of her friend being exposed to the same kind of scorn didn't sit any better. The whispers, the stares, the judgment. . . "You don't deserve that." *I do.*

"I'd rather face gossip than a gunfight." Her friend's tone was light, but she meant every word. "But I feel so. . ."

"Alone?" The thought broke out before Midge could button it up.

"Yes. That's it, exactly. But more than that"— Opal finished pouring the last of the wine into the final tin—"as though I won't be good enough anymore."

"I understand that." Midge flicked the final bits of salt from her fingers and picked at her nails. "Felt like that when I came here."

"I'm so glad you came!" The hug caught her off guard. "Thank you for coming to see me even though I've been disgraced."

"Yours is a fake disgrace." Midge angled out of the hug to grab Opal's shoulders. "Listen to me. I know your secrets, and I won't abandon you or tell a soul, no matter how people treat you. But you have to let me help."

"You're too good." Opal headed for the small grove of cottonwoods bordering the apiary and sat down.

"No." Midge stayed standing when they reached the scant shade, rooted by the enormity of what she was about to do. "I'm anything *but* good. And that's why I can help. Listen, Opal. I have something to tell you, but you can't tell anyone. Only Saul and Clara know. I'm only letting you know because I can't help you win Adam without you knowing why I know some things."

"What's this about?" Opal tugged her hands. "Sit down. I've already gotten the picture that you know more about things no one else notices than I can even imagine!"

"That's because I learned to look." Midge reached down the front of her dress and pulled out the only link to her past. The battered brass locket had to be coaxed open to reveal its tiny portrait. "This here's my mom, but my sister, Nancy, looked just like her. I take after my dad."

"She's lovely." Opal traced the rim of the locket. "They both are."

"Were." Midge snapped it shut and thrust it back down her dress front. "I'm the only one left, that's true. And I met Dr. Reed on the streets of Baltimore, and he did save me."

"Yes, that's what they said. That he couldn't save your sister, but he took you in." Opal frowned. "There's no shame in living, Midge."

"There's shame in *how* we lived." She closed her eyes and could smell the dank stench of the alleyway, feel the cold creeping along the edges of their small fire, taste the terror when Randy looked at her. . . "The fever took Ma and Pa when I was about eleven and Nancy fourteen. I always looked younger, but Nancy seemed older than her years. She got a job at a factory but lost it when the foreman found me in her room. We just about starved until Randy came along."

"Randy?" Sudden wariness darkened Opal's gaze, showing she understood where the tale turned.

"You saw how pretty Nancy was. He turned her head, gave us a home. And in a week, he turned Nancy out. Either she worked the streets and served the gents, or we'd be back in the cold. Nancy refused, but Randy's fists did the convincing his mouth couldn't." Midge shivered. "Randy's fists did a lot of talking."

"Oh Midge."

Opal reached out as though in comfort, but Midge jerked away. "I ain't done." She sniffed back tears. "For two years Nancy worked and I took in odd jobs sewing. I still looked too scrawny to catch a man's eye. Then the day came Nancy's luck and potions failed her. She found herself expecting."

Opal's quick indrawn breath somehow gave her more determination to plow ahead.

"Randy didn't hold with that. He sent for one of the butchers to get rid of the problem. Nancy fought him—and fought hard. So did I, but it didn't do any good. The quack ripped the babe from my sister's belly, but something went wrong. Nancy didn't stop bleeding. So the next day, Randy made me take her place. Dr. Reed was the first man I stopped. Saul noticed the bruises on my neck, how young I looked, and offered to help me find a better life. He even tried to save Nancy, but she'd already passed by the time we got to the room. And then he whisked me away from that place and brought me here."

She spread her arms, palms out, shrugged, and waited for Opal's reaction. Now she'd find out if she'd made a mistake. If she'd lose a good friend and the respect of everyone else in Buttonwood to boot.

"You're amazing, you know that?" Opal's gaze held no disgust, only compassion and—could that be admiration? She reached out to snag Midge's hand and clasp it tight. "I never suspected you'd gone through so much. To think how the Lord brought you here, it gives me hope."

"It wasn't the Lord." Midge snatched her hand away. "It was Saul. Dr. Reed brought me here. God didn't answer Nancy's prayers, and He didn't hear any of mine on her behalf, either. Don't give Him credit for what Saul did!"

"I'm glad Saul came to Buttonwood. I'm thankful you approached him before anyone else." Opal leaned forward. "And most of all, I'm glad you're my friend."

Something hard inside Midge seemed to soften at Opal's complete acceptance of her. "You're sure? I'm not good like you."

"No. I came from a safe home and managed to spin a web of lies to land myself in trouble. You grew up surrounded by danger and evil and are here to help me." Opal gave a laugh. "We're not much alike."

"That's not what I meant!" But that didn't stop a secret part of her from liking to hear it. "And we're a lot alike. For one thing, neither of us gives up easy."

"True." The light of battle entered her friend's gaze. "Especially when so much depends on seeing something through."

"Tomorrow will be crucial." Midge watched as dozens of bees zoomed around the hives, dipping into the tins of water and honey stuff they'd laid out. "The ambush yesterday set you back a good deal. You can't rely on Adam as an ally anymore. You've been cast in the role of a sneak, and the way things stand, Lucinda's better at it."

"This isn't helping." She raked her fingernails through a stalky clump of purple buds.

"It should." Midge caught Opal's hand before she could shred any more of the emerging wildflowers. "You can learn from this—the best kind of sneaking is done right out in the open, so no one suspects it."

"People always suspect things." Her hand clamped tight. "They will tomorrow."

"That's where being sneaky comes in. You have to make them suspect what you want them to." She stood up. "And I'm going to teach you how."

Just in time for church.

Opal marched out the door of the Grogan soddy the next morning girded for battle. As she dressed, she kept in mind the armor of God.

For the breastplate of righteousness, she slid on Mama's pin. She felt that simply going as a Grogan counted as shodding herself in preparation for peace—standing as the link between their two families. The shield of her faith couldn't be seen, but she carried it as surely as she did Ma's Bible—her sword of the Spirit. Her best bonnet didn't quite classify as the helmet of salvation, but it would have to do since no decent woman left her head uncovered in God's house. Which left one missing piece.

Ephesians 6:14 kept running through her mind, mocking her with its impossibility. *"Stand therefore, having your loins girt about with truth. . . ."* Because no matter how she tried, Opal couldn't convince herself she lived up to that spiritual standard. In fact, a virgin trying to seduce her husband to prevent an annulment on the grounds she wasn't carrying an illicit child seemed the very antithesis of truthful loins.

It took all the wash water and a trip to the well to stop her blushes after the realization that her virtue now made her the worst sort of fraud. A *sneak*, Midge called it. *My only chance to keep things together.*

Opal raised her chin high and accepted Adam's arm as they walked to town. *I'll do my part to convince everyone this is a happy marriage, that our families cried peace, and no one needs to get hurt.*

"Adam?" She deliberately slowed her pace until they were a good distance behind the others. Not too far, or they wouldn't arrive together, but far enough for her to speak her piece. "We both know the importance of today."

"Yes." He hadn't spoken a word more than absolutely necessary since handing down his punishment.

205

"Then you know that standing stiff as a board and looking like you're nursing a sore tooth will make people think you don't want to be my husband." *In other words, they'll catch on to the true state of things.* "My family will see it as an insult to me."

He let loose a drawn-out breath and made a visible effort to relax.

"Better." She swallowed and pressed ahead. "Our families won't be able to hide their displeasure. The town will see it's a mask. But the two of us can show the picture of a happy couple united and uniting others or—"

"Let everyone know we were forced into it and provoke the type of speculation that will cause our families to snipe until they snap." A grim nod. "You're right. No one need know of the shotgun wedding since Parson Carter agreed to simply say he married us in a private ceremony with Pete and Midge as our witnesses. Will Pete pull through?"

"Oh, Midge will make sure of it." Opal gave a small chuckle at the thought of what awaited her brother if he didn't act as though he thoroughly approved the match. "She plans to stay near Pete and make sure he doesn't forget his role and scowl at you."

"Pete doesn't stand a chance." The tight lines around Adam's mouth faded. "I won't forget my part either."

"Is it such a hard role to play?" A wistful note crept into her voice before she could prevent it. "That you enjoy my company?"

"No." He threaded his fingers through hers. "That's the problem."

THE BRIDE BACKFIRE

Before she could explore that intriguing comment, the clapboard church came in full view. Or rather, they came in full view of the church. And the entire town.

Folks typically gathered around outside, shooting the breeze until time came to shuffle to their seats. Today proved no exception. The Fossets stood chatting with the Calfrees on the left side of the whitewashed building. The Warrens exchanged pleasantries with the Doanes farther right. The Reeds caught up with the Burn men and the Dunstall women front and center.

The parson and his wife stood in conversation with newlywed couple Sally Fosset and Matthew Burn. Young men and women clustered near the well, pretending disinterest in one another while the children of the town made merry mayhem while trying not to dirty their Sunday best. Pa and her brothers headed to meet them, and suddenly it seemed as though the entire scene froze.

Conversations ceased midsentence. Mouths hung agape. Children stilled. And Opal started to pray.

CHAPTER 24

Lord, protect my family. From the Specks. Adam caught sight of Ma's glower and the bulging vein in Pa's forehead. *And themselves. Don't let any of us do something that lights the tinderbox we stand on.*

"Pa?" The quaver in Opal's voice matched the tremor in her hand. The fabric of her sleeve shook.

Green. The color called forth a memory of her talking to God in the fields of her farm. *"If I had to pick a color to represent hope, I'd pick the pale green of a new blade of grass. . . ."* And she'd worn it today.

What do you hope for, Opal?

The realization that he cared didn't surprise him. He'd wanted her when she was the daughter of his father's sworn enemy. He'd wanted her when she trapped him into marriage. He'd wanted her though she planned to pass off another man's child as his and refused to reveal the identity of the father. Even after she'd stooped so low as to put rocks

208

in his mother's bed to cause petty discomfort, he hadn't even considered washing his hands of Opal.

Shaking her until her teeth rattled, kissing her silly, or sweeping her away so it was just the two of them and nothing else for miles until she spilled her secrets and saw sense—now those, he'd considered. But giving her up now that she'd crashed so completely into his life? Never.

Not while Opal needed him. Not when that child needed him. Whether she wanted to admit it or not, she couldn't do it alone. He'd see through the promise he made to provide for both of them. *For better or worse.*

Adam could wait for the "better" part, so long as Opal wasn't hoping to get out of it.

"Grogan." Murphy Speck didn't even acknowledge his daughter's greeting. The man gave a curt nod and kept walking.

"Opal." Elroy stopped a few feet away, his tone low and urgent. He looked at Adam and back at his sister. "You all right?"

"Yes, Elroy." Opal nestled closer against his side as though happy to be there, but her gaze followed her father's retreating figure. "Adam treats me well."

"Let me know if that changes." The man narrowed his eyes and followed after Murphy, the two Specks cutting a wide swath through the townspeople who didn't make any pretense at doing anything but gawk.

"Of course he treats her right!" Pa's yell jerked them to a halt. "Don't insult my boy by suggesting otherwise, or you'll answer to me!"

"Anytime a woman weds, her family keeps an eye on things." Ben, the Speck who'd been gone four years and only just returned, seemed to have donned the mantle of peacemaker after Opal's defection. Whatever else he said got lost in the gasps and sudden swell of excitement as everyone heard him.

Adam's wife shrank into him as though seeking protection. He looked down to find her staring up at him, eyes wide, offering a hesitant smile. Before he knew it, he could feel himself grinning back. A fresh wave of murmurs swelled around them.

"I'd say we have plenty of eyes on us." He went ahead and chuckled at the scrutiny, unleashing a townful of titters. But the sweetest sound was the ghost of a giggle as Opal joined in.

Has she laughed once since our wedding? Adam fought to keep his smile.

"Everyone can congratulate the happy couple after the service," Parson Carter called from a safe distance—the church steps. "Let's remember where our attention should be."

Despite the reminder, his flock was slow to straggle into the house of worship that morning. It seemed everyone waited for. . .something.

"Ready, honey?" The endearment came easily, though he hadn't planned it. Adam thought how well it suited his beekeeper as he led her past the avid gazes of everyone they knew and to the bench where his family always sat.

Ben and Pete Speck followed closely, a silent show of support stronger than his own family bringing up the rear.

210

Adam registered this peripherally, instead pouring his focus into meeting the eyes of every man he passed. Every man in town. It should have been easy to find the man who wouldn't meet his gaze or looked too thunderstruck.

Somewhere among this tight-knit community lurked the scoundrel who'd taken advantage of Opal. Did the man even know of his impending fatherhood? Opal hadn't said one way or another, and Adam hadn't asked. He figured it'd be an issue to take up in person. When he made it clear that the reprobate would never come near his wife—or their child—in the future.

Young or old, tall or short, squat or spare, didn't matter. Adam eyed anyone in britches. And to a man, each eyed him back. Some with speculation; others didn't hide amusement. He might even have caught a flash of pity from one misguided soul.

Even Brett Burn, the youngest blacksmith and the man Adam most suspected, showed only good-natured resignation. If there'd been hostility or even envy, his hackles would've gone up. Instead, even the young man who'd shown an interest in Opal joined the town's main reaction. The great majority seemed to be anticipating something.

Probably for the mother of all fights to break out between our families, Adam guessed. *Truth be told, I'm waiting on that myself.*

If the old adage held any truth—that an over-abundance of curiosity counted as sin—Opal hoped all the sidelong glances and outright gapes of disbelief aimed her way were paired with a little shame. The weight of all this scrutiny should splinter the Grogan bench into toothpicks long before Parson Carter finished his opening prayer!

It certainly felt heavy on her shoulders. Or maybe that knot came from her working so hard not to crane her neck to see Pa. Outside he'd acted as though looking at her would taint him. Pain wrapped around her midsection so tight she'd not drawn a full breath since then, and she knew seeing Pa send her one of those special smiles he'd always managed whenever she needed one would make the air right again.

But she wouldn't give anyone in town cause to think she pined to go home. No matter it was truth to rival the Gospels the Parson preached from, she wouldn't disgrace Adam that way. Instead, she kept her spine straight and her shoulders tilted as far away from Larry as possible. Somehow her brother-in-law seemed to take up more space than a body had any right to, making her press closer to Adam than even she'd planned on this morning.

His solid warmth at her side sent a physical message of reassurance she craved almost as deeply as she needed the parson's reminder of God's sovereignty.

"This morning, I'd like us to think about something we, as Christians, are freely given and called to extend to others. The greatest gift, but we have trouble accepting it and even more trouble offering it to the people in our lives: forgiveness."

Parson Carter caught the gaze of each parishioner, but it felt to Opal as though he could see the anger staining her soul.

"Forgiving other people is the step most of us admit we struggle with. When someone wrongs us, it's all too easy to sit on our anger and stew about it, when we're supposed to give it to God and show our fellow man the same acceptance God shows us."

Opal closed her eyes for a moment, refusing to wince at the truth of the message and longing to shut out the realization she needed to forgive Lucinda for the horrible trick she'd played. *Lord, I know I need to. I know I'm supposed to. I know I'm flawed and have no right to judge others because I'm not anywhere near perfect, but at the same time, knowing something and feeling it are very different! I feel she deserves to be exposed for the vicious conniver she is and made to suffer for it. I feel as though she doesn't deserve my forgiveness for what she's done in driving a wedge between me and Adam and keeping me from my family.*

Loneliness crashed over Opal afresh as she sat in the wrong pew, away from the comfort of her father and brothers, with no one beside her but a husband who never wanted her. And, thanks to the machinations of his mother, may never want her. She swallowed a sigh and admitted the worst part of her struggle. *Lord, there's a part of me that is so angry I just don't want to forgive her. It makes me sad to think of how she hates me and how her ploy succeeded to the point it almost overwhelms me. I'm afraid if I give up my anger in favor of grace, I'll be swamped in*

213

all the things that weigh me down with nothing to give me the strength to fight it.

"Our ability to forgive should come not only from knowing that we don't deserve the grace we've been given but also from our certainty that our Lord is just and it is not for us to seek vengeance or hold grudges. He tells us in Exodus, 'The Lord shall fight for you, and ye shall hold your peace.'"

Opal's breath escaped in a whoosh as the verse hit her like a blow to the ribs. Strength wasn't supposed to come from anger—it came from resting on faith. Another area she'd failed.

But how do I stop fighting when I'm plunked in the midst of the battle?

Midge struggled to keep her expression calm throughout the sermon. She'd read a description of a heroine in a novel once who'd been serene and liked it. Sometimes words carried flavors for the mind, and Midge figured "serene" tasted cool and smooth, like peppermint.

So that's how she kept her face now. Smooth, as though any hint of a scowl or a frown would wrinkle into a thousand cracks and shatter the mask she'd put on that morning. The mask she always put on before church, where she sat still and quiet as though it came natural not to move, and didn't voice the waves of questions and objections pummeling her thoughts as Parson Carter spoke about the goodness of God.

"How can you do it?" she'd asked Nancy one

night while Randy drank away the money her sister earned from cheap men who dared treat unfortunate women as worthless. "How can you smile and go along when you're screaming on the inside?"

"I smile because it doesn't matter and because I'm not screaming on the inside anymore, Midgelet." Nancy smoothed the hair back from her forehead and tucked her close. "I'm praying."

Her sister prayed for everyone. Even the men who used her body. Even Randy. Even Midge, when it was all Midge's fault Nancy lost her mill job and ended up in that awful alley in the first place.

Today in church stood Parson Carter, who'd probably never gone hungry a day in his life or seen someone he loved beaten or killed, talking about how God would fight their battles. Problem was the other guys fought dirty, and good people who prayed still died.

So Midge sat tall and straight, screaming silently behind the smile she wore so well.

Chapter 25

Lucinda tried to ease some of the stiffness in her neck by turning it first to one side then the next, only to find all of blessed Buttonwood staring at her family's bench! Maybe a few glances darted in the other direction, toward the Speck seats, but Lucinda felt the scrutiny of her neighbors as though pinpricks of fire broke out all over her body. Like a rash.

Of course they stared. Everyone in town knew about the wedding. At least, they knew there'd been one. Parson Carter wouldn't breathe a word about the shotguns that had forced her son into Opal's clutches.

No one will. Adam's honor won't be smirched like that. Oh, people will talk. People always talk. They'll guess there's a child on the way. But the girl will be gone long before she proves them right. Long before she makes Adam known as a fornicator and binds him to her so tightly he'll never escape!

There was time yet, so Lucinda could wait. Hadn't she proven she was good at waiting? Even as young as eleven, when she came to the Grogans, second cousin and poor relation of Diggory's mother, hadn't she laid plans with the expertise of a master mason?

Look at me now. Diggory's wife, just as I planned. Mother of four beautiful children, head of a fine homestead, successful in every way.

Except one.

The Speck gal had more gumption than she'd reckoned on. An entire week's worth of snide remarks, sly jabs, backbreaking work, and deepening aspersions cast on the girl's character hadn't been enough to drive her out.

We'll see how she does after another month. Rocks in the mattress made for a nice start to show Adam his bride's true colors. *Next time, I'll shade them darker. And keep layering things one on top of the other until her character is so blackened Adam can't stand to look at her!*

She curled her fingers around the edge of the bench, welcoming the sharp jab of a splinter poking through her gloves. The minor nuisance fed her irritation over the situation, and she nursed it all through service as she thought up ways to drive the interloper from the ranks of her family. Specks and splinters ruined fine things, but both could be removed with the right technique.

Her thoughts caught her so completely that the closing prayer took her off guard. Service never seemed so short before this morning, but Lucinda offered thanks that the ordeal had almost ended. Whisk the family back to the farm to avoid curious questions, and she'd breathe easier again.

"Before everyone gets up," Parson Carter's voice snagged her when she would have risen and started to make her escape, "I'd like to invite you to a surprise wedding reception. No sense pretending the whole town didn't notice Opal arrived with Adam Grogan, so I'm happy to announce that I married them in a *very* private ceremony early this week. My wife's cooked up a storm and bought out the Dunstalls' café for their ready-mades. It's time to celebrate the joining of two families who've finally laid aside their differences to come together in love!"

Love? Lucinda wrestled with the urge to claw at her bonnet ribbons, which suddenly seemed to choke her. *Lies! Lies of the Specks snaked out to snare my son in this sham of a marriage, and now the parson tightens the bind. But the tauter the rope, the greater the snap when it's severed.*

Lucinda contented herself with certain knowledge that she'd make the Speck girl snap long before the Grogans gave way. But for now, she'd play the part of reluctant mother-in-law of an enamored groom. Anything to preserve Adam's reputation and keep the family as whole as possible.

Standing, she hid her face behind the brim of her bonnet and plucked the splinter from her palm, dropping it to the floor. One step forward, and it crushed beneath her heel, lending her pasted-on smile a measure of sincerity as Lucinda prepared to meet the many well-wishers and scandal-sniffers of Buttonwood.

Forgiveness. A concept Christians chased like a cat batting at dust motes glinting in the morning sun. The tantalizing glimmer made them rear up and lunge, only to have what they sought lose the sparkle on those rare occasions they nabbed it.

Because it can't be earned or even caught and held. God's gifts to us can only be appreciated. Adam savored the warmth of Opal pressed close to his side throughout the service. He thought of all the times he'd made mistakes or wished petty things on his brother and knew himself to be no better than the woman he now called his wife.

It wasn't his place to judge her actions or even forgive her for them. Forgiveness wasn't something a man could give—it was a blessing to be shared.

Just one of the blessings I'd like to share with Opal. Lord, I believe You gave me this woman as my wife with the intent that I keep her. I lay down my anger over the paltry trick she played with the mattress. I want to move on with my marriage. Jesus, please work in her heart so she will confide in me the name of the father of her child so that we can begin afresh and without any looming threats to the life we build.

Parson Carter's announcement of an impromptu dinner came as a surprise. If not welcome, it struck Adam as a good opportunity to solidify their marriage in the eyes of the town and show everyone he didn't regret his choice of wife. When they all stood, it seemed only natural to slide his hand across her back and steer her through the throng of people crowding the aisle.

Opal showed no inclination to stop and clog the narrow passageway to chat. The small church, filled with townspeople for the morning and shut against the chill of the spring morning, began to grow stuffy. Some soul impervious to the curiosity plaguing the rest of Buttonwood had the good sense to throw open the door, sending a welcome breeze through the structure.

Everyone else seemed determined to be the first to reach him and Opal, pepper them with questions, and roast them on the flames of speculation until their lives could be picked apart.

Expressions of disappointment and thwarted determination painted the faces around them as he swept his wife past and toward the open door offering freedom.

They broke through into the fresh air almost at the same time, and for one moment Opal's gaze found his and they shared a smile at their small victory. That smile settled the matter in his mind as they hurried to the open grassy area where they couldn't be hemmed in again. Past mistakes would stay behind them, and they would continue as they were now. United.

He skimmed his hand to her waist and tucked her to his side as the crowd behind them caught up. Her soft gasp at the unexpected closeness made him want to catch her eye again, but he found his view blocked by her bonnet as she focused on a gaggle of women babbling their well wishes to her. Something inside him stretched restlessly as the townspeople kept Opal's attention from him, but the warmth of her waist through the cotton layers of her clothing beneath his palm kept him reasonable.

"Never thought I'd see the day." Old Josiah Reed, owner of the town store, clapped him on the shoulder. "Grogan married a Speck. Took a lot of guts to nab her from her family like that. . .and a lot of determination."

"She's worth even more than that." Adam didn't have to think about his answer before he spoke. *No lie there.* His comment sparked a round of giggles and elbow jabs among the folks clustered around.

"Thank you." With her head tilted back, Opal's bonnet didn't block her pretty face from his view any longer. Genuine gratitude shone in her eyes before she turned to another one of the women. Brim blocked her from him again.

"Snuck in and beat us all." Brett Burn's good-natured acknowledgment confirmed Adam's impression that he hadn't been the man to play Opal false. Some tension eased from his shoulders as he discarded that threat.

"*Snuck* is right." A grumble sounded from a tight group bunched off to the side of the jubilant crowd.

Adam's eyes narrowed as he surveyed the men and distinguished two distinct knots of fulminating family. The Speck men eyed the Grogan men, with less distance between them than ever before with no bloodshed.

The comment sounded like one that should, by rights, have come from Murphy Speck or even one of Opal's brothers. *Why, then, did that sound like Larry?* Adam shook off the notion. Not even Larry would try to cause problems today.

"Adam is no sneak." Opal's declaration took him off guard—almost as much as the hand she slid behind him to curl around his waist. If a woman could bristle like a porcupine, he got the feeling that's what she'd be doing. It was etched in the straight line of her back, the way the awful brim of that bonnet quivered in outrage. "Our wedding may have been hasty and private due to the tensions between our families, but I'm proud to call this man my husband."

"I gathered the bouquet myself." Midge Collins pushed through the crowd to stand alongside them, dragging Pete Speck in her wake. "Pete and I stood as witnesses, and it's been a positive drain to keep it to ourselves all week!"

"Was it romantic?" A sharp-eyed matron, whose name Adam couldn't recall as she was newer to the town, poked her long nose right in.

"A secret wedding in a spring clearing." Midge waxed poetic to a rapt audience, and Adam had the good sense to let her weave her spell. "I'm sure Parson Carter would tell you it was one of the most memorable ceremonies he's ever performed."

All eyes shifted to the pastor, whose enthusiastic nod sent heads bobbing back to focus on Midge.

Adam figured it was time he joined into the spirit of things. He reached up and quickly tugged free the small bow in Opal's bonnet strings with his free hand.

"She wore this same dress, knowing it's one of my favorite colors." He grasped the back of her bonnet and tugged, sliding it from her hair and sending wisps dancing along the breeze around her face. "And no bonnet so I could see her face as we spoke our vows."

A flurry of wistful sighs greeted the gesture, but Adam only cared that his restlessness faded when he could see Opal's face again.

Her eyes widened when the covering slipped from her hair, but the surprise changed to mischief in a twinkle. His bride opened her mouth to speak, and Adam knew he was in trouble.

From the moment they escaped the church into the fresh air and Adam gave her that conspiratorial grin, Opal knew today would mark a new beginning for them. Hope blunted the rage she felt toward Lucinda, whom she couldn't profess to have completely forgiven yet, and even muffled the cry in her heart from the way Pa still wouldn't look at her.

The armor of God protected her and held her up, allowing her to accept the greetings and exclamations of her neighbors and friends without arrows of guilt piercing her too deeply. She even kept in mind Midge's advice to make the most of today's opportunity to demonstrate affection.

More importantly, Adam outdid her. Oh, he'd sucked in a breath the first time she'd scooted over and pressed against his side in a bid to avoid Larry's remarkable ability to intrude on her space, but afterward Adam hadn't protested the proximity one bit. Better still, he must have sensed how she dreaded getting trapped between the church benches, caught up in stifling interrogations before she made it outside.

When the weight of his hand settled on the small of her back, the pressure of his palm firmly encouraging her to surge toward the freedom of that open door, she'd felt grounded for the first time since she'd seen him surrounded by her family's shotguns. If a smile could stretch through eternity, Opal would've kept the moment he'd grinned at her as though she were his partner in truth, not pretense.

A mistake, because then she would have missed his arm sliding around her waist, nestling her against his side in the crook of his arm as they greeted Buttonwood as man and wife. She never would have seen the gleam in his gaze when he slid off her bonnet, looking as though he'd uncovered a treasure. And she would have lost her chance to make up for the kiss she'd missed by the chicken coop.

Heat rose from her neck to her ears, and Opal knew that for once her bemoaned tendency to turn red over anything would serve her well. After all, how better to convince the townspeople she was a blushing bride than to blush?

"Midge!" Opal made sure her whisper carried over the bunch of people. "Adam! No one need know any other particular part of the ceremony. Stop discussing the details. Those are"—she met Midge's eyes and nodded meaningfully—"*private*."

Immediately the swarm buzzed, demanding more information, just as Opal depended they would. All the attention increased the heat flushing her cheeks, making her blush brighter.

"She's blushing!" Several people noticed and speculated as to why.

"C'mon, Midge," Alyssa, the sixteen-year-old town belle, implored. "Tell us what's making Opal turn ruby red!"

"Nothing to make her turn red," her friend protested. Obviously, Midge caught on to Opal's scheme to mention the wedding-day kiss, and now whipped the people into an expert froth of nosiness. "Only what's natural for a new bride and groom. . ."

Avid stares heated Opal's blush to boiling, and she began to regret her impetuous course of action. Her boldness fled, her downcast gaze no longer a role to play but a way to avoid meeting her husband's eyes.

"They kissed." Her youngest brother's voice rang with impatience and even a little disgust as Pete sidestepped a sharp elbow from Midge. "No big secret there. Happens at most weddings." His blunt words and obvious disdain did nothing to bring the residents of Buttonwood in line.

Guffaws from the men eddied alongside titters from the women on the afternoon breeze, but a huddle of humanity on the edges of the crowd didn't join the laughter. *Finally, the Specks and Grogans agree on something.* Yet Opal found no joy in the discovery. If all their families shared was rage over this marriage, the tension would escape to consume everyone.

"Kiss her again!" Josiah Reed's voice rose above it all as though on cue. Come to think of it, the man most likely knew exactly what he did, given his history of meddling in relationships. Clara and Saul turned out the better for it, so Opal reckoned she shouldn't complain.

Her thoughts screeched to a halt when Adam's hand moved at her waist, turning her toward him. Her husband didn't waste a word, simply angled his body closer and cupped her cheek with a large, rough palm as he leaned forward.

"I know you did that on purpose." His undertone floated to her ears as though imagined, but Opal knew Adam had figured out her little game. But he kept playing.

Her breath hitched when his lips brushed against hers. Once, a featherlight whisper. Twice, a silky murmur. A third time, and his mouth captured hers for a second of stolen sweetness before he drew away.

When her breath and brains returned, Opal started scheming. She needed another one of Midge's lessons on how to snare the attentions of her reluctant spouse. By sheer force of will, she didn't press her fingertips to the tingle in her lips. *Because next time, I don't want him to stop.*

226

Adam fought a brief but powerful skirmish with his own unwillingness to release Opal when the guffaw got loud enough to tell him he shouldn't offer any more "proof" of their shared affection.

He'd seen the look in her eyes and known she plotted some mischief, but never anticipated what she had in mind. In one fell swoop, Adam learned two very valuable lessons about his firebrand of a bride. No matter her determination to lead the town by the nose, Opal's acting skills wouldn't fetch much on the market.

Those overblown protests about Midge revealing the "details" of their wedding couldn't be more obvious. Only her blushes—that becoming rosy tinge creeping up her cheeks as she got the reaction she'd sought—saved her from the whole town catching on to the more important discovery of the day.

Opal wants me to kiss her. The realization rang through him. He planted his boots on the ground and snagged her in his arms. Once he nabbed her, he couldn't resist taunting her with his knowledge that she'd put them in this position on purpose.

But the soft feel of her pressed lightly against him, the warmth of her breath when his lips grazed hers, the elusive hint of honey that hung in the air around her, turned the tables in an instant. Adam snuck a second taste. Then he knew he should let her go—but she swayed into him, and he sampled her sweetness a third time before gathering the fortitude to pull away.

The refreshing breeze that enveloped them when they left the church died away, offering no help to cool the urgent heat racing through his veins. Adam swallowed, trying to make his mouth and mind work as a team again while good-natured friends teased and sour onlookers muttered.

No use. His mind and mouth were hitched in harness to one idea, and wouldn't budge from it. He wanted another kiss.

CHAPTER 26

Midge Lorraine Collins-Reed!" The hissed whisper offered no advanced warning, as it hit her ears the same moment Clara's hand clamped around her elbow.

Midge might not have minded were it not for a few facts. First, she'd just drawn that selfsame elbow back for a much-needed jab to Pete's ribs when Clara nabbed her. More important, she'd almost forgotten that there'd be a reckoning with Clara once her friend/adoptive mother—although Clara, at only six years older than she, could hardly stand as her true mother—discovered the incredible secret Midge had been sitting on all week. Now the skirts of Opal's secret were billowing in the breeze and doing a fine job of exposing what Clara would see as a betrayal of her and Midge's friendship. And last, she hated her middle name. *Lorraine.* Sounded so snotty. Not like her at all.

Midge wrinkled her nose and allowed herself to be dragged a safe—or not-so-safe, depending on how upset Clara turned out to be—distance from where the rest of the town speculated over Opal and Adam's hasty wedding. Raised eyebrows and lowered voices carried theories ranging from star-crossed love to unwanted children, just as she and Opal expected. So long as no one hit on the real reason for the marriage, things would stay manageable.

"I can't believe you kept something this important from me! Did Opal ask you not to say anything?" Clara's large green eyes just about swallowed her face this afternoon, swimming with questions and hurt.

"Pete came to find a witness to the ceremony, and he made me swear not to tell a soul if I wanted to find out what was going on." Midge didn't have to squash any guilt over heaping the blame on Pete. Not only was it true, but he'd escaped that second elbowing. "He said Opal needed me, so I gave my word to keep my mouth shut and went with him and Parson Carter."

"You could have trusted me." The protest escaped as though pushed through by a grudge, and her friend showed the grace to look somewhat ashamed of herself for voicing it. "But if you gave your word, I understand."

"I knew you'd understand, even though you wouldn't like it." Midge heard a light footfall behind her and knew Aunt Doreen joined them. "*Both* of you."

"We can waste breath harping on her about why she didn't tell us what happened," Doreen said quietly as she came alongside them, "or we can get to the good parts and just ask what happened!"

"Parson Carter married Opal and Adam, and Pete and I stood as witnesses. I couldn't breathe a word because Pete swore me to secrecy." Midge kept it simple, matter-of-fact, and honest. Even if something deep inside her didn't lurch like a drunken sailor at the thought of lying to the Reed women, she didn't want to be scrambling to remember what she said. It's why she'd planned for this moment days ago.

"Obviously." Doreen's keen gaze didn't leave much room to wiggle. "Everyone knows that much. What we want to know is the reason behind the wedding."

"Love." Not so much as a blink while she uttered this proclamation. Sure, she knew Doreen and Clara would think she meant that Opal and Adam were in love with one another, but the wedding went on for the love of their families. Opal sacrificed her standing with her family to avoid a feud and save their lives, after all, and far too much rode on making this makeshift marriage a success for Midge to jeopardize it with something as tawdry as specifics.

"Adam all along! Not even two weeks ago I tried to speak with Opal about Brett Burn, and she went pale as a ghost and said something about ignoring a man who chased after her." Clara practically bounced over the discovery. "Surprised her when she realized

I meant the blacksmith. Shocked me she wouldn't tell me who she thought I'd meant but wouldn't say another word about it. Now I know why!"

"Sounds reasonable." *But you're wrong.* Midge started to wonder how much biting one woman's tongue could take. She contributed nothing more than a few absent nods to the conversation.

Adam wasn't the Grogan Opal wanted to ignore. Midge sucked in a breath. *I knew I didn't like how Larry looked at her but didn't know he'd made such a pest of himself. And Opal wouldn't tell a soul, for fear of the fighting between their families.*

The more she fiddled this strange piece of information into the puzzle of Opal's sudden marriage, the more certain Midge became. *Somehow, this whole mess is Larry's fault!*

≈≈≈≈

Lucinda's stomach roiled as she watched her son pull away from Opal's clutches. Adam wore a befuddled expression, as though the hussy addled his brains with nothing more than a smooch.

No. Terrible fairness compelled her to acknowledge that Opal wielded far more than a simple smooch to snare her son. *A kiss marked the beginning long ago. How long?* The questions skewered her. *Weeks? Months? Seasons? When did that baggage first cast her eye on my boy? When did I fail to see the danger?*

She eyed her daughter-in-law's trim middle. *Too trim. Any child far enough along to erase all doubts would begin to show about now.* The back of her throat burned with restrained rage. *Opal lied. She's not carrying Adam's child. He need not have married the scheming whore.*

"You must be soooo proud." Griselda West, overly fancy in her East Sunday costume, sidled up and cooed at Diggory. All that sweetness didn't fool Lucinda one bit.

Sugarcoat a chicken bone and it'd still choke a body, after all. Griselda's avid gaze shone with her true intent. The woman waited for someone to spill even a hint that Adam and Opal weren't a true love match so she could lap up the gossip and spread it across the town.

Choices didn't come easy some days. Champion Adam by making it sound as though he and Opal struck up a forbidden romance, as they spoon-fed to the town, and watch it all come unraveled when her son discovered his wife's lies? Or let it slip that Opal acted no better than she should be, a hoyden with no mother and a godless upbringing, tempting upstanding men into the ways of sin? Adam may seem a fool for succumbing, but most would brush off the lapse with a chuckle at his manly ways— particularly since he'd done the honorable thing and married the chit. This way, when she rousted Opal and got rid of the girl, no one would blame her boy.

"Of course we're proud." Lucinda tilted her chin upward in a haughty show as the newlyweds walked over. "Adam could charm a bird from a tree, but even we didn't know he could manage to woo a Speck from her family loyalty."

A strangled cough rasped from Murphy Speck at that comment, making the rest of the Speck men go ruddy in fury.

So unbecoming, with all that red hair. Lucinda bit back her first smile of the day, pleasantly surprised with the effort it took once she noticed Opal's reaction. It seemed almost as though the crimson flooding her family's faces leeched all the color from her own, as she went ghostly pale.

The moment passed all too quickly as Parson Carter came and fetched them all to sit at a makeshift table for the celebratory "wedding" dinner. The rest of the town would fend for themselves, more or less. In the end, Lucinda perched on the end of a bench, narrowly avoiding being shoved to the ground by Diggory's enthusiastic shoveling of his food. With all eyes on the "happy" couple, nothing she said made much of an impact.

Lucinda relied on Larry to share her sentiments. Her middle son had always been the one most eager to scrap with the Specks, always the most in tune to her moods. Usually, he took his place at her side, but in the hubbub of Parson Carter's arrangements, somehow both her grown sons flanked her family's intruder.

Adam to her left, Larry to her right, Opal lorded it over the town as though some sort of Buttonwood royalty. She and Adam—acting along—bore the only partially convincing smiles at the table. Murphy and Diggory glared daggers at each other. Lucinda didn't think it coincidence that the Carters settled on serving stew. Spoons made for the least amount of damage in a brawl. Dave sent scowls winging toward Pete Speck, who ignored them in favor of doting on that upstart Midge Collins.

Larry's brows almost met in the middle, disapproval radiating from his every move. Anytime Adam and Opal spoke to one another, his lips grew thinner. But Lucinda's brief spurt of pride died into a dry throat when she realized his searing glances weren't directed at Opal. Larry aimed all his fury straight at Adam.

A gust of memory blew away Lucinda's anger over the town dinner. *Adam and Larry arguing in the barn. Over Opal.* No matter how hard she swallowed, nausea crept up the back of her throat. *Larry saying he had his eye on her. Adam threatening to deliver his own brother to the Specks if he came near Opal. . . . I should have known then, but I didn't see Adam's involvement with her.*

As though detached from the scene, she watched Larry angle his arm so his elbow pressed against Opal's arm. The girl's uncomfortable avoidance offered no reassurance. Having lured Adam to her side, that trollop encroached on Grogan land but wasn't satisfied. Now she worked her wiles on Larry.

It's so clear what she plans to do—turn brother against brother and destroy us from within. But this time I see what she's up to. And I'll stop it. Lucinda's knuckles whitened, and she felt the metal of her spoon easing from its rigid mold from the pressure under her fingers. *No matter what I have to do.*

CHAPTER 27

Folks filed by throughout the meal, and Adam lost track of how many times men clapped him on the shoulder. He kept busy trying to look every male in the area in the eye, hunting for any glint of anger, regret, or relief to mark the man who'd taken advantage of his wife. *The man who could still lay claim to her.* Mrs. Carter's stew didn't set well at the thought.

As though sensing his discomfort, Opal pressed tighter against his side. The wordless reassurance enabled Adam to keep hold of his grin as Dr. Saul Reed approached. Not that he need have worried about Reed—the man wouldn't have noticed half the townspeople were female if he hadn't been medically trained. That's how strong a bond he'd made with his wife, Clara. Adam didn't fix the label of friend to just anyone, but Reed made the cut.

"Grogan." His friend's grin stretched too wide

for show as he hauled his wife and their baby to the table. "You and your new missus proved something I've wondered about for a while."

"What's that?"

"If Clara hung up her matchmaking bonnet after our marriage or if she kept quietly scheming." Laughter greeted the pronouncement, as almost everyone knew by now that Clara had taken a wild bargain and tried to marry Saul off to any eligible woman in Buttonwood two years ago before taking him on as her personal, permanent project.

"Clara didn't plot to bring us together." The supple warmth at his side vanished, replaced by Opal's sudden rigidity as she defended her friend.

"I didn't even know." Clara almost choked on the admission. Surprise, hurt, concern, and suspicion chased each other across her face.

"I'm sorry." The stiffness leached from his wife's spine, and Adam felt more than saw Opal slump beside him. The posture of defeat.

It demanded action.

He slid his arm around her waist to bolster her up, jostling her just enough so her head leaned toward him, sun-warmed hair spreading across his shoulder as much as her pins would allow. A small sigh escaped her, but Adam didn't take the time to classify it as sad or satisfied.

"A world of truth survives in silence." Doreen Reed—Clara's aunt and now the wife of Saul Reed's father—intervened. "Kept in quiet and dependent upon discretion."

Mine does. Adam resisted the urge to swallow,

all too aware that it would give away his discomfort. *Discretion lays the foundation of our marriage, because if the truth we bury is ever unearthed, our families will destroy one another. Survival itself depends on that silence.*

"Whoa." Dave's nine-year-old voice piped up from down the table. "Somebody real impressive must've said that."

"Thank you." The older woman's acknowledgment made Clara, Opal, and everyone else smile as they realized Doreen hadn't been quoting anyone at all. Just sharing her own insight.

"That was beautiful." Willa's voice, seldom heard outside the family, caught everyone's attention.

For the first time, Adam looked beyond Opal to see where the rest of their families had settled. No surprise to see the Specks to the left of the table and the Grogans monopolizing the right half. Midge Collins made a useful placeholder between Dave and Pete on the opposite bench, but otherwise things had gone awry.

Seated in the center of the bench, Opal should have been the connector to her family, easing tension and uniting what had been antagonistic clans. Instead of this natural order, someone jumbled the arrangement in a way guaranteed to provoke tempers.

How did Willa come to sit next to Benjamin Speck? Adam knew the exact moment Pa and Ma made the same realization. No one blinked. Willa ducked her head under the weight of their stares, obviously regretting drawing any attention to herself.

238

After Benjamin's ill-advised notice of his sister the previous week—Adam could scarcely believe only a week had passed—his effrontery in sitting beside Willa couldn't go unremarked.

"Daughter," Ma's voice sounded thin, as though she spoke from far away, "how did you come to be so far away?"

"Halfway down the table isn't far." Midge's comment, reasonable though it seemed, made no impact.

"Leaving family land to settle with Grogans—that's far." Ben, who Adam noted took care not to let so much as an elbow brush against Willa, kept both his tone and expression even. Nothing to give offense but just enough to show he wouldn't be cowed.

Adam felt Opal go ramrod straight, physically bracing against an emotional blow. He kept his arm wrapped around her, refusing to relinquish his support. Or his claim.

"Just far enough for a fresh start." He gave his bride a squeeze and a smile to diffuse tension. *Today is the most difficult.* He willed her to remember that.

"Says something when a woman needs a fresh start away from her own family."

Adam couldn't say whether Opal's squawk came from indignation over Larry's idiocy or as protest over the way his arm tightened around her in his own reaction. He loosened his grip immediately and started to push away from the table. If he had to knock down his brother to keep the peace, so be it.

"Don't be a ninny, Larry!" Willa's outburst stayed him. She glowered at their troublesome brother, only the way she wrung her hands in her lap identifying his normally shy sister. "Opal and Adam's marriage means a fresh start for all of us, and we don't want needling comments like yours trying to prick pride and draw blood."

"Well said." Admiration shone in Ben Speck's gaze. More than enough for everyone at the table to notice it.

Pa's eyebrows drew together. Ma reached out a hand as though to snatch Willa to her side then made poor cover of the gesture by reaching for a roll. A sudden jerk from Dave told Adam his younger brother attempted an unsuccessful kick beneath the table.

The Specks showed signs of displeasure as well. Elroy muttered beneath his breath. Murphy gave a swift, short shake of his head. Young Pete looked as though he sorely wanted to make an unwise comment, but a well-timed poke in the ribs from Midge kept his tongue between his teeth.

In fact, the only person at the entire table who showed no reaction was Willa. Having said her piece, she'd ducked her head back down and resumed staring at her hands, oblivious to Ben's all-too-apparent regard.

Well, at least Willa didn't return Speck's interest. Adam rolled his shoulders in a futile bid to relax. They'd still avoid disaster so long as his sister kept her head.

Wait. No. I didn't see that right.

Opal felt her eyes widen and didn't even bother trying to fix it. She stayed busy keeping her jaw off the ground as her new sister-in-law gave Ben a timid smile.

Until a fingernail dug into her shoulder blade, an unsubtle signal that Clara wanted to make sure she wasn't missing the byplay. Then Opal's wide-eyed wonder turned into a wince. Her friend needn't have worried. *After spending my whole life trying to keep Specks and Grogans apart, I'm more sensitive to their interactions that anyone in all of Buttonwood!*

The strong hand resting on her waist clenched into a fist, making her amend her thoughts. *Except, maybe, for Adam.* Opal accepted the possibility that her husband made a good match for her in this area, at least. She slid one of her hands atop his fisted one and gave it a light pat to let him know she understood the implications of Ben and Willa's camaraderie.

Strange how this new threat to the fragile truce between their families didn't shake her nearly so much as it should have. Or, at least, as much as it would have before the events of the past week.

Maybe because there's a much bigger threat looming above us. She closed her eyes against misgivings over her hasty marriage. *No. I'd rather think it's because God's brought us this far without bloodshed. Surely another Speck and Grogan getting along will ultimately do good. Like me and Adam.*

Somehow, her fingers had laced with his, and

she breathed more easily as she felt some of the strain ease from his muscles. If she wasn't mistaken, her husband had been about to stand after Larry's foolish comment and take care of matters. *Which, of course, would have made everything worse. Lucinda would blame me for turning her sons against each other.*

"Fresh starts are for fools who make mistakes, and there's been enough foolishness to last both our families a lifetime." Diggory Grogan's statement, if retold by a neutral person with a kind voice, might be mistaken as the equivalent of an olive branch offered to the Specks.

But no one at the table, nor any one of the occupants of Buttonwood clustered around it with ears open and minds racing, would interpret it as anything but malicious. Venom coated Diggory's words as surely as the fury in his gaze refused to be held to one person. It spread from herself to Adam, then Ben and even Willa, infecting them all and poisoning all her efforts to keep their families from outright war.

No! The bitterness welled up until it threatened to choke her. *Lord, help me. I didn't betray my father's trust and wed a Grogan only to see it all fall apart now!* The bitterness eased enough for her to draw breath. Even as she asked for strength to fight the hatred surrounding her, Opal knew the answer. Hadn't Parson Carter shared it earlier that morning?

" *'The Lord shall fight for you, and ye shall hold your peace. . . .'* " Fighting only made things worse.

"My father-in-law is right." Opal leaned across the table to pat Diggory's hand, relishing the surprise seeping across his features. "Both Specks and Grogans have wronged one another, made enough mistakes to stop now and never be in danger of committing the blasphemy of claiming perfection." Clara, Midge, and Doreen laughed, and the rest of the town reluctantly joined in. Opal waited for it to die down before she finished. She kept one hand atop Diggory's, anchoring him to her words even as she held her father's gaze with her own. "I'm glad the parson preached on forgiveness this morning... so we can leave the past behind and move forward as the neighbors we should always have been."

"Amen!" Parson Carter hastened to offer his support. "The Lord tells us we've all fallen short."

The town erupted into murmurs and even out-bursts of hearty agreement as folks besieged the table with congratulations, forcing Parson Carter's hopes of a truce into reality. With the entire town not allowing tensions to break free, and a wedding to cement connection between the families, Opal started to wonder if today might truly be the end of the feud that had threatened her loved ones for so long.

"Well done, girlie." Diggory leaned forward, reluctant appreciation in his gaze as his hand slid from hers. "A worthy move."

"Yes." Lucinda's agreement rang bright and loud before the hissed accompaniment. "Just remember, Opal, that some people fall far shorter than others."

CHAPTER 28

Y ou don't mean it?" Opal's gasp pierced something in Adam's chest.

"A fresh start." He repeated what he'd just told her. "After the way you smoothed the path for our families to reconcile yesterday—especially in the face of Pa's and Larry's aggression—I've decided to put the past away."

"All of it?" Shrewdness sharpened her features.

"We'll forget about the cause for our wedding." *I can afford to be generous when it saved my skin.* "And even dismiss the rocks in the mattress."

Her sudden hug caught him off-balance. Almost literally. One minute his wife stood before him, face bright with hope, and the next instant warm woman filled his arms with softness and his breath with a tantalizing hint of honey. His arms skated around to hold her closer.

It takes little enough to make her happy. Adam

didn't even try to dredge up a protest, just savored the sensations. *I'll remember that and be sure to do it more often.*

"Rank ewe." Opal's murmur puzzled him.

"We don't keep sheep." He lost her response when he felt the heat of her breath through the cotton of his shirt. *I'll buy her some sheep if she wants them.*

"Mmffm." Her hands pressed against his arms, pushing the realization that he'd been holding his wife too tightly.

He immediately released her, jamming his hands in his pockets as she took a great gulp of air. Oops.

"Sheep?" She looked confused. "I said, 'Thank you.'"

"I misheard. It's no matter."

"It matters." The shiny happy look came back. "More than you know. After seeing Pa and Ben and Elroy and Pete yesterday, it made me miss them even more. Knowing I wouldn't see them again for so long made me wretched. I can't say how much it means that I can go over there tomorrow."

"I don't want you to be wretched, Opal." *Will she ever look like that when she says my name?*

"Wouldn't have lasted. What really makes me happy is that you're letting us start afresh. Completely new." One smile shouldn't be capable of containing such radiance.

Adam blinked to clear his mind. "Opal, there's one matter that must be laid to rest before we move forward entirely."

"Yes?" The smile faded, though her glow remained. She reached out and clasped one of his hands in both of hers.

"Opal, I know you don't really want to discuss it, but I think we both know that he left town a while ago." He spoke carefully, trying to upset her as little as possible as he broached the topic of the man who'd impregnated then abandoned her. He'd come to the conclusion the day before that the fellow didn't remain in town. "You must have thought he wouldn't come back?"

"There were times when even I began to doubt." Her openness touched him. "But he's a man of his word, Adam. I knew he'd return to us."

Us. She's known she was with child for months now. Opal will begin to show the pregnancy anytime. And she still believes he's returning for her and their child? It seemed as though all the moisture in his throat crisped to ice.

"Is he worthy?" *Will you want to leave with him if that day comes?*

"I've never known a more worthy man." The earnestness of her expression felled him. "He'll make a good provider, Adam. You don't have to worry."

"People will talk." He grasped at anything to keep her from slipping away. "Our families will declare war."

"No. Another marriage will only strengthen the alliance between the Specks and Grogans." She squeezed his hand. "Benjamin made a lot of money in the mines, Adam. He'll more than do right by

246

Willa. Your Pa will come around."

"Ben." He all but shouted her brother's name. *How is she talking about Ben?*

"Yes." Opal squeezed his hand tighter, as though to make him focus. Maybe he needed it. "I know you and your family think Ben was flighty for going off to the mines, but he and Pa made the decision together. He always planned to come back. Even if he didn't write as often as I'd like, he tried. You can depend on Ben to stand by Willa, and, like I said, he has the money to keep her more than comfortable."

Her flurry of words penetrated his confusion. *When I asked about the man who'd left awhile ago, she thought I meant her brother?* If biting back a bellow didn't take his concentration, Adam might have struggled against laughter. *I'm trying to coax my wife to confess the name of her lover, and she's trying to convince me that her brother will make a good husband for my sister!*

"No." He placed his free hand over both of hers as the consequences of what she suggested sank in. *Pa will take blood in exchange for his only daughter.* "I can't let that happen."

"What do you mean?" Opal went ahead and asked the question but already knew the answer. As she'd spoken of Ben, she'd watched Adam's expression grow increasingly impassive. *Why did you ask about my brother if you'd already made up your mind?* She wanted to cry out but knew better than to push this new husband of hers.

Already this morning he'd rescinded the punishment for Lucinda's ploy with those rocks in her mattress. Questioning his judgment about allowing Ben to court Willa might set her back more than she could afford.

"I mean that we've more than enough difficulties surrounding our marriage to even consider assisting another one." His hands beneath and atop hers put forth an astonishing amount of heat. "We can't waste our time or energy trying to keep track of Ben and Willa when there's so much riding on our relationship."

"Our relationship." She liked the sound of that far too much, but he said it as though they made a team. *I've always been a Speck but didn't really fit in as the only woman and the one trying to keep everyone from fighting. But Adam's talking as though I could belong.*

"Keeping everyone believing we chose each other. . .it takes a lot of work." His flat comment squashed her silliness.

"Of course it does." She tugged her hands away but only managed to free one. *It's obvious a man like you would never choose a nothing like me unless forced into it. You speak of fresh starts, but really you're just making the best of a bad situation.* Her eyes stung at the thought.

"Especially when we aren't in it together." His grip tightened, as though trapping her.

"What do you mean?" A welcome wave of anger rolled away the loneliness for a moment. "I've stood alongside you to help avert bloodshed from the very beginning. No, even before the beginning. Back before our wedding day. How can you imply anything less?"

The same way Pa figures I'm not loyal to the Specks. The idea floored her. *It doesn't matter how much I do or how many times I prove that I'll sacrifice my own needs for the best interests of others, in the end I'll still be the outsider.*

Sorrow crashed over her, dousing the flames of her indignation. But only for a moment, when she realized Adam was talking about unanswered questions and an uncertain future.

"When you won't tell me who the father is?" He finished as though he'd built up to this last question, though Opal hadn't caught most of what he said.

"You're asking me why you should move forward with this marriage when I can't tell you who is going to be the father of my child?"

"Exactly."

"Perhaps because this marriage saved your life." Opal jerked her hand from his when another light tug didn't immediately free her. "And therefore the lives of your entire family."

"Yours, too." His jaw hardened.

"That's why I'm ready to go ahead." She jumped on the opportunity. "If I'm able to, why aren't you?"

"I'm not the one who would be seen as unfit for society when my babe entered the world without a father." Adam's usual use of diplomacy vanished right along with hers. "You're the one who only wants to go forward so she can leave secrets buried in the past."

"You, you. . ." Opal clenched her teeth together to keep the words from escaping. *I can't tell him I'm a virgin. I can't tell him my secret is that I have no secrets. If he knows before the marriage is consummated, he'll annul the marriage and get us all killed.* She reminded herself of the facts over and over again. *He only thinks you're carrying a child out of wedlock because you allow him to believe so.*

"I what?" He folded his arms across his chest. "I deserve to know the name of the man whose child I'll be raising?"

"You're a hypocrite!" The accusation bled from her thoughts before she could staunch the flow. "No one forced you to claim me or my future child. You could just as easily have denied me to my family, admitted Larry's guilt in writing the note you should have burned, and taken the penalty. You may even have lived long enough to seek vengeance for the punishment my father dealt your brother. The secrets of which you speak aren't mine, husband." She took a deep breath. "They're *ours*."

"True." Adam closed the space between them. "I don't like it but won't deny it. At least we can share our secrets and the common purpose of safe-guarding those we love, Opal."

"Yes." She kept her gaze fixed on his shoulder, knowing somehow that if her eyes met his she'd be undone. "We share those things, if not a bed or a life."

His hissed intake of breath let her know the remark hit home.

"Marriages are based on trust, and trust on truth.

There will be truth between us, wife." His forefinger crooked beneath her chin, tilting it upward until she faced him fully. "Tell me his name."

"You're wrong."

She tried to back away, but he held her fast, his thumb coming to rest almost tenderly on her chin.

"How so?"

"Trust is based in honesty, not truth."

"Two branches of the same tree. I'll take either one." The slightly rough pad of his thumb traced her lower lip. "We'll start our marriage in full when you answer. Tell me."

"So be it. Honestly"—she closed her eyes against the hot pinpricks of tears as she gave him the only answer she had—"there's nothing to tell."

CHAPTER 29

Tell me everything." Midge barely waited until they reached the edge of the apiary before demanding information. Opal wore the look of a woman with too much on her mind.

With a fake illicit pregnancy, a hidden shotgun wedding, a pending family feud, and an evil mother-in-law, there's plenty to keep her busy. Even without me asking if I'm right about Larry making a pest of himself and somehow bringing that farce of a wedding on her and Adam. . .

Today called for a tall order of talk followed by a dose of scheming. *If God really existed, maybe He did well to get me here for Opal, like He put Dr. Reed in Baltimore to save me from Randy.* The thought caught her off guard, so Midge shoved it to the back of her mind. She had more important matters to delve into right now.

"We spoke yesterday after church."

"That much to cover?" Midge gave a low whistle. If Opal's reluctance proved any gauge as to the level of difficulty they could expect, at least boredom wouldn't creep up on her. "And don't try to brush me off. The whole town besieged you and Adam so much the two of us didn't have a moment together."

"Did you bring woolen gloves?"

Opal's question seemed senseless until Midge remembered that her visit bore an actual purpose. Today they had to move the apiary from Speck land to the Grogan clearing Adam marked for it. "Yes. Though leather's easier to work through."

"Not when you're working with bees." Her friend's expression turned serious. "If a bee feels threatened and stings, leather will trap him and he'll die. With wool, he can usually remove his stinger and survive."

"Will you kick me out of your apiary if I say that the bees who sting me aren't my highest priority?" Midge tugged her sleeves down over her wrists.

"I won't, but only because you said 'who' when you talked about them, and that shows you think of them as individuals." Opal passed her a misshapen brown lump. "Put this in your pocket, just in case."

"Looks like tobacco." Midge inspected the texture of the thing then sniffed it. "It *is* tobacco! I don't want this."

"You will if you get stung. It's an old trick my mother taught me. Warm some tobacco in your hand until it's moist then rub it on the site of the sting until the pain and swelling lessen. It works better than even ammonia does and won't take your skin off." Opal passed her a straw hat. "You'll be especially glad since the hotter the weather, the worse the swelling."

"This starts to sound like you assume some bees will sting me." Doubt niggled through her. "They never have before."

"Before, we fed them. Today we're going to move the hives. They'll see that as an attack." Opal pulled out yards of netting. "It's why we take extra precautions like the gloves and netting and make sure we smoke the hives to lull the bees to sleep as best we can before we start jostling them around."

"Is there anything else I should know?" *Now that it's too late to back out.*

"Keep your ears open. One of the first alerts will be the sound the bees make. When they're making that buzzing hum, they're happy and busy. When they're agitated, it takes on a shrill pitch. That's when they're more likely to sting."

"I've only ever heard them hum, but that's good information to have."

Midge watched as Opal put on her straw hat and began layering netting around her head. Opal wound yards of white netting around her face, covering her head and hair completely all the way to her shoulders. Midge mimicked the motions, insulating herself with the light, gauzy fabric that made the world seem softer. Then they pulled on their gloves.

A brief tutorial on how to handle the smoker, and they cautiously approached the first hive. Movable-frame, Opal had called the 12"x12" boxes. She'd gone on about it being the ideal size and such forth for reasons that seemed too specific to Midge. Right now, though, how to secure the bottom boards and close the openings while smoking the bees definitely seemed important.

They got through the first five hives, loading them into the small wagon, with Midge suffering only two stings for her trouble, before they headed toward Grogan land. The mule before them—Simon—plodded as slowly as a creature could move and still count as moving, but Opal said that was the idea. Jostling the bees would upset them and maybe wake them up.

Midge drove Simon while Opal kept the smoker ready to subdue any irritated insects. It was only hours later, when after painstakingly driving over the last of Opal's twenty hives, that Midge found an opportunity to steer the conversation back to personal matters.

With the hives in place and reopened, the contented, buzzing hum Midge found strangely soothing blanketed the new apiary. She watched as Opal unwound the netting from around her face and followed suit.

"Something like this stuff may work to keep the bees from penetrating your defenses, but we both know I see through such flimsy tactics." Midge handed the netting back to her friend. "You haven't distracted me."

"How do you give the impression your attention is fickle, wandering to new interests before most folks could ever guess, when really you're as single-minded as a bloodhound?"

"Maybe because my fickle attention only wanders when it's not fixed on something important." Midge pulled the loosely woven fabric away and tucked it back in the wagon so she wouldn't have to see Opal's reaction when she said the next part. "You're important to me."

"Oh Midge." The hug came almost as a tackle. "Thank you for that. I needed to hear it today."

"Why today?" She didn't see any reason to bother with repeating mushy sentiments. Unearthing information so she could make plans, on the other hand, registered high on her list.

"My progress with Adam seems more going backward than anything else." The admission made her friend seem more fragile somehow.

"Of course." Midge snorted. Aunt Doreen's lady lessons sank in deeper than she expected, but sometimes even a lady needed to indulge in a solid, dismissive snort. Quickest way to let someone know she sounded ridiculous. "That's exactly what the whole town will buzz about all week—how you and Adam can't get along."

"We made a good team yesterday."

"You two have made a good team for much longer than that, from what I can tell." Midge scooted her rump back until she perched on the back of the wagon. "It went unnoticed on account of your families, but you've worked in tandem to keep the Specks and Grogans away from the others' throats for years."

"Holding a common cause doesn't make two people a team."

"Call me crazy, but I think doing something alongside each other is exactly what makes two people a team. Some teams are temporary and dissolve after a short task. Some last a lot longer. You and Adam share a burden neither one could pull alone and have for so long you take each other for granted."

"No one wants to marry a horse." Opal sounded positively morose—which meant deep down she wanted Adam to want her. Good.

"Except another horse." Midge gave her shoulder a friendly nudge. "Especially since you two have been hitched together since long before your wedding."

"Maybe you're right." A small laugh burbled from her throat as Opal envisioned her and Adam tied together, each pulling in opposite directions. The laugh died abruptly, as the thought of her husband trying to escape their binds grew more prominent.

"What's wrong?" Midge sensed the change in her mood.

"Hitched together in desperation and driven apart by lies. That's me and Adam." The dark pit of her situation yawned before her, inescapable and bottomless. "How long before the whole thing gets destroyed?"

"Stop it!" Her friend nudged her into the back of the wagon, where Opal sat with little grace. "You're both heading for the same goal, and that's keeping everyone together. So I don't see how you can be torn asunder so long as you keep on that way."

KELLY EILEEN HAKE

"Lucinda's suspicions and little games, for one." Opal didn't want to think about what her mother-in-law might be hatching next. "Though this morning Adam rescinded his decree that I can't visit home."

"That'll give the biddy more to cluck about." The glee in Midge's voice livened Opal's spirits a little. "And shows Adam's more alongside you than ever. Why so gloomy?"

"Adam asked about two other things this morning, and those didn't go well at all. Since you seem to have all the answers today, you can probably guess." She raised a brow in challenge.

"Ben and Willa?"

"You're downright spooky."

"Nah." Midge made an abrupt gesture with one hand. "That one's obvious. Anyone who went to church yesterday would've come up with it, which means every blessed soul in all of Buttonwood knew the answer."

"Adam says he can't allow it." *As though it's for him to allow.* Opal barely kept the disloyal thought to herself. *Wait. Disloyal? Since when is wanting happiness for my brother disloyal?* Foolish question. *Since I pledged my life to Adam.*

"Who made him king of Buttonwood?" Midge's huff made Opal grin.

It may be wrong for me to voice such things, but that doesn't mean I can't appreciate another person's perspective!

"No one governs the heart, save God."

258

"Not to argue, but I think we choose who we love. Some people make poor choices is all." Midge shrugged. "Hearts can be won, but they have to be given. If Willa wants to give hers to Ben, nothing Adam can do will stop it."

"He and his family would keep them apart, a big mistake. Even if Ben hadn't returned from the mines with a handsome sum, he bears half of Speck land. The Grogans would have to go far to find another who works half as hard or would do so much for those he calls family. He'll be a good husband and even better father someday." The more she thought about it, the more insulted she became. "Willa would never regret choosing my brother, but the Grogans act as though he isn't good enough."

"They treat you as though you aren't good enough." Midge's interruption stopped Opal in mid-stew.

"I know."

"You accept that."

"Because I can't change it, and we're supposed to forgive when others wrong us." Opal needed the reminder as much as Midge did. "Turn the other cheek."

"I read that." Her friend absently rubbed her now much smaller lump of tobacco on a small red bump that marked her fourth and final sting of the day. "It makes me wonder, though. . . ."

"Wonder what?"

"How many times?" Past pain shadowed Midge's

normally avid gaze, turning it fierce. "How many times do you turn your cheek before it turns you into someone you don't even recognize?"

CHAPTER 30

They killed your grandfather!" Ma's voice thinned to a shriek. "Adam, you can't let her bring them here. You can't!"

"Opal won't bring them near the house. Pa and I designated the south clearing for her new apiary." Adam refused to acknowledge Pa's abrupt gesture indicating that he not mention his involvement.

After all, we wouldn't be in this mess if Pa hadn't mentioned Opal moving the apiary today. When Ma commented on her absence at the dinner table, all he need say was that she tended to her bees and mentioned she might run long.

"Diggory Ezekiel Grogan"—Ma rounded on her husband—"you're involved in this?"

"Now. Lucy." Pa used the pet name he only brought out under duress. "You know I'd make sure those bees stay as far away from the house as possible."

"Don't you 'Lucy' me!" Ma clutched Larry's shoulders. "Not when you've put us all in danger. Our children..."

"They won't go near the apiary." Pa made it both an assurance and a command for Larry and Willa.

"Opal won't move any of the hives any closer either." Adam joined his father's attempts to placate his mother. "It shouldn't pose a problem."

"Bees killed your grandfather when that cursed apiary remained on Speck land." Ma sank onto the bench between Larry and Willa, an arm around each as though to ward away death itself. "Less distance means more danger."

"Bees didn't fly over here and sting Grandpa." Willa seemed to fold in on herself as she said it, although whether from the strain of using enough nerve to speak against Ma's will or the pressure of Ma's physical grip, Adam couldn't tell. "He went over there."

"They never proved it!" Larry's snarl made Willa shrink even more. "Those Specks could've planned the whole thing and made it look that way. Everyone knows they wanted the border pasture so bad they could taste it."

"Old arguments." *Senseless arguments.*

"Pa didn't get himself trussed up by any Specks." Pa's expression when he spoke of his own father painted a portrait of exasperation and admiration. "Though the bees is what killed him."

"How can you know?" The hairs on the nape of Adam's neck stirred. A piece to the mystery of the origins of the feud lay within his grasp, if he could seize it.

"He told me his plan." A shrug far too casual accompanied the admission. "Specks weren't the only ones angling for that border pasture."

Have the Specks been right all along? Was Grandpa on their land to strike the first blow? Suspicion started to simmer in Adam's chest. "What did Grandpa plan to make the Specks rescind their claim?"

"Burn a few hives, just to show what Grogans are capable of when it comes to protecting what's theirs." No shame shaded the words. "A good plan, if he hadn't been caught."

"Caught." *Just like he told Larry. The problem wasn't in behaving without integrity; it was in getting caught.* "No piece of earth is worth a man's honor."

"He only meant to deliver a warning." Pa's eyes narrowed. "Nothing to harm a living soul, mind. Just enough to send a message to those Specks to keep away."

"Like the message you dispatched with Larry?" Adam's fingers curled around the note he kept in his pocket—a tangible talisman of his wedding. "Not enough harm to prick your conscience but just enough to inflict damage?" *Enough to spark a feud and destroy generations. Enough to trap two people in a marriage neither wanted.*

"Don't start sounding so high and mighty with your morality, son." Pa's jaw jutted out. "Sneaking around behind everyone's backs with the Speck girl. . .what you did far outstrips any note of mine and Larry's they never even found."

"Wrong." Something uncurled within him, smashing against the wall of caution he'd built around every decision he made. "I went over to remove it and had to ask Opal's help with the search. She found it."

"She did." A reptilian smile slithered across his brother's face as Larry processed the news that his note found its mark after all. "Good."

"I took it with me." His hand plunged out of his pocket, revealing the note. "Heaven knows I should have burned it but thought I might need the evidence of Larry's scheming someday. Like his grandfather before him, Larry's message went terribly wrong." He thrust it toward his father. "Read it."

The soddy seemed strangely airless as Pa surveyed the message he'd scripted. The defiant nonchalance slid from his features once he reached the last sentence.

"Larry Bartholomew Grogan, what is this addition?" For once, their father's volume didn't rise.

"Nothing important." Larry noticed the change and registered the inherent threat. He made an attempt to take possession of the note. "Just a last-minute thought."

"You expect me to believe a single thought rattled around in that skull of yours when you wrote this?" Pa's mustache quivered with the force of his inhalation. "Murphy would have the right to slaughter every last one of us for this. Had they ever threatened Willa, they'd not have drawn another breath."

"Opal found it, not Murphy." Larry stood up

and took a few steps away. "No harm done."

"No harm." A snort of what might have been laughter, if anything about the situation struck him as funny, escaped Adam. "Murphy read it, all right. That one sentence brought about my wedding, little brother."

"No." The blood drained from Larry's face, and he groped for the edge of the table. "That note didn't force you to marry Opal. You lie."

Lucinda couldn't tear her eyes from the strip of parchment in her husband's hands. That such a small scrap could so thoroughly devastate all she'd built...

"Please." Her hand trembled as she stretched toward Diggory, the one word both asking for the note and imploring him to somehow stop a horror already passed.

Her fingers curled around the parchment without conscious decision as Diggory handed it over. Lucinda wondered if she should sit down then realized she'd never stood. She set the fragment on the table before her with great care, splaying her palms on either side to flatten it.

She recognized Diggory in the looping letters of the first sentence. The open lines of his writing betrayed the friendly boy he'd once been, before life and loss taught him better.

NEXT TIME WE LOSE A COW, WE TAKE A SPECK IN PAYMENT.

Simple, fair, impossible to misunderstand. Nothing there to ruin Adam's life. Below, more words seeped into their lives, the ink darker where the pen slashed across the parchment. The angry script could belong to none but Larry.

And I got my eye on your only heifer!

A muffled sob burst from her lips at the irrefutable proof of her second-born's guilt. The only sound since Diggory passed her the note. If Adam said this message caused his marriage, no doubt remained. Only questions. "How?"

"I discovered Marla missing the morning after I retrieved that note and tracked her to a broken fence in the southeast pasture bordering Speck lands."

"'The next time we lose a cow. . .'" Lucinda quoted, tracing the letters before her. "So you went after it." *Of course Adam wouldn't allow the slightest chance of the threat coming true. He knew it would mean the end of us all.*

"Southeast pasture." Diggory caught Larry by the collar. "I told you to mend that days before! Too busy skulking around the Speck place causing trouble?"

"Stop!" Willa's cry froze everyone. "Let Adam finish. We don't know when Opal may come back. Yell at Larry later, when you can yell at him for everything."

"You know Murphy and Elroy came over the week before to address Larry's wandering. His trespassing increased tensions, so when Pete caught me looking for Marla, the Speck men felt obliged to treat it as a serious matter." Adam kept his face impassable—a sure sign he felt strong emotion. "They searched me and found that note."

"It didn't matter." The shout didn't even sound like Larry, it came out so hoarse. "They'd already decided on their course of action. The Specks planned this from the start!"

"Be quiet, Larry." Lucinda's own voice sounded strange to her ears. "The Specks didn't want Opal with Adam any more than we did. We'll hear no more lies from you."

"When they found the note, they assumed I meant to carry it out and decided they couldn't let it pass. Not when it left Opal at risk."

"Can't blame them." Diggory shook Larry a bit but stopped himself.

Lucinda found herself wishing her husband kept on.

"Opal intervened to save my life." Adam fixed his gaze on Larry. "When logic didn't work, she reminded them I'd pulled her from the fire at Reed's house. When that didn't work, she told her father the only thing that could stay his hand—that I was to be the father of her child."

"Until then she hadn't breathed a word?" Awe underscored Willa's question.

"She never so much as told me." A rueful shake of Adam's head punctuated that statement. "Opal would never have told that to a soul."

"It's true." If anyone asked, Lucinda couldn't

have told them whether she spoke the words aloud or simply whispered them to herself. But she knew the truth of it down deep in her bones.

Opal wouldn't let her family feel the bite of betrayal under any but these circumstances. She would have kept the secret of her indiscretion at all costs. No matter if she blamed a man who came through town once. Could even have claimed she was unwilling and her family would keep her. You can't say much for Opal Speck, but she would protect her own.

"Larry couldn't have known what one remark would do." If she lost loyalty to her children, she'd lose everything. Lucinda watched the corners of Adam's mouth tighten.

Besides, Adam is the son who took up with the Speck girl, after all. Never mind Larry wanted to. Who knows how many men she's lured with her wiles?

As quickly as that, her perspective shifted. Everything came back into clear focus. *The hussy probably took up with untold weaklings, and I've been right all along. She doesn't carry Adam's babe. She just saw an opportunity to grab a good man and took it.*

Lucinda felt her breath come easier. *Of course my Larry's a victim same as Adam. Opal's the villain here, no matter if she fools everyone else!*

CHAPTER 31

W ait." Her sister-in-law's call stopped Opal as she tried to slip from the door of the room they shared the next morning. "Please, Opal. I want to go with you."

What is going on? Since she'd arrived back from moving the apiary yesterday, there'd been a strange mood over the Grogan farm. Granted, Opal thought the feel of the place always seemed somewhat odd compared to the easygoing environment of the Speck home, but even after the usual allowances, things felt different.

"You want to come to my family's farm?" Opal left the *why* part unspoken out of sheer politeness.

"Yes please." Willa slipped from the bed and hurriedly pulled on a heavy dress. "We both know Ma tries to keep us apart as much as possible, but I'd like an opportunity to talk with you about a few things and get to know you better." As though a speech of this unprecedented length taxed her, the slightly younger girl busied herself with washing her face and brushing her hair, pulling it back in a loose bun.

"I'd like that, too." A surge of warmth toward her sister-in-law had Opal resisting the impulse to hug her.

Willa had scarce spoken a word to her since Lucinda revealed those rocks in the freshly stuffed mattress. This made for a welcome change, even though Opal wondered at the reasons for it. Perhaps Willa returned Ben's interest?

Opal nibbled on her lower lip as Willa laced her boots and fetched her bonnet. Bringing her sister-in-law with her on her first visit to the Speck farm would do wonders to show her family that the Grogans didn't mistreat her. *She'll also get to spend more time with Ben.* A fact that wouldn't go unnoticed by her in-laws. Or Adam.

"Perhaps this isn't the best idea, Willa."

"Ma won't like it, I know." She paused with one hand on the door, a study in solemnity. "It's rare I do anything Ma won't approve of. It keeps things the most peaceful, you see, and I put a premium on peace."

"Then why would you choose this as your chance to do the unexpected?" *When Lucinda will point to me as a bad influence.*

"You always seemed a good person to me." The door opened to let in the weak rays of morning's first light. "Those rocks seemed out of character, but on Sunday the Opal I respected came back.

Then, after yesterday, I knew my family has been wrong to misjudge yours. It's long past time for us to be friends."

"Yesterday?" *I knew something changed; I just knew it!* Opal followed her out the door, abandoning the idea of trying to convince Willa to stay at home. "What happened yesterday?"

Her new ally wouldn't answer, just lifted a long finger to her lips and snuck past the house and beyond the yard with quick strides. Obviously, Willa didn't want her mother halting her adventure.

For her part, Opal could be content to wait. Not long, though. Once they reached the fence marking the boundary between Speck and Grogan lands, she dismissed the easy silence that had accompanied them so far on their walk.

March mornings reminded Opal why spring days fed so heartily on the glory of the sun. Only then did they escape the cold bite of winter that still lingered in the early hours. Snatches of birdsong broke through air thick with moisture and the promise of life. Dew clung to every blade of grass— some cold enough to show touches of ice.

"Ma's scared of your bees." Of all the things Willa might have said, Opal wouldn't have predicted this. "When Pa told her you missed dinner on account of moving your apiary, she went pale as the inside of a potato peel."

"The place Adam selected suits all my needs perfectly." Opal spoke cautiously, sure to praise her husband and clarify that she didn't intend to move the hives closer to the homestead. "The hives will stay on the far edge of the farm, for your mother's peace of mind. . ." *And mine.*

"Do you know I never stopped to consider you an optimist?" Willa's question left little possibility for reply.

"I give up. Should I take that as a compliment?" Opal doubted Willa would ever deliberately insult anyone, but the thought seemed out of place.

"Yes. Seems I should have noticed it before, since you go out of your way to keep our families from tearing each other to bits. Adam's the same way—always believing the time will come when we'll put aside our differences." Willa gave her a considering look. "You two have a lot in common."

"Don't most people want to keep their families alive and whole?" She kept the words light, but Opal picked up her pace. Suddenly, getting to the house and having things other than Willa's observations to occupy them seemed like a very good idea. "So I should have a lot in common with just about anyone."

"My hinting that you and my brother match each other makes you uncomfortable." A shrug. "Then I'll let it go for now. Would you like to hear about what you and I have in common?"

I want to hear more about what happened yesterday! The desire for a solid friendship won out over impatience. "Yes."

"Both of us grew up with families involved in a feud, though we each refused to take active part in it. Neither of us has a sister who survived infancy." A deep breath braced Willa to keep speaking, leading Opal to wonder whether Willa's silence wasn't actually a preference so much as a habit after being raised by Lucinda. "Men in town won't court us because of our families, and we won't look at men who plan to move away from Buttonwood, so both of us have remained unwed a long time."

"A considerable list." Opal debated for a moment about whether to add to it. "Long enough, I think, for me to presume to ask if we share another quirk?"

"Yes?"

"Is there a chance both us may end up marrying the son of our father's enemy?"

"No." Adam broke in. "Enough nonsense."

"Adam!" Willa's guilty flush didn't assure him that her answer would have matched his. "You followed us?"

"And we didn't notice?" His wife's incredulous murmur almost made him grin.

"I caught up with you in time to hear that last question. I'd thought to escort you back to Speck land to make sure things went smoothly." *To be there if your Pa hurt your feelings and show him I stood beside you in all things.*

"Didn't realize you planned to do that, Adam." Genuine surprise—even a little bit of pleasure—filled the statement.

"Willa doesn't belong here." He shot a look of rebuke at his sister. "Go home, sis."

"The time has arrived for me to trust my own judgment instead of blankly relying on Ma's or even yours," his sister announced. "At eighteen, I believe it's more than proper for a lady to visit her in-laws in the presence of her brother and his wife."

"That's—" he broke off, unable to finish any logical protest. "Different." Adam squinted at his sister, noticing for the first time how much she'd grown, the calm that surrounded her. *When did this new Willa emerge?*

"Yesterday I came to realize the Grogans aren't always right, in spite of how we claim to be." Her raised brows were mirrored by Opal's. "So I've decided not to let disproven prejudices determine my future."

"What disproven prejudices?" Opal didn't exclude Willa, but her eyes found his. "About my family?"

"Not the time or place." He cast a look around, half-expecting Murphy or Elroy to appear at his side. "Reviving old grudges serves no purpose."

"If I've not shown by now that I don't hold grudges," Opal turned away as she spoke, "you'll never understand." With that, she marched in the direction of the Speck soddy, leaving him and Willa to watch her.

"Poorly done, brother." Willa watched him instead. "Either Opal's earned your trust, or you've grown stingy."

"She and I discussed the matter of Ben. Opal knows I disapprove, yet she went behind my back to encourage your interest." He shook his head. "This behavior doesn't call for trust."

"Did Opal agree with you that I shouldn't indulge in so much as a passing curiosity regarding her brother?" When her pause grew pointed, he shook his head. "Then she didn't break her word or change her stance. Nor, may I add, did she encourage anything. Simply asked as to my thoughts on the matter. Which"—his sister's gaze saddened—"is more than you took the time to do."

The hurt in her face pinched at him. "Willa, I know you well enough there's no need to ask. You sat beside Ben instead of Ma on Sunday without any reason."

"Another assumption." The words lacked heat but not power. "Ben barely returned home before Opal married you. He tried to sit beside his sister. In part, I think, because he's missed her, in part to make sure she's all right, but mostly to help hide the fact that their father didn't want to because he's too stiff-necked to forgive her yet."

"Why didn't you let him?" *And keep at least one problem off my list. As it is, sounds like you two got awful cozy at that table.*

"Larry shoved his way next to Opal, rude as could be. I saw him eyeing Ben as though considering how best to goad him."

"Likely." Adam closed his eyes. Larry again. *Every time I turn around, my brother creates difficulties.*

"So I politely asked if I could sit between them and did my best to buffer the two." Having finished her explanation, Willa fell silent. She seemed relieved not to have anything more to say.

"Thanks." He figured that part of the conversation ended when she nodded. "Did you come with Opal today hoping to see more of Benjamin

Speck?" Aloud, the suspicion didn't sound as ridiculous as he'd hoped.

"I hope to help put the animosity between our families behind us once and for all." With that, his sister followed in the direction Opal had struck out moments before, leaving Adam alone. . .

To notice that Willa hadn't said no.

CHAPTER 32

The nerve of the man, to follow her and Willa, hint about secrets involving her family, then refuse to tell her! Opal all but stalked to her family's soddy. *Oh, very well. I am stalking. But it doesn't make him right. There's a difference between a moment's anger and a grudge.*

Opal didn't bother to hold grudges. For now, though, the anger had her pumping. It carried her into the soddy, where she noticed Pa and her brothers had apparently already left for the fields. The rapid beating of her heart slowed as she surveyed what had been her home for nineteen years.

Father, how can this be the way my family lives?

Dishes slopped over one another across the table, remnants of old biscuits and older gravy crusting them together. Ashes mounded before the fireplace, a source of the dust disguising her wooden cabinets. A pair of empty pants sprawled in Grandma's rocker, mate to the shirt slumped alongside.

A soft keening surprised Opal when she realized the sound came from her. Guilt kept up its assault, only to be driven away by a pair of strong hands clamping her shoulders, bracing her. She drew in her first real breath since stepping past the threshold, the pungent odors of stale coffee and musty clothing strong enough to fell an ox.

"It's not your fault." Adam's whisper made itself felt more than heard. "Things change in time."

"We didn't live like this." She blinked to clear moisture from her eyes, looking up at the roof of the soddy to keep the tears away. Pages from catalogs she'd so painstakingly collected no longer marched in neat rows across the ceiling. Now, advertisements for shoes sagged beneath the weight of debris. Edges of the pages curled down to catch in the hair of those unfortunate enough to wander close. Dark splotches obliterated drawings of bicycles and fanciful dolls.

"This *is* my fault." *For leaving.* The accusation hung everywhere she looked. The entire soddy sat as one dank, wordless recrimination.

Adam nudged the empty pants from the rocker and settled her inside it as though she'd be content to stay there.

The sound of one dish hitting another as Willa cleared the table snapped Opal from her grief and into action. *Face it.* She took inventory of what needed to be done. *I can fix it.* Opal headed for the barn, unearthing the large wooden washtub from the corner and rolling the heavy container back toward the house. *Keep working.*

"What are you doing?" Adam put himself at risk of being trampled by a runaway washtub, planting his feet in her path.

"Washing." Opal rolled around him. *No time to waste.*

"Stop this." He moved as though to block her again, so Opal sped up until she had the tub just between the house and the well. "Let me help you."

"Thank you." Her easy acceptance took him off guard. She could tell by the way he stayed quiet. "If you start filling the tub, I'll help Willa bring out the dishes. Letting them sit in water for a while will make them easier to scrub."

By way of response, her husband began lowering the bucket to the well. No words were needed when he showed support. The panic that had gripped her since she walked into the soddy and saw what had become of the place after a single week of her absence began to fade. The alarm served its purpose and got her moving, taking control of things the way she always had.

She and Willa heaped dishes and soap shavings into the rising waterline of the washtub, filling it full. With that done, she took rags from the bin she kept tucked away, intent on attacking the dust and grit built up in her absence. If she could finish the dishes and get everything dusted and wiped down, she could do a week's worth of baking. She'd also make the men a dinner they'd be glad to have in their bellies when they went to work again, with the memory and promise of more to come for supper!

Working felt right. Seeing results made it worthwhile. Having Willa and Adam alongside her, giving their time and labor for her family, made the day precious in a way Opal couldn't put words to. She tried anyway. "You didn't have to—"

They didn't let her get any further.

"I wanted to. How else to repay you for your help stuffing mattresses and cleaning out that chicken coop?" Willa halted briefly when she mentioned the mattress but rallied. "I dreaded doing that then escaped it entirely!"

Adam cleared his throat at the mention of the chicken coop, his eyes going intense in a way that made Opal wonder whether or not he remembered that day as well as she. Whether he remembered that he'd almost kissed her...

She bit back a sigh.

"Opal," a gruffness caught her attention when he spoke her name. "I'll be back before noon. Don't ring the dinner bell before you see me."

Where are you going? She nipped back the question, refusing to be impertinent today of all days. Not when he'd let her see her family. Not when Willa chose now to assert herself.

"Understood?" For the first time, he made it a question. They both knew Adam wasn't offering her a choice, but the acknowledgment made a difference. Somehow.

"Understood." She watched as he exited the dark confines of the soddy and plunked his hat on before heading off.

Lord, what if Pa finds him on Speck land? Or Elroy? Ben won't do much now that he bears interest in Willa, but he'd bring him to Pa for trespassing. Possibilities seared her. *With the town apprised of our marriage, Pa would consider the babe to have a name and respectability, and Adam's death would bring me home.*

Opal made it halfway out the door, lips open to call Adam back to her side, when something caught her.

"Stop." Willa gripped her elbow with surprising strength and pulled her back inside. "If you call my brother back because you're afraid, he'll take it as you doubting his ability to take care of himself and you."

"It's not that I question his manhood. . .but men are mortal."

"Trust in Adam and in God to bring him back this afternoon," her sister-in-law warned, "or poison another part of your marriage."

Opal stilled. *Our marriage scarcely survives as things stand. I can't afford to take the chance.* She turned away from the door, toward the cook fire, and started working.

Keep him safe, Jesus. Please. Oh please.

Adam kept one hand at the pistol on his belt as he made his way through Speck land. He combined a stealthy pace and steady eye to keep away from any sign of Opal's family, not so foolish as to test their tempers so soon.

Soon enough, he passed the fence he'd mended on his wedding night—the fence that led Marla into Speck land and Adam himself into the most muddled marriage Buttonwood would ever see. Back on Grogan land, he usually breathed easier.

Not today.

Not when Opal remained on Speck land, not within quick reach. Her family wouldn't harm her, but Adam didn't like her being so far away. For one thing, the father of her child may return. Where would that leave him?

He walked past the clearing he'd designated for Opal's apiary, giving it wide berth. Adam took note of the twenty hives, placed in neat rows, looking almost as though they'd sat in such an arrangement for years, and acknowledged a sense of satisfaction. Here he saw the beginning, the first outward sign of his and Opal's coming together as a wedded couple ought.

The satisfaction ebbed as he continued on his way. Willa's presence caused both comfort and concern. Comfort to know Opal kept company with someone he trusted. Comfort to know his wife wouldn't run off with some scapegrace under his sister's watch. Comfort to know she would fetch him should anything go wrong. He'd told Willa where to find him. That alleviated some of his concern.

Home. He arrived in front of one of the few large hills on Grogan land, stopped, and surveyed the site. The mound of earth topped him by about two feet—a good size for a dugout. Adam stepped into the depression he'd begun hollowing out days ago. Every moment he could spare from the farm, he came here. This would be the house where he and Opal lived as man and wife, once they'd overcome the most pressing obstacles before them.

Right now, he struggled with the idea of his sister remaining unguarded on Speck property. Willa, determined to stand alongside her sister-in-law in a show of support Adam couldn't bring himself to undermine, placed herself in the path of danger. In the path of Benjamin Speck's all-too-interested gaze.

And in so doing, pitted them all against a threat he couldn't avoid. His formerly quiet sister made that clear enough. The more he protested, the more she dug in her heels. Shotguns and shouts, Adam could hold his own against. But this gentle defiance resisted all weapons in his arsenal.

The rough outer leather of his work gloves faded into pliable softness as he slid his hands inside and grabbed his tools. Time and earth caved beneath the bite of his spade. Each stroke lessened the tumult in his chest and brought him one shovelful closer to building a future.

He kept a close eye on the progress of the sun across the sky. Adam judged it to be before eight when he began digging—a good time. The frost of the morning thawed, leaving the earth moist and soft. As the temperature rose and shadows shortened, he determined it time to head back to Opal and Willa. He planned to make it long before any of the Speck men—the only reason Adam had been able

283

to leave the women for even those three hours was his certain knowledge that the Speck boys would be out working the fields and surely not beat him back. Well, that and the certainty he'd finish the home by week's end. But the main thing was knowing he'd beat the Specks back.

Which didn't make him any less cautious during his return. Adam kept to whatever scant shadows the prairie provided, be they the occasional cottonwood or large rock. Not even the burbling call of a small creek tempted him to halt his progress. Stooping down with his back to the open made a man an excellent target.

Besides, Adam washed up in the stream running close to the site he'd chosen for his own home before he set out. All the same, by the time he got within smelling distance of the Speck place, his mouth watered and stomach rumbled as though competing for attention. Two cold biscuits at the crack of dawn didn't hold a man used to a full breakfast.

"Smells good." He let the compliment precede him, so as not to startle the women as he walked in the door. Adam couldn't even pinpoint what all tickled his nose so well, just that there seemed an array of good things to tempt a man.

Foremost among them stood right next to him. His wife rushed away from the cook fire the moment she heard him, barely stopping before running into him. Adam found himself wishing she hadn't put the brakes on in time. Even in the dim interior of the soddy, her eyes sparkled. "You're back." A smile the likes of which he hadn't seen since before their wedding day lit her whole face. "I'm glad."

"You are?" Not that he doubted her. It just took him off guard to find his wife so pleased to see him. Her blush tattled that the significance he placed on her greeting embarrassed her.

"You're safe." Opal didn't give any more explanation than those two words as she turned back to the table and shifted a few dishes to make room for something Willa carried over.

"I see." And he did. *She worried.* The rumbling in his stomach stopped, despite the wealth of food arrayed before him. The warmth spreading through him left no room for hunger. *Opal cares about me.*

CHAPTER 33

W hat on earth is going on?" Pa burst through the door first, gun in hand, scant minutes after Opal rang the dinner bell. His sudden stop just inside the house almost made them pile one atop the other as Ben, Elroy, and Pete skidded to a halt right on his heels.

"Good to see you, Pa." Opal fought back the impulse to rush him with a hug. No sane person rushed a man with a gun—kin or no. Especially when Pa still hadn't shown any signs of forgiving her for her hasty marriage. "Adam thought to let me come over and make you all some dinner as a surprise today." She gestured to where Adam stood at her side, a polite warning of her husband's presence where no Speck had presumed to enter uninvited before.

"Opal?" Pete's voice came through accompanied by hopeful sniffing. "You cooked for us?"

"You don't surprise a man by trespassing in his home, Grogan." Pa raised his gun with more specific purpose. "Dangerous habit you've picked up, boy."

"Pa!" Opal made to step forward and shield Adam, but her husband's hand clamped around her arm and jerked her behind him, next to Willa. "Willa and Adam came in friendship and kindness!"

"Willa?" This from Ben. "Pa, lower that gun and let us inside." He didn't really wait for his father to agree, instead elbowing his way inside. It didn't seem to matter much to him that Elroy and Pete still loitered on the doorstep, but Opal wasn't about to quibble.

"He trespassed."

"Opal invited him." Ben's gaze darted to hers before moving to Willa's. "And her sister-in-law."

"Opal don't live here anymore." Pa's words sliced her soul, and she might have sunk to the floor from the pain of it were Adam not in such jeopardy.

"Would you shoot me, Pa?" This time, she found the power to resist Adam's pull and remain at her place by his side. Her heart couldn't give her voice any more strength than a whisper. "You have my love. If you don't want it, you may as well have my blood. It's the only way to stop me from being your daughter."

"No." Adam stopped trying to force her behind him and stepped in front of her, putting his chest scant inches from the barrel of her father's rifle.

For a frozen moment, no one moved. Opal saw everything from behind the arms her husband spread to cover her, processed Adam's protection, and waited. Pushing him out of the way might startle Pa into pulling the trigger, so she could do nothing but pray.

Lord, please watch over those I love. Don't let them be hurt or killed for my foolishness. Please.

"No." The gun lowered. His face pale, Pa stepped forward and reached out a hand. "Opal, you'll always be my daughter."

A flood of tears broke from her even as Elroy and Pete pushed inside. She squeezed beneath Adam's arm and into her father's embrace for the first time in far too long. "I'm so sorry, Pa." The words came out broken, but it didn't matter. She knew he understood what she meant.

"Me, too." Rough words almost swallowed by her hair, but so precious. When he pulled back, with a suspicious gleam in his eyes, Opal felt better than she had in ages.

The part of her heart that pulsed with hurt since her father turned his back on her began to beat with hope once more. She turned to her brothers and embraced each of them, still able to notice the way Ben went to Willa the first possible moment, murmuring as though to ensure she remained unharmed by the dramatics.

"Speck." Adam extended his hand, and if his gaze seemed a bit wary, none could blame him.

"Grogan." Pa looked down at the friendship offered, glanced at Opal, and took her husband's hand in a firm shake.

Thank You, Lord. It's a start.

"More than a start, I'd say." Midge finished sprinkling salt around the edges of the hives and straightened up. "For more than one thing, even."

"I know." Opal's excitement came through loud and clear as she hastily filled Midge in on the events of the morning. After all, she didn't have much time before she had to get back to where Willa baked on the Speck homestead. If Midge hadn't brought the suppers by, she wouldn't have left. But surely this had to be God's timing. "Pa and Adam can forge peace between our families at last, and maybe Ben and Willa have a chance at a genuine romance. They're good for each other."

"So are you and Adam." She didn't bother to mask her exasperation. "Why is it you notice all the good in and for everyone except yourself?"

"You know Adam doesn't want to be my husband." The quiet response contrasted so sharply to her friend's earlier happiness, Opal's feelings for Adam must run deep. "Even now he'd annul the marriage should he learn the truth."

"Don't be so sure. He put himself in front of you, shielded your body with his." She got no reaction. "A man who doesn't care for his wife doesn't offer up his life in exchange for hers without a second thought, Opal!" *Same as you did for him when your Pa aimed the gun at Adam. But I won't point that out just yet.*

"Without thought is exactly right. His sense of honor won't let him see anyone else hurt. I'd make a huge mistake if I thought anything more about it."

"If someone aimed a shotgun at Ben, do you think Adam would step in front of it?"

"Most likely not." Opal's answer came slowly. Reluctantly. Wonderingly. As though Midge got through. Then, "But Adam made a vow to protect me, so that's that."

"What are these?" *Time to change tactics.* Logic couldn't sway the heart, and Midge didn't bother with losing battles. She pointed to the whitewashed boxes they'd tumbrel sledged over to the apiary.

"Supers." She picked up one of them. "We affix one to each of the hives so that the extra bees have space in the spring." She demonstrated how to set it up, and the two of them worked in silence for a little while.

Midge did it intentionally, knowing that working with the bees gave Opal time to clear her thoughts and, more importantly, lower her guard.

"Why are there extra bees in the spring?" She asked only once each hive boasted a super.

"Some die in the winter, but in the spring the honey supply becomes so low, the queen lays up to hundreds of eggs a day so they'll have enough workers to replenish the food stock. They need places to go." They retreated to the stand of three scant cottonwoods nearby, where they always relaxed and talked.

"Then they die?" Sounded like bees used other bees just like people used other people. Midge frowned.

"No. When the hive supply is restored, another

queen bee hatches, and the current queen bee flies away. About half the bees follow her and find a new home and start a different hive. It happens in May, usually." Opal clasped her hands around her knees. "You watch for bees to be unable to get inside and hover around outside the hive, especially in the evenings. Then you come early in the morning and try to catch them. I've ordered ten new hives."

"How do you get the bees to choose your hive?"

"You'll see when the swarming starts." Her friend grinned. "For now, I think it's time for you to be teaching me some lessons."

"You did beautifully at church—maneuvering for that kiss. . ." Midge raised her brows. "I'm glad I caught on to the ploy."

"So did Adam."

"Really?" Midge stopped plucking at the grass at her side. "How do you know?"

"He told me—it's what he whispered right before he kissed me." If her cheeks got any redder, it might be permanent.

"And he still did it. *Three* times." She tapped her fingers together. "Excellent."

"He did it to play along."

"The first time, maybe. Here, you're flushed." Midge passed her friend the canteen of water they'd brought. "The second time would persuade the most stalwart doubters. But the third time, my friend, the third time Adam kissed you because he wanted to."

Glugging greeted her proclamation as Opal all but emptied the canteen in great gulps. When her friend finished, she had to take a minute to gulp in about the same amount of air. At least her flush faded to a dull rose, and determination defended any vulnerability in her gaze. "So what's the next step in seducing my husband?"

"Obviously, he needs to kiss you again." Midge figured she'd need to start out slow with Opal. Her friend may be a farm girl, but her innocence wasn't just physical. "The next time, without an audience."

"Then there's no pretext." Shoulders slumped, her friend exuded hopelessness. "How can I convince him to kiss me without any reason?"

"You *are* the reason, Opal." Shaking the woman would do no good. "You convince him to kiss you because he *wants* to kiss you again. Just like that third time on Sunday."

"Oh." Opal fiddled with the pocket on her apron. "How do I convince him to kiss me the first two times to get him to the third time, then? I can't very well ask everyone to kindly leave after the second try!"

"Stop being silly!" This time, Midge bumped her friend's arm with hers. . .and none too gently, either. "He wanted to kiss you in front of the chicken coop, too. And kissing you after the wedding was his idea. You don't have to inspire an attraction; your husband already fights one. You just have to convince him to stop fighting it!"

"Half the battle's done?"

"The half that can't be taken for granted is over. Now comes the march to victory."

"Sounds promising." The slumping stopped.

"How do I march?"

"Easily enough." Midge sprang to her feet and gestured for Opal to follow her. "The first step to master has to do with walking. . . ."

CHAPTER 34

Step, sway. Step, sway. One foot exactly in front of the other. Don't look down any more than absolutely necessary. Shoulders back. Stomach in. Step, sway. . .

Opal kept the litany in her head, wondering whether she'd hear Midge's voice every time she took a step for the rest of the day. Or longer. Oh, she'd laughed when her friend told her she needed to learn to walk. Hadn't she been walking since her first birthday?

Yes, Midge explained. Opal could walk. Serviceably. Which, obviously, would never do. Mules and boots strived to be serviceable. Women needed to embody seduction. At least, Opal did. For now.

Because, Opal vowed, as she placed one foot in front of the other as though walking atop a log, she couldn't manage this seduction business for very long. The very mechanics of it were liable to kill her.

For example, when she stepped forward with

her right foot, moving it in front of her left foot, her natural inclination seemed to be to have her hips follow toward the left. But nooooo. Midge instructed that when she stepped across the left, her hip pushed to the *right*. Her friend said it exaggerated the curve and increased the sway of her skirts.

Opal said it increased her chances of falling flat on her face. Although, she couldn't argue with Midge that this gait did make her skirts swing in a saucy fashion she'd never managed before. Between that and holding her shoulders even farther back, the new stride almost lent her a feeling of power.

At least, it would if she weren't afraid of ruining it. She shoved the doubts aside, refusing to let them trip her up—in her thoughts or in reality—and kept on toward where she knew Adam mended fences that afternoon. Yes, he mended fences because fertilizer was setting into the fields, and the smell hardly made for romance, but Opal couldn't afford to be choosy about timing. She could catch him alone now.

There. Not too far away, he bent low, resting on his heels, mending a joint in a fence. No sound alerted him to her arrival. No inexplicable sense of her presence like some couples shared made him look up and send a smile her way. *Because we aren't really a couple. We share no connection save a willingness to pretend at love to save our families.*

She shook off the defeatist attitude, heading toward the first clump of plants that were her pretext for coming here. Opal stooped at the knees, reaching for the bright yellow flowers that already began to close in the afternoon sunlight. Squash blossoms bloomed wide open in the morning and shriveled up as the day wore on—almost the way she felt as she spent time with Lucinda.

Opal plucked the majority of the flowers, leaving enough not to strip the plants, and straightened. A quick glance around showed that Adam moved slightly closer but demonstrated no awareness of her. She took a deep breath and used her new walk to mince toward the next grouping of blossoms, closing even more of the distance between them. She began to stoop and suddenly remembered Midge shaking her head.

"Ladies bend at the knees to retrieve something. It's as demure as a woman can be. Holds all the parts of the body tight together, puts nothing on display, practically begs everyone not to notice that you're there. When you are around your husband, Opal, you don't want him to think of you as a lady. You need him to see you as a woman."

Heat crept up her throat and suffused Opal's cheeks as she realized what she needed to do. Thankful Adam hadn't yet looked up, she slowly bent at the waist, poking her bottom into the air in a shameful manner and stretching her arm out so she could reach the flowers. The first time, she straightened up so fast her head rushed a little.

"If you go up again too fast, the effect is wasted." The caution sprang to her memory a moment too late. *"You lose the appearance of grace and have to start all over."*

She peeked to see whether her husband noted

her presence yet. No. Opal breathed a sigh of relief that her clumsy attempt escaped a witness, used her new walk to move on, and tried again.

This time, she decided to get into the spirit of the thing. She put one foot in front of the other—the better to exaggerate any curves—and leaned down with her arm extended as elegantly as possible. After plucking several blossoms, she snagged a final one and, pleased with her success, gave it a celebratory swirl as she gracefully began to rise.

"Opal?" The deep voice right in her ear startled the poise right out of her, making her jump.

Unfortunately, when one leg is crossed over the other and a body is half bent over, jumping is a bad idea. *The only thing I can say for the whole mess,* Opal decided, *is that at least I didn't have far to fall.*

An abrupt movement to the right caught Adam's eye. He reached for his gun and pivoted in one smooth motion to get a clearer view of the threat. Instead, he saw a woman.

Slightly backlit by the afternoon sun, her face obscured by her bonnet, she floated toward him. The vision of femininity swayed a few steps before stopping. Only then did awareness shiver up his spine. *Opal?* Were it not for the calico dress she wore, he wouldn't have recognized his wife.

He opened his mouth to call to her then closed it again. What would he say? More importantly, when would he have the opportunity to observe her when she thought herself completely alone? Adam thumbed back his hat for an unobstructed view as she moved once more, this time the shift so subtle it might not have caught his eye.

A basket half filled with yellow flowers dangled from one of her arms as she bent to gather more. But she didn't bend as he'd ever seen her. No. This secret Opal, the surprise bride who thought herself far removed from any eyes watching her, moved freely. She folded at the waist, her backside a shapely curve extending into the air. She reached toward the flowers in a smooth motion, long and lithe as she stretched.

He sucked in a sharp breath and found himself at her side before he decided to take so much as a step. From the closer vantage point, he could smell the lingering trace of honey that always clung to her, see small wisps of the red-gold hair that escaped her bonnet to dance in the breeze.

"Opal." This time, he said it aloud.

She offered no soft smile in response. No, this vision of grace, so imbued with the innate allure of woman, gave a strangled shriek and some sort of aborted hop. . .just before she fell right on those curves he'd admired moments before. Which might have done him a great favor and lessened her appeal. If, that is, he hadn't tried to catch her and she hadn't fallen into his knees, knocking him down along with her. They ended in a tangled tumble, her bonnet dangling by its strings, his hat knocked away.

Immediate awareness hit Adam harder than the impact. He lay half atop her, his chest pressed to the softness of hers as she struggled to draw breath. It was her gasp that brought him to his senses. He levered himself onto his forearms, putting some distance between them.

Not enough. Opal's eyes went wide in surprise, her lips parted in an attempt to catch her breath. One of her hands clutched his bicep, another lay flat against his shoulder, but she made no move to push him away. Her warmth seeped into his shirt, beckoning him closer.

"Opal," he murmured her name this time, a one-word question if she was all right.

"Adam?" She tilted her chin slightly, just enough to bring her lips closer. An invitation no man could resist.

He dipped his head to taste her. Softness swept against him, yielding and sweet. *She is mine. My wife.*

She pressed upward, sending heat surging through him, demanding...

More. He pulled her bonnet away and sank one hand into the silky strands of her hair. *More.* Adam urged closer, tracing her lips with his. *More.*

"Baby." He no sooner uttered the endearment than he pulled away. *The baby. How could I forget?* He moved back, bent almost double in an effort to keep away from her.

"Adam?" Confusion dampened the dreaminess of her gaze. Her lips full and rosy from his kisses, her hair mussed from his caress, she looked the very image of a woman who'd been thoroughly kissed. And wanted more.

It was enough to drive a man mad.

"Get up." Harsh, shallow breaths made the words rough, but so be it. He gained another measure of control when she sat up and smoothed the wrinkles from her dress, restoring some appearance of propriety.

"I'm sorry." Her lips—still invitingly pink—must have bothered her as much as they did him, because she raised her fingertips to them and pulled her hand away as though burned. "I didn't mean to be so clumsy."

"Doesn't matter." The thought she found his kiss distasteful soured his stomach. *What? For a moment did she forget it was me? Did she think it was the real father of her child?* If blood could boil within a man, surely it did now. He thought of the way she'd moved when she'd thought she was alone.

I was wrong. She didn't move in freedom, away from prying eyes. Those were the motions of a woman putting on a performance. Only her imagined audience is long gone, and she's dissatisfied with her substitute.

"It matters to me." Her words verified his thoughts. Of course it mattered to her that she'd fallen into his arms when it was the last place she wanted to be.

"Fine. But I say you can be as clumsy as you like." Adam snatched his hat from where it had fallen and turned away. "So long as you remember not to do it with any other men."

CHAPTER 35

*D*anger. Lucinda's hands shook as she washed the dinner dishes. Dishes used by too few that morning, as Willa abandoned her to join Opal at the Speck place.

Danger surrounded her family, creeping closer every moment. Closing off any means of escape. Tightening the noose. Specks were their greatest enemies. . .always had been. Ever since the greedy gudgeons dared try to claim land Diggory's father staked out.

As though their protests that no markers meant no claim mattered. Everyone knew the land between two runoffs of the Platte could flood. No, instead there'd been bitter battles. Blood and bruises on both sides over a scrap of earth where they'd all end up buried because the Specks wouldn't be honorable.

Lucinda put away another dish and reached for the next. Her mind worked in tandem with her hands, scrubbing circles into the problem in an attempt to shine up a solution. Hadn't Diggory's pa tried to stop the madness? Hadn't he come up with a plan to send a little warning to the Specks to make them see reason and end the fighting once and for all?

Instead, Opal's grandma bid her bees to punish him. Lucinda bore the knowledge deep in her heart. *Moving one hive wouldn't kill a man. She must've used some pagan ways to summon the bees from other hives to do him in. I saw it.*

What other explanation for how she'd found her adopted father in that field? When he didn't come back after their secret plan, she'd gone in search of him. And found the horrible truth obvious in his body.

The hives covering every inch of his hands, arms, face, and neck. The terrible way his eyelids puffed up and out. The horror of his swollen mouth and protruding tongue as though screaming even from death for her to run. . .

And so I ran, and never let on that I'd seen. But I didn't forget. I seen the evidence of murder that day, and I won't let it near my family again.

Lucinda looked down when she realized she'd been groping for the next dish for a while. With none left to clean, she hefted the basin of rinse water and carried it outside. A few steps around the house brought her to Willa's flower garden, and she flung the water across the carefully cultivated expanse.

Ephemeral bluebells rose to dangle their buds in the breeze, ranging from soft pink to bluish violet.

A white blanket of low larkspur provided lovely contrast until the red flowers and notched leaves of bloodroot made an appearance. Star-shaped spring beauties basked alongside white-and-purple shooting stars, the drops of water she'd flung on them catching the sun in a kaleidoscope of colors.

"Too bad Willa's not here to see that." Larry gestured toward the garden of wildflowers. "But it's even worse she's missing it because she's on the Speck farm."

"This will be the last time." Lucinda knew she'd erred in not specifically forbidding her daughter to return, but typically one hint of displeasure sent Willa scurrying in the proper direction. "If it weren't for the influence of that girl, Willa wouldn't have gone today."

"Probably has more to do with Opal's brother." Her son's gaze all but snapped his irritation. "You know how Ben looks at our Willa. It can't go on."

"It won't." Her jaw ached from clenching her teeth.

"She needs to learn she can't disregard the wishes of the family and put her safety at risk, Ma." Larry's expression changed to one of deep concern. He reached out and fingered a damp bluebell. "So many risks around here."

"You know better than to mess with Willa's garden." Some things were sacred, after all.

"She knows better than to consort with Specks." Larry straightened. "Willa's been making those choices, Ma. Choosing the Specks...and their bees."

Her throat went dry at the reminder that the

hives currently rested on Grogan land, inching ever closer. Making it easier to kill them all.

"Ma, do you know that bees are attracted to flowers?"

"What?" Her eyes fell on the colorful garden she'd been admiring moments before. "No. These are far away."

"Not far enough. I've been reading up." He plucked the bluebell and crushed it between thumb and forefinger. "These could bring the bees. Just like Willa brings Benjamin. And, given a choice, she'd keep things that way."

"Then she doesn't get a choice." Lucinda fell to her knees, blindly reaching among the colorful petals and yanking plants out of the ground in heaping handfuls.

She'll understand someday, my Willa, Lucinda promised herself. *But first, I have to protect her. I have to protect her so she can learn.*

⁂

"So old Grogan did mean to set fire to one of the hives." Opal could hardly believe what Willa told her as they headed back from the Speck farm. "All that claptrap about Specks dragging him to be attacked by bees. . . Diggory knew the truth all along?"

"Papa had to protect his pa's memory," Willa said by way of explanation. "He knew Grandpa would turn in his grave if Specks got that land, and Papa wouldn't let him die in vain, so. . ."

"So he's ruined all of our lives, caused bitterness

and false enmity for decades?" Anger almost choked the words before Opal forced them out. "Blackened my family's name? Where is the honor in that, Willa?"

"I'm sorry. You know the rest of us only discovered the truth days ago."

"Days ago." *But Adam didn't tell me. Was he afraid I'd be so foolish as to tell Pa? I know better than to give him any more cause to resume hostilities when things are going well!* "And none of you trusted me enough to share this information."

"I thought you should know. I thought…" Willa trailed off, and Opal knew her friend was thinking that Adam should have been the one to tell her.

"The hatred between our families ends one way or another, Willa. Pa wouldn't react well to this information even if Diggory apologized now. It's best to let things gradually mend, as it's begun. With you and Adam reaching out to the Specks, things are bound to keep improving." *I hope.*

"Surely mercy and goodness shall follow us," Willa paraphrased the psalm with a smile, only to pull up short with a gasp. The smile shrank from her face as she stared before them.

Opal followed her gaze and let out a cry of her own. There, where that morning had stood Willa's beautiful flower garden, sat a bare patch of earth. Completely denuded of its colorful carpet, bald dirt turned raw by the careless piles of uprooted plants scattered around, the sight made her want to weep.

Even worse were the silent tears rolling down Willa's cheeks. Her friend's mouth hung agape, but no sound emerged. It was as though the new confidence and vitality she'd found had been ruthlessly cut off along with her flowers.

"Now you see?" Lucinda's sharp voice pierced the air. "You see what your new friend did to you?"

She's blaming me. Disbelief washed over Opal. *Just like with the mattress.*

"How could you?" Willa didn't turn, simply kept staring at the destruction of the love she'd lavished on those blossoms.

"Well Opal?" Her mother-in-law's demand inspired an urge to do bodily harm.

"What's going on?" Adam sauntered around the side of the soddy to get his first look at the damage.

"Look at the trouble your wife caused now!" Lucinda clawed at her son's arm, dragging him farther away from Opal than ever before.

"Opal didn't do this." Adam took one look at the garden and shook his head. "She helped Willa tend it."

"How could you?" Still not facing anyone, Willa stooped to lovingly gather the limp plants into one pile.

"Willa, I didn't." Opal knelt beside the woman who'd become her friend and sister and wanted to weep. "I'll help you replant, I promise. Anything to make it better."

"You can't make it better." The hiss of a snake. "You've made things worse since the moment you married my son."

"Stop, Mama." Willa stood, her arms full of desecrated plants. She extended the corpses of her beloved flowers toward her mother, tears still streaming down her face. "How could you?"

"It's her fault!"

"No Mama. You did this. Opal and I left and spent the whole day together."

"Why?" Adam put his hands on his mother's shoulders. "Why would you do such a thing, Ma?"

"It *is* her fault! If it wasn't for her bees, I wouldn't have to get rid of the flowers. Flowers bring bees, Adam." Fear filled the older woman's voice. "I had to protect us all. And Willa has to learn the Specks are dangerous. Don't you see?"

"No." Diggory strode onto the scene and took Lucinda away from Adam. His gestures remained controlled, but that very control bespoke great anger. "You don't punish my little girl like that without my say-so, woman."

"She's consorting with that Benjamin, Diggory."

"Not anymore." Diggory glared at the daughter he'd championed scant seconds before. "Willa, you're not to talk to that boy again, do you hear me?" He didn't even wait for a response before pulling his wife toward the house.

Adam went to put his arm around Willa, leaving Opal reluctant to intrude just to get to the room she shared with her sister-in-law. Instead, she turned and headed toward the barn. The smell of hay and horse never failed to soothe her.

She opened the door and took a deep breath, feeling the weight of sorrow start to ebb. But peace didn't take its place. Instead, a sort of energy crackled, making the hairs on the back of her neck stand up. *Danger.* Opal turned to leave.

Too late.

"Hello, Opal." Larry lounged between her and the door. "Rare to catch you alone these days."

"I'm just heading back." She made as though to step around him, but he blocked her.

"Of course. After we settle a little business between us." He straightened, his body too close to hers.

"We have no business, Larry. I'm Adam's wife."

"Only because of the child." Fury distorted his features. "But if there were no babe, you wouldn't be tied to Adam. Isn't that right?"

"Larry," she could scarcely squeak his name past the terror in her throat. *He can't know. Oh Lord, please don't let him know!* Then the world narrowed to a pinpoint and she doubled over, gasping. Larry pulled his fist from her middle and pushed back her shoulder while she fought to draw breath, desperate for air. He drew back and slammed another punch to her stomach, this time letting her collapse on the floor while he stood over her.

"We can be together now." The smile on his face made her blood run cold. "That should have finished the brat."

CHAPTER 36

Pounding on the barn door woke Adam the next morning. Larry, of course, remained dead to the world—and the knocking.

He pulled on his pants and a shirt, leaving it half unbuttoned in his haste to see what needed attention, and threw open the door with gun at the ready to find his wife, clad in nothing but a night rail and a cloak. Adam reached out and clasped both her arms, pulling her inside. He thrust her behind him and looked to the left and right to find what disturbed her so.

"Willa's gone." Her whisper stopped his search.

No. He shut his eyes against the news, but nothing could shut away the truth of it. His eyes flew open once more when he felt her hands on his chest, doing up his buttons.

"We have to go after her." Opal kept quiet, obviously trying not to wake Larry. "Maybe it isn't too late. I don't know when she left—I slept closest to the wall."

"Put on clothes, Opal." Adam grabbed his boots and sat down. "We'll head over to your family's place, but I'd stake everything I have they're long gone."

She left in a whirl of cotton and cloak, muttering something about having to try.

Opal stood ready in a blue calico dress, still wearing her cloak against the coldness of the pre-morning. Dawn didn't yet lighten the sky as they left.

With Daisy and Dusty as their only draft horses, and mules or oxen notoriously slow, they made their way on foot. Adam's stride ate the distance in long stretches, but it seemed to him Opal lagged like she hadn't before.

"I'm coming," she gasped. One arm curled protectively around her stomach, and it seemed as though hurrying cost her great effort. "Keep on, Adam."

The baby must be moving. Wistfulness panged through him. Any other time, and he would've asked to feel it kicking so he could share part of the joy of their child's growth. *But now. . .* It was all he could do to remain thankful his wife trooped on.

When they arrived at the Speck doorstep, Adam's pounding put Opal's earlier efforts to shame. A bleary Elroy opened the door gun-first.

"Grogan." He peered past them. "Just you and Opal, or the whole clan come for vengeance?"

"Been expecting us, I see." Adam didn't bother to

keep the anger from his words. "Only us. For now."

"Let 'em in, boy." Murphy's order came just as Elroy started to open the door anyway. "They're too late to stop Ben and Willa now. Might as well enjoy a visit."

"Might be the last thing you enjoy when my pa catches wind of this." Adam rubbed a hand over his face and sank onto a seat, mind racing.

"Tit for tat." His father-in-law wore the broadest smile Adam could remember since their wedding. "Willa came to Ben, so Diggory's got no call to vent his spleen."

"He will if you can't prove it."

"Willa left a note." Opal reached into the pocket of her cloak, retrieved it, and passed it to him.

My Beloved Family,

I love you all but am tired of living caged by past disappointments and false discord. Ma uprooted the flowers and tried to blame Opal, who's done nothing but good since she married Adam. I don't believe anymore that she put rocks in the mattress. I've gone to be with Ben. We planned to elope anyway, but Pa forbidding me to see him hurries things along. Opal doesn't know anything about this—I go as my own woman and will return as Ben's.

All My Prayers,
Willa Grogan Speck

"Well, at least this proves she went willingly." Adam carefully folded it and placed it in his own jacket. "Without this note, Pa would've gone after your heads for sure."

"I've been doing some thinking." Murphy leaned forward. "Why don't we come with you to break the news? It'll show we've got nothing to hide. Better yet, I'm willing to agree that the delta land should go to Ben and Willa for them to establish a homestead, if he's amenable. With our families bound by two marriages, it's time to bury the hatchet."

"I'll go in first," Adam decided. "If I think Pa won't shoot first and listen later, we'll all talk like civilized men."

"Best anyone can hope for." A small smile tugged at the corners of Opal's mouth as they all headed back to the Grogan farm.

Adam kept her close as they neared home, wanting to order her back to her room but certain she wouldn't abandon her family under any circumstances. *Not fair to ask her to when I wouldn't either.*

By the time they got back, he found Pa and Larry in the barn. He closed the rolling door behind him, offered a prayer, and cleared his throat to get their attention. "Pa. I need you to hear me out on something. You aren't going to like it, but it's too late to do anything to change it." He took a deep breath. "I already tried."

"What?" Larry's eyes narrowed in that calculating way of his, but Adam simply passed Willa's note to their father.

"No." He crushed the note in his fist, went pale white then livid purple. "We'll get her before it's too late."

"They left last night. By the time Opal discovered Willa gone this morning, fetched me, and we got to the Speck place, they were long gone."

"Willa ran off with that Speck boy?" His brother surmised the situation. "That girl doesn't have the sense God gave a goose. When we catch up to them, she'll regret the day she ever—"

"We won't catch up." Pa smoothed the note. "By the time we reach them, they'll have reached Fort Laramie and be hitched right and legal. It's over, Larry."

"Murphy, Elroy, and Pete would like a word about the matter." Adam cautiously laid the groundwork for a meeting. "If you want to discuss it, Pa."

"What's to discuss?" The light of battle gleamed once more. "If those feckless Specks think I'll agree to give Willa a dowry, they've gone mad."

"No Pa. Actually, they've offered to give Ben and Willa their claim to the delta land, if you'll agree."

"Well, now." Pa stroked his beard. "That might merit conversation."

~~~∾⊙∾~~~

"You've forgotten how to walk." Midge tsked as she watched Opal's stiff movements. "In less than three days, you've lost everything I taught you. If anything, it's gotten worse!"

"I tried your walk; you didn't warn me of the time limit."

"Time limit?"

"Apparently I can only be graceful for so long

before I topple like poorly stacked sacks of grain." The grim tone, coupled with Opal's stiff walk, left no room for doubts.

"Not. . .not in front of Adam, surely?" Her mind started whirring ahead to how far that would set them back.

"Oh no. Nothing so humdrum as falling in front of my husband." Opal waved a hand. "I, of course, fell beside him in such a way I knocked him over as well."

"Wait, this could be good." Midge switched gears. "Did he fall right beside you, or maybe even on top of you?"

"Kind of perpendicular to me. His chest knocked the wind out of mine." The nonchalant tone stayed, but now Opal didn't meet her eyes.

"I hope you made the most of it!" *Well, really, at that point it's Adam who should make the most of it.*

"He kissed me."

"And?" The abruptness of the admission told of things left unsaid.

"Ran his fingers through my hair."

"Good. And?"

"Suddenly stopped and acted like he couldn't stand the idea of being within ten feet of me."

"Wait. What?" This didn't make much sense. At this point, Midge fully expected to hear that Adam wouldn't be able to annul the marriage. Once a man got that carried away, Nancy had told her, he didn't stop.

"He called me 'baby' then just froze." Misery painted the words. "Pulled away, told me it didn't matter, and implied I did such things with other men."

"That's it!" Midge stopped even pretending to pull weeds around the hives. "Baby! It made him think of the one you're supposedly carrying and made him think about the real father, and it didn't sit well."

"You think?" Hope brightened Opal's countenance for a moment then faded. "But I can't fix that until after he beds me, and he doesn't want to."

"He wants to. In fact"—she reached out and grabbed her friend's hand to share the momentous realization—"Adam's in love with you. Otherwise he wouldn't care about the 'father.'"

"No man likes to be cuckolded—even before his wedding."

"Bah. He married you, he wants you, it's time to raise the stakes. I even know how to do it. . . according to the Bible."

"Really?" Her friend stopped working to sit back on her heels and eye her askance. "You found somewhere in the Bible where it explains how to seduce the man you tricked into becoming your husband for the sake of your family?"

"Almost the same thing." Midge held her pause until she could see Opal squirm then still kept quiet.

"Midge, don't make me do something rash!"

"Well Opal, what do you know about the book of Ruth?"

"The Moabite whose husband died, but she followed God even after his death and stayed with her mother-in-law when Naomi returned to the land of her family?"

"Yes, that one. What *else* do you know?" *The important stuff!*

"She went to glean in the fields to provide for herself and Naomi and caught the eye of Boaz, who owned the field." Opal obviously had a good memory, as she recited the story. "And Naomi told her that Boaz stood as her next relation, which in biblical times meant he could be her kinsman redeemer and wed her. Which he did when she asked, because she had impressed him with her faithfulness and loyalty to Naomi."

"What about the most interesting part?" Midge didn't bother holding back any longer. Folks always tried to hold back the scandalous bits, and they were the best ones! "The part about *how* Ruth asked Boaz to be her husband?"

"She lay at his feet while he slept after the harvest." Opal didn't exactly blush, but a pink tinge crept up her cheeks. "So she could speak to him alone."

"What you mean is she went to his bed."

"He slept on the floor, probably on a pallet...." Opal's protest sounded feeble.

"I used to sleep on a pallet, and I called it my bed. Lots of people have and still do, Opal. When Naomi told Ruth it was God's will for her to seek Boaz as her husband, she went to him in bed."

"You aren't suggesting I go to Adam's bed..." The pink turned to crimson. "I couldn't."

"You can."

"No. For now, Adam shares a room with Larry. And you know I can't change that—the man is the head of the house."

"You're forgetting what women do best." Midge allowed herself a wide grin. If Opal spouted particulars, it meant she considered going through with it.

"What do women do best?"

"Men may be the heads of households, but women turn heads."

CHAPTER 37

"Adam." Lucinda stopped her eldest before he left for the fields. With Willa gone, it was more important than ever that she roust the Speck chit and restore order at home. After nights of thinking, she'd found a way to destroy Opal's hold.

"Yes Ma?"

"Son, there's something we need to discuss." She looked around as though afraid of being interrupted. In truth, she knew Larry left for an overnight hunting trip, and Diggory had gone to look over the delta land he held even dearer now that their daughter would settle on it. Even Opal made herself scarce on the pretext of weeding around her beehives—as though such a ridiculous thing could possibly be necessary!

"What is it?"

"Come inside." She led him back to the table, where she poured him a cup of coffee and set it before him with a deep breath, as though certain he'd need the strength of it. "A suspicion has plagued me for quite some time, though I feared to give voice to it." She sank down opposite him and lowered her voice. "Now, I'm more afraid not to."

"Suspicion regarding what?"

"Opal's babe." She watched her son square his jaw and knew finding a hole in the wall he'd built around this issue wouldn't be easy. But knowing the particulars of the past paved her way. "Adam, there's no way for you to be certain it belongs to you."

"We've already discussed this." He put down the coffee and started to rise. "Opal's child belongs to me, and that's the end to it."

"But son—" She reached out a trembling hand to stay him. She didn't even have to fake the tremble, anxiety so overwhelmed her. "What if the babe isn't yours but should still bear the name Grogan?"

"I don't know what you mean." Adam's eyes warred with his words.

"Son, think." She shut her eyes as though in horror at the prospect. "We both know Larry skulked around the Speck place—we both saw what he wrote on that note. He's never said a word against her since she arrived but has been terse and tense with you the whole time. What if Opal played you false with your own brother, and he blames you for taking her away?"

Silence stretched beyond her carefully scripted speech. Lucinda waited. If she tried too hard to convince Adam, he'd see it as a ploy. As it was, even she couldn't say she hadn't hit upon the truth.

She watched as Adam's eyes darkened, his fingers clamped around the mug.

In spite of what Adam said to her, she considered her work accomplished. She'd sown the seeds of doubt, and it wouldn't be long before they took root.

Kinsman redeemer. The phrase wouldn't leave her throughout the day. *Ruth had Boaz. I have Adam.* Midge even missed one of the key reasons why Boaz stood in the position to become Ruth's husband. Why, really, Ruth *needed* Boaz enough to creep into his sleeping place and pursue him.

A child. Ruth's husband died without giving her a child, leaving her and Naomi destitute. Her lack of child spelled disaster. And back in Old Testament days, the nearest male relative could be recruited if he met the requirements.

For here and now, Adam is my husband. And my lack of a child threatens to destroy my family, too. Do I have the courage to crawl into my husband's bed?

She pondered this as she made her way to the shielded grove on her family's farm, where she used to bathe on hot summer days. There, in a little crock on a rope, she found the supplies she'd placed long ago. Some of the honey-scented soap she always made, a lump of fired beeswax, and a comb.

She checked to make certain no one loitered nearby or had followed her—though she'd been confident no one would. Midge sent her off to bathe as soon as she'd learned of the possibility, and everyone else expected her to be with Midge.

Opal set the beeswax on a rock to warm while she washed then stripped down to her shift. First, she lathered her hair, luxuriating in the bubbles and rinsing it clean before everything else. It would take longest to dry. Then she made short work of bathing before clambering onto the flat rock where the sun would warm the moisture away from her skin while she worked the comb through her hair.

As a final touch, she took the beeswax and lightly rubbed it over her skin, smoothing it in for extra softness the way her mama taught her so many years ago. By the time she finished and dressed and walked back to Midge, her hair dried enough for her to put it back up.

"Ready, then?" Her friend's grin did nothing to calm her nerves.

"As ready as I can get."

With Larry gone on an overnight hunting trip, it took Adam extra time to complete the evening chores. He didn't mind.

Not only did it give him time to think without going mad for lack of something to do, but it meant Larry wasn't around. Because when Adam thought about it, really thought back on his conversation with his brother about whether Larry'd been with Opal, he couldn't come up with a single solid statement to reassure him.

Only a bark of laughter and his brother's taunt, *"What do you think?"*

Back then, he'd thought Larry'd never gotten to Opal. Now, when he considered his original suspicions, the fact that no other man in town showed any signs of anger or shame at his marriage, that Ma cottoned on to Larry's behavior, he couldn't remember why he'd decided his brother didn't count as a concern.

Tiredness tugged at him by the time he made it to his room, lit a tin-covered safety lantern, and disrobed down to his drawers. But when Adam turned back his covers, he found far more than his pillow.

There, resplendent in nothing but a thin night rail, lay his wife. Her hair flowed down her back and around to cover the curves of her chest like a blanket of fiery silk. Her skin seemed to take on the glow of the scant lantern, a siren's call to make him lean closer. Opal's eyes stayed closed, long ginger lashes giving her an innocence he wished with all his heart she actually possessed as she drew the deep, even breaths of one completely asleep.

She came to my bed. The finality of it staggered him. Everything inside him demanded he slide beside her. That he pull her close, cover her mouth with his, and watch her lashes flutter with awareness at her sweet awakening.

Everything but the warning that his wife might, in reality, belong to his brother. *I should wake her up and send her back to her room.* But all the reason and logic in the world couldn't alter the truth—if he touched her, he'd be lost. If he watched her wake up, stretch, walk to the door in so little, he'd be lost.

So Adam sank onto his brother's bed, wound the covers tight around him, and tried to forget about the woman dreaming only feet away. The woman he'd been dreaming about longer than he'd any right to. The woman who—

The woman who is sliding into Larry's bed alongside me this very moment. Adam didn't move a muscle as his wife snuggled up to him and tugged at the blankets. Didn't so much as breathe when she leaned over and dropped a featherlight kiss on his cheek, sending soft strands of her hair to tickle his neck.

"Adam?" When she couldn't free the blankets or elicit a response, she spoke. "I know you're awake."

"Can't be."

"You are, my husband." Her breath warmed his ear. "And I am your wife."

One man should only be asked to withstand so much temptation, Lord. Adam turned, keeping the covers whipcord tight around himself. "What else are you, Opal?"

He almost would have sworn he saw a flash of uncertainty in her eyes, but she recovered quickly.

"In your bed."

"Wrong." It came out curt, but that suited him just fine. "You're in Larry's bed. Question is, have you been here before?"

"Never." She moved as though to push away from him, but he caught one wrist and kept her connected to him. "Let me go."

"No. You came to my room, you'll answer my questions." He kept his grip loose enough not to hurt. "When Larry kept trespassing onto Speck lands, did he go to see you?"

She swallowed, hard. "I'm afraid so."

Suddenly it seemed as the air turned to lead. Adam fought to keep going. "Do you want to be with my brother?"

"No!" Opal didn't struggle, just stared up at him with pleading eyes. "I'm here to be with you, Adam."

The air thinned slightly but not enough. He still had one more question. "Has my brother touched you since you married me?"

"Don't ask." A broken sob escaped her lips, one arm curling around her middle as though to protect the babe his brother sired within her.

"Then go." He flung her arm from him and turned his back. "I don't want you."

Opal stumbled back to the room she used to share with Willa and sank down onto the bed.

Lord, what am I to do now? She relived the time she'd spent with Adam that night and saw no ways left to make their marriage work. *There's nothing. If a man won't take a woman who climbs into his bed, he doesn't want her. I should have known that even before he said it.*

After all, Adam didn't choose to marry her. Adam never said he wanted to be with her. Adam didn't arrange for them to room together after Willa left. Nowhere along the way had her "husband" done anything to demonstrate the slightest interest.

She wrapped her arms around herself in a bid

to hold herself together and ward away the rejection but found herself wincing once more. Opal lifted her nightgown and peered at the purples and blues smearing her stomach.

At least that's one thing I don't have to worry about—his seeing the bruises and asking what happened. She couldn't work up a smile. Truth be told, Adam might not even care what happened. *But I care.* She blinked back tears that owed nothing to the soreness in her stomach and everything to the ache in her heart. *I care.*

Adam doesn't want me as a woman, doesn't want me as his wife. He deserves better than to be trapped this way. Now I know Pa will forgive me—he'll forgive me more readily for not having betrayed him the original way. Ben and Willa can be the ones to unite the Specks and Grogans.

Opal rose to her feet and slid her satchel from beneath the bed to start packing.

Tomorrow, I'll see Parson Carter about that annulment.

Chapter 38

Adam woke early the next morning. At least, he would have if he'd slept.

In any case, dawn found him already up with most of his chores done and him ready to head to the fields. Which is where he went. Without breakfast. His appetite left at the thought of facing Opal over the table, so he got a great start hand-casting oats.

It wasn't until he ventured back to the well to refill his canteen that he spoke to another living soul. Seemed Pa'd had the same idea at the same time.

"Today another day for Opal to help her Pa and brothers?" The question caught Adam off guard.

"No."

"Must be with the hives, then." Pa closed his canteen and used the tin cup they kept by the well to take a long swig. "We haven't seen hide nor hair of the girl today. With Willa gone and Larry not back yet from hunting, place seems empty."

Unease gnawed in the pit of Adam's belly. "I'll check the apiary to be sure."

A few minutes later, the unease grew to concern when the apiary produced nothing more than humming hives and busy bees. Adam headed back home. He made for the main door but swung around the side, toward the entrance to Willa and Opal's room, at the last minute.

The door stood ajar.

He pushed in but didn't see anything wrong at first. Bed was made neat and tidy, nothing out of place, nothing to cause worry, nothing—nothing. *That's what's wrong.* The realization hit him in the gut. No clothes hung from pegs. No bonnets waited to be worn. No signs told of any woman's presence, save a piece of paper on the writing desk.

Adam walked over to find an already-opened letter. He'd worry about who opened it later. For now, he concentrated on the small, sweet letters whose lines slanted upward at the end.

Dear Adam,

First, please let me apologize for all that's gone wrong. I never meant to mislead you, but when I shouted in the clearing that you would be the father of my child, I chose the words knowing Pa would force a shotgun wedding. I grabbed at my only chance to save your life that day. When you mentioned the possibility of annulment being lost only due to

*my pregnancy, I knew I couldn't tell you the
truth until we consummated our union.*

Here, he lowered the letter for a moment, stunned
by the revelation. *Does this mean my wife is untouched?*
Unable to keep from grinning, he kept reading.

*After last night, and in light of Larry's
interest, I know we can't be together. By this
point, the volatile nature of our families'
interactions has been largely contained.
Ben and Willa may take up as the new
peacekeepers. This sham of a marriage is no
longer necessary to keep bloodshed at bay,
so you may rest easy. Please know that I'm
leaving this morning to speak with Parson
Carter about seeking an annulment, which
will certainly be granted upon the supremely
provable grounds of nonconsummation.*
   *Many apologies for the difficulties I've
brought you,*

Opal Speck

Adam didn't take the time to fold the letter
before heading to the barn, instead creasing it on
the way. He had Daisy saddled—draft horse she
may be, but she pulled double duty in a pinch—
before Ma or Pa could catch up to him.

*Opal hasn't been with Larry. Opal never lay with
any man.* The certainty flooded him like a song of
praise. *She chose to save my life. She married me because
she wanted to.* Memories of all the times they'd

worked in tandem to keep peace jumbled in his mind until there was only one thing he could keep straight. *Opal and I have a chance at a real marriage as long as I can convince her I don't want an annulment.*

He urged Daisy to move faster as he remembered finding Opal in his bed last night. *No annulments for us.*

When he arrived at Parson Carter's, the older man hadn't seen Opal. Adam bit back a grin. Perhaps his wife didn't feel so anxious to end things as her letter let on. Maybe she waited at the Speck farm even now for him to show up.

But when he showed up, he found no trace of Opal there either. Worry clawed its way into a frown, but Adam persevered. Perhaps Opal had gone back to the Grogan farm, hoping to find him? He pressed Daisy harder than ever to get home, fighting his growing unease.

Pa said they hadn't seen her at breakfast, he recalled. *By now she should have visited Parson Carter and been back at the Speck place many times over.*

So it didn't surprise him when he got home and found no Opal. Only his mother remained at the Grogan farm, and even she sat, weeping at the table, raising a tearstained face to him.

"Oh Adam," she sobbed. "I think Opal ran off with our Larry!"

Lucinda couldn't stand. She wanted to fling herself at her eldest son, to comfort him over the betrayal of his wife and brother and wring out what comfort she could in return. But instead, she seemed affixed to the bench.

"Why do you think she's with Larry?" His footfalls sounded slow, as though the news weighed heavy on Adam.

"She ran out on her chores this morning. Then Larry came tearing through here like a man possessed." She pushed her handkerchief to her mouth. "He demanded the cash box, took everything, and left. Said he had someone waiting. I know it's her."

"Opal doesn't want Larry." Certainty rang in Adam's voice. He pushed a letter toward her. "Though Larry wants my wife. . .badly enough to do something foolish. Which way would he go, Ma?"

Lucinda read the note and had to swallow back the bile that swelled past her throat.

I knew it! I knew that girl didn't carry my son's child. She tricked him into marriage. She threw my Willa at her no-good brother. She turned Adam's head, and now she's addled Larry's wits.

"Ben." She reached past the nausea into her memory for anything useful. "Larry said something about Ben's mine being a good place for a new start."

"I'm going to bring them home, Ma."

"Adam?" Her call scarcely made him pause in the doorway he was so intent on racing to his hussy. "Be merciful to your brother. Remember your blood."

"Yes Ma."

Opal awoke to find herself trussed up and slung over a saddle, every step the horse took sending new aches streaking through her bruised middle. She worked her dry mouth and tried to remember what had happened.

The humiliation of last night's rejection rose to the front of her mind until she shoved it down. *I wrote the letter, packed my things, and set out for Parson Carter's.* She strained to marshal her thoughts or even clear her vision but kept seeing spots.

Then it came back. *Larry.* He intercepted her on her way to Parson Carter's and tried to convince her to leave Adam. Hoping to get to safety, she'd told him the truth of where she headed and why, but it backfired. Instead of escorting her to get the annulment, Larry trussed her up like a turkey and went to go read the note she'd left for Adam.

He returned with his whole face lit up, swearing he'd make her happy. But no matter how she played along, she couldn't convince him to take her to Parson Carter's nor her family's farm. The more she insisted, the more he resisted, until he said something about being sorry, but it would be easiest if she slept. Then he raised the butt of his pistol. . .

Which must be why her head throbbed even more than her stomach. She concentrated on drawing a few deep breaths and praying.

Lord, please give me the wisdom to handle Larry and the strength to take whatever opportunities You send. I ask for peace to clear my thoughts so I may be wise.

The one small mercy Larry afforded her had been to not gag her. Although, having knocked her unconscious, he probably hadn't needed to. At

331

any rate, she tried to use her teeth to loosen the rope around her wrists, contorting her hands and compressing her fingers in a bid for freedom. No use. She decided against trying to rear back and lunge off the horse.

Not only did she gamble a bad fall, but it wouldn't do her any good with her legs bound together. At best, the attempt may slow Larry's progress by a few moments. At worst, he might strike her unconscious again. Opal shuddered at the thought and refused to risk it.

But she did try to angle her arms beneath her enough to maneuver her stomach off the horse a little. Not much, just enough to bear some of her weight and relieve the pain. It didn't work, but it alerted Larry that she'd awoken, and she felt them come to a halt.

The saddle leaned as he slid out. His hands sent revulsion up her spine when they settled on her waist and pulled her down, but her much-abused midriff sighed with relief. He didn't say anything, just stared at her for a moment before cupping the back of her head, feeling where he'd bashed the back of her skull. It made her wince.

"I'm sorry, sweetheart." His use of the endearment made her skin crawl. "But I had to do it. I knew you wouldn't leave without saying good-bye to your pa and brothers. Am I right?"

"Yes." The urgency in his voice acted as her cue, even if she hadn't already decided the smartest thing would be to agree with him unless he asked something of her. "I wanted to see them."

"Don't be sad, baby." He smothered her in a hug. "You know if you saw them they wouldn't let you leave with me. I couldn't let that happen." Larry kept one arm around her but pulled back enough to look down at her. "You would've been so upset if they stood in our way."

"I'm sure you would've found a way." She kept the words sounding sweet. *A lying, thieving, sneaking, conniving, abusing, kidnapping, no-good jerk always finds a way to take what he wants.*

"Of course I would've found a way for us to be together." He smoothed her hair back—right over the tender knot that made her wince again. "After how hard I've been working to get them out of the way, you know that. Even if it backfired and you wound up having to save Adam."

"I'm the reason you wanted to spark the feud?" It clunked into place but made no sense.

"Yes. Your family wouldn't let me have you, so they had to be taken out of the picture. We're destined to be together, no matter what I have to do to make it happen." A beatific smile made sinister by the scar bisecting his face. "You know that."

CHAPTER 39

Adam followed the tracks from the Burn smithy due west. Sure enough, they said Larry'd rented the fastest horse they had. With cash up front.

But that horse carried two passengers, and his trusty Daisy only carried one. Together, they pushed as quickly as possible, the tracks growing fresher the farther they got. Hours of riding saw the scenery change, sending them into a land of reddish soil and spiky desert plants that didn't seem to bear much thirst.

It was here, behind a small stand of bedraggled trees that looked more like twisted bushes, Adam caught sight of his quarry. Lickety-split, he slid off Daisy and snuck closer, taking stock of the situation.

There stood the horse—munching on a tuft of grass so dry it looked as though it would cut a cow's mouth. Larry faced Opal a few steps behind. From this side view, Adam could see that his brother had bound his wife's hands and knees, keeping her completely under his control.

The beast within him that claimed Opal as its own gave a mighty roar when he saw Larry's arm around his wife. When he heard Larry telling her he'd do anything to make them be together, the roaring became louder, rushing in his ears when he saw Opal wince.

"Step away from my wife." Adam gave the order from less than four feet back. He crouched, ready if Larry sprang at him.

"Adam!" Opal made as though to move toward him, but her bindings brought her up short. She fell to the ground with a painful thud as Larry released her and turned.

"Brother." The sneer mocked him. Mocked their blood tie. "You read the letter. She's left you. Be gone."

"Noooo. . ." A low moan from Opal negated Larry's taunt.

"Larry, come back home. Opal and I will move out. Things will go back to normal. You'll never go near or even see my wife again." He inched forward, attempting to reason with the unreasonable man. "We'll put this all behind us."

"No. Opal's mine." Larry pulled out a knife. "You tried to take her from me once. You're my brother, Adam, and it took me a long time to figure out how it happened. Now that I know it was a mistake, I can forgive and forget it. But I won't let it happen again. Leave us in peace now."

"Put away the knife and come home." Another step toward subduing Larry. Another step toward saving Opal.

"Get back." His brother waved the knife, moving to stand over Opal. "She and I are meant for each other. Leave us in peace."

"Larry, I have to bring her back. She's my wife. She belongs with me."

"No!" Larry lunged forward, slicing through the air—and a part of Adam's shirt—with his knife. It would've done more damage, but he stepped in some sort of depression in the earth and his balance faltered. He quickly righted himself and attacked again.

Adam grabbed his brother's knife arm with both hands, keeping it poised away from his body, twisting until Larry dropped the knife. He kicked it far from where they stood, evening the match.

No matter, Larry wouldn't give up. He came after him, fists flying, face full of fury. They had the knock-down drag-out of the century.

Until Opal screamed.

Larry, as the one closest, processed the problem first. The depression his foot sank in when he wielded the blade hadn't been mere loose earth. While they'd fought, the deadly force he unleashed crept toward Opal.

Each about a foot long, two snakes slithered to where Opal lay, bound and helpless to escape. The yellow background and gray dorsal pattern, with two light diagonal stripes along their faces, clearly marked them as prairie snakes. The usual warning rattle hadn't alerted them, as these youths each boasted only a single rattle, producing a soft sort of sizzling sound to express their anger at having their nest disturbed. Having grown so long, it seemed likely that these two had driven off or eaten most of their siblings.

336

"Opal!" Adam scrambled to his feet and began to charge for his wife, knowing he wouldn't make it in time.

"Opal!" Larry dove in front of her, directly in the path of both snakes.

Out of the corner of his eye, Adam saw the snakes dart toward his brother while he dragged Opal to safety. He raced to pick up the knife he'd kicked away earlier in the fight, falling upon the creatures still attacking his brother with a vengeance. In seconds, neither snake's head could find its body.

"Larry." Puncture wounds covered his brother's arms, hands, and chest. Young prairie rattlers were known to strike multiple times, with venom more concentrated than that of grown snakes. With two of them... Adam couldn't swallow past the lump in his throat as Larry struggled to sit up.

"Opal." His brother's dying request had Adam untying his wife and bringing her to her kidnapper's side. He might have worried that she'd shy away, but not his wife.

"You saved me." Opal dropped to her knees and drew Larry's head in her lap, her tears falling in a gentle rain. "Thank you."

"See?" A sweet smile transformed Larry into the brother Adam had grown up with. He reached one shaking hand to trace the path of one of Opal's tears. "I was right, Opal." He fought to breathe. "You do care."

His words only made her cry harder and hold on tighter as Larry took his last breaths, his heart giving out from the poison.

Adam didn't move. Couldn't move. Not until all

Opal's tears were shed and she stood up. Together, they carefully wrapped Larry in a blanket and tied him to the saddle before setting out for home.

Opal didn't speak and neither did he.

He thinks it's my fault. Opal kept her arms wrapped around Adam's waist to keep from falling off Daisy as they started home.

Oh Lord. After this, there's no chance for me and Adam, is there? The death of his brother. . . He'll blame me. Or he'll blame himself, which is even worse. His parents had barely begun to tolerate me. Now that will end entirely.

Despair bogged her down, rooting her in misery. The best she could hope for now was that their families didn't kill each other over this incident, that Larry's death would be the last. Her thoughts pulled her in so deep, Opal scarcely noticed when the sky turned dark. Not until they came within sight of the Grogan house.

Then she struggled not to tighten her hold on Adam. Funny how she'd thought she'd given him up entirely this morning, but now she felt as though she couldn't let him go. He swung out of the saddle them lifted her down. She followed him to the other horse, which Daisy had led the entire way, and helped him untie Larry's corpse. Adam carried the bundle inside, where his parents and little brother waited.

"No!" Lucinda's anguished scream rent the night the second she saw Opal walk through the door behind her son and knew the figure masked by the blanket must be Larry. "No!" She grasped Larry's shoulders and sank onto the floor, where Adam carefully placed him.

"What happened?" Diggory's eyes didn't look hard tonight. No greedy glint or angry gleam lit their depths. Instead, his expression seemed strangely flat.

"He kidnapped Opal on her way to Parson Carter's." Adam didn't so much as glance her way as he spoke. "Ma says he then came and took the cash box, which I assume is still in the saddlebags. Opal didn't go willingly, so he tied her up, which is how I found them."

"Anything you want to add?" Her father-in-law interrupted Adam and turned to her.

"No." Her saying anything would be out of place.

"Tell me everything anyway." Diggory Grogan demonstrated a greater understanding of her than Opal would have credited him with. "Best to have all the details now."

"He knocked me out with the back of his pistol"— Opal flinched at the angry sound from Adam as his hand settled directly on the tender spot at the back of her head—"when I didn't agree that we were in love and I belonged to him."

"Lovesick." Lucinda had freed Larry's head from the blanket and tenderly fixed his hair. "Just lovesick for the wrong girl. That's all he was. He didn't mean no harm."

"He said he's been trying to provoke the feud to kill my family and get rid of any objections." Opal wouldn't meet anyone's gaze as she repeated Larry's words, all too aware how ridiculous it sounded.

"I should've seen it." Diggory lowered himself

onto his haunches and looked at Larry's face.

"None of us did." Adam sounded so hoarse, Opal wouldn't have known his voice if she didn't see his mouth move.

He blames me for not telling him. I thought he wouldn't have believed me, but would he? Do such questions even matter anymore? She reached up and curled her fingers around Mama's brooch.

"When I found them, Larry told me to leave them. I wouldn't, so he pulled a knife and sprang at me." Adam recounted how he disarmed his brother, how Larry's step faltered, how the two fought until Opal cried out.

"Tied up, she couldn't get away. Larry threw himself in front of Opal when he realized the situation."

"It should have been you." Lucinda's hiss seemed oddly akin to that of the snakes from earlier as she stared at Opal. "You should be wrapped in this blanket. Not my boy."

"Larry kidnapped Opal, bashed her skull, tied her up, and put her in the path of those snakes." Her husband spoke more loudly now. "It shouldn't have been Opal, Ma. It shouldn't have been anyone, but Larry created the problem."

"No." The hatred in Lucinda's stare made Opal's blood run cold. "*She* created the problem when she seduced you and wormed her way into our household, playing brother against brother."

"Opal misled her family, and myself, into believing she carried a child on our wedding day just to save my life. She's never been with any man, so don't call her a seducer or one who pits men against each other."

"No grandchild?" Diggory's face went duller. "Well, at least we know you got yourself a good wife, son."

"A good wife?" The scream should've brought the town running. "She murdered our Larry and disgraced his name!"

"Larry saved my life." Opal didn't care that Lucinda hated her, but she wouldn't stand by and let her affection for Larry's memory fade to nothing. "I honor him."

"As do I." Adam moved to stand alongside her.

"Same here." Diggory straightened up. "He may have gotten things mixed up, might have caused trouble, but by taking on those snakes, Larry proved himself a good man in the end. I'm proud of him."

"You have reason to be."

"Don't speak about my son." Lucinda lurched to her feet. "Get out of my house. Take her out, Adam. Now!"

"I'll take her home."

Home. Opal bowed her head. *He's returning me to the Speck farm. Of course he is. The only thing that's changed is that his brother died—over me. No wonder he wants to be rid of me.* She followed as he stabled the horse, not protesting when he grabbed her satchel.

Neither one of them uttered a word as they trudged toward the Speck farm.

It wasn't until they stood on her father's doorstep that Adam asked a question Opal hadn't imagined weighed on his mind. "What's wrong with your stomach?"

"Oh." The memory of Larry's fist made her close her eyes, but not before she glanced down and registered that her arm braced her stomach, as it had for most of the walk. "Being thrown over a saddle and jounced around takes a toll."

"No." His eyes narrowed at her shrug. "You hurt before today. I noticed when we went after Willa—but thought it was the baby. Now I know better." He angled closer. "What happened?"

"Doesn't matter anymore." She braced herself more tightly and reached for the door, the obvious escape. "I'll be fine."

His body blocked the door—solid, powerful, and far too close for comfort.

She fell back a step.

"Tell me, Opal."

"Larry."

The *smack* of knuckles splintering wood muffled her husband's curse as Adam gouged her father's door frame with a vicious jab before stalking off into the night.

Even though the door opened to reveal her entire family, Opal couldn't help but feel isolated. Adam didn't even see Willa and Ben had returned. How could he?

He never looked back.

CHAPTER 40

W ake up, Lucy." Diggory shook her awake, and for a blessed moment, Lucinda didn't realize why she lay half sprawled on the kitchen table instead of snug in bed.

Then she saw Larry—just as she'd left him when the tears finally carried her to oblivion. Dressed in his Sunday best, arms folded across his chest, freshly shaven, and looking every inch the wonderful son she'd raised. And lost.

She lost the distance she'd gained upon waking, when she'd half risen before reality came crashing back upon her. Knees seemed such flimsy things to stand up to such a blow. But somehow they managed the task when her husband scooped Larry's body into his arms and headed for the door.

"No. . ." The cry emerged as a raspy whisper, her throat too raw from sobbing the night through to manage any volume now. So she followed, stumbling a little in the bright morning light as Diggory carried their son away.

Lucinda blinked away the bleariness by the time her husband stopped—carefully laying Larry in a wooden box he must've cobbled together the night before. Parson Carter stood at the ready, a whole group of people surrounding a freshly-dug grave. *A funeral. Larry's funeral.* Recognition dawned.

An insane urge to throw herself over her son and demand he be given back warred with gratitude toward her husband and friends for arranging the respectful farewell Larry deserved. The battle lasted only as long as it took for her to identify those gathered to mourn him.

"What is *she* doing here?" An aching throat lent itself well to her hiss of rage as Lucinda threw away polite manners and pointed at the Speck murderess, only to realize the entire contingent of Specks surrounded the dealer of death. "What are *any* of you doing here?"

"Paying our respects." Willa's was the last voice she expected, but her daughter stepped forward, and she realized belatedly that Ben's presence meant they'd both returned. "To my brother."

"So now you remember your family?" Somehow, the words snapped out before Lucinda could snatch them back. Now it was too late to rush to her only girl and envelop her in a hug that would never end.

"I never forgot." Willa didn't recoil or even have the grace to look abashed. Even worse, Ben reached out and clasped her hand while she spoke. "But I remembered that we're no better than anyone else.

The Specks are a part of our family now, Ma. Between Ben and Opal, we're joined forever."

"The pair of them aren't worth Larry! The whole Speck family isn't!" Her voice broke through the soreness in a screech. "I won't have it. I won't have Larry's murderer attend his funeral when inside she's laughing at our loss. Willa, come home. Adam's annulling his sham of a marriage. We can all be together again." She stepped forward and reached a hand toward each of her errant children. "Don't let Larry's death be in vain."

"Larry died to save Opal," Dave piped up, walking up to his sister-in-law. "Pa says it was brave."

"It was." The cause of all their woes smiled down at her youngest son, sending a shaft of fear straight through Lucinda's heart as neither Willa nor Adam moved to join her. "I'll never forget Larry's selfless courage."

"No." Lucinda grasped Dave by the soft, fleshy part of the arm, just above the elbow, and hauled him to her side. "I won't lose any more of our family to Speck machinations. Dave isn't permitted to speak to any Speck!"

"Not even me, Ma?"

"You're still a Grogan, sis." Dave wriggled in an attempt to break free, but Lucinda held on tighter. "Ma didn't mean you."

"Yes, I did, Dave. You aren't to visit your sister if she stays with the Specks. Only if Willa comes back home." Willa's gasp sent a surge of satisfaction through her. *There. Let her see what she's given up. Nothing comes without a price.* Lucinda's gaze fell on the makeshift coffin cradling her middle son and fought a surge of dizziness.

"No." Diggory pried her hand off Dave's arm, letting him rush to hug Willa. "Larry died to make amends, Lucy. I won't let it be for nothing. The Specks are here to honor what he done right, and I won't take that away from any of us. Davey can talk to any of the Specks anytime he wants."

" 'Hatred stirreth up strifes: but love covereth all sins,' " Parson Carter broke in. "Your son's death epitomizes one of my favorite verses."

"I won't support this." Another sob caught in her throat, swelling until she thought it would swallow her whole. "You know where to find me when you come to your senses." Lucinda headed back to the house, stopping only to plant one last kiss on Larry's cheek before losing herself in the loneliness she'd dreaded so long.

During his mother's outburst, Adam slid one arm around Opal's waist. It felt right, and her wordless acceptance eased some of the tension from his neck. Opal's nearness affected him that way, relaxed him, put him at peace. Question was, had he discovered it too late?

The night before, when she'd revealed Larry's abuse, he hadn't trusted himself to speak. Hadn't trusted himself to keep from scooping her up and taking her home, where he should have taken her long ago. *But it wouldn't have been right to ask her to be my wife after all she'd been through yesterday.* Instead, he'd gone back to the dugout and thrown himself into the finishing touches. Too little too late, when he should have protected her all along, but he had to make it perfect before he would show her that he offered her more than he'd given so far.

"Can I have a word?" Her nod had him guiding her across Grogan lands, knowing she expected him to take her to her father's farm.

She hadn't protested when he took her to her father's last night—didn't ask to stay. Why would she? Opal busily did everything in her power to fit in on the Grogan farm, only to have it flung in her face. She'd made every possible move to make their marriage work. . .and he'd rejected it.

Because I didn't understand. But will such a woman as this give a fool a second chance? God, please help me to do this right.

"I'd like to show you something." He waited for her nod before picking up the pace. Adam knew he shouldn't move faster, shouldn't do anything that could scare her. But his Opal didn't scare easily, and he didn't want her changing her mind.

The dugout looked much like any other hill from a distance. It wasn't until they drew closer to the structure that they could make it out for what it was. The hollowed-out hill stood, at its tallest, about eight feet high, with natural earth for three walls and the roof. A stovepipe stuck through the top.

Adam made earth bricks for the fourth wall out of the dirt he'd excavated from the hill. Into this one, he installed the door and covered the window openings with leather flaps until he could order glass.

"Adam?" Her voice made his name a question. "What is this?"

"Home." He swallowed. "If you want it to be."

"You built this?" Her eyes caught the brilliance of the sunlight. "For us?"

Adam couldn't manage much more than a nod. But she didn't say anything either, just stared at the dugout, and he knew now was his last chance. "Opal?" He took both her hands in his. "Now isn't the ideal time, but I'm coming to accept that there will never be an ideal time. And if I don't say something now, I may lose my chance."

"Your chance for what, Adam?" If words could carry color, hers sounded like they'd be the pale green of hope.

He shoved aside the fanciful thought and plowed ahead. "Weeks ago, I didn't choose you to be my bride." He held fast when she made a small sound of distress and tried to pull her hands away. "But I should have seen it as a gift. I should have watched over you more diligently. If you can forgive me for being so slow to realize how blessed I am to have you as my wife, Opal, I ask you to choose me as your husband."

"Truly?" She stopped trying to pull her hands away, her fingers curling around his. "You want me as your wife?"

"I want you, Opal. I want you in my house, I want you by my side." His voice dropped. "I want you in my bed, without any misunderstandings between us. I want what you said that day on your family's farm to be true—I want to be the father of your child, Opal Grogan. What say you?"

"I say. . ." She tilted her head and bestowed upon him the loveliest smile he'd ever seen while she drew out her answer. "We have a lot of lost time to make up for husband."

"Then let's get started"—Adam swept her up into his arms and headed for the door—"wife."

ABOUT THE AUTHOR

KELLY EILEEN HAKE is a reader favorite of Barbour Publishing's Heartsong Presents book club, where she released several of her first books. A credentialed secondary English teacher in California with an MA in Writing Popular Fiction, she is known for her own style of witty, heartwarming historical romance.

JOIN US ONLINE!

Christian Fiction for Women

Christian Fiction for Women is your online home for the latest in Christian fiction.

Check us out online for:

- Giveaways
- Recipes
- Info about Upcoming Releases
- Book Trailers
- News and More!

Find Christian Fiction for Women at Your Favorite Social Media Site:

 Search "Christian Fiction for Women"

 @fictionforwomen